ISBN-13: 978-1-7333949-4-9

Cover design by: Sarah A. Wagner for RadSarah Art

Printed in the United States of America

A FAINT REFLECTION
OF RIDDLES
BOOK THREE

TEARS IN A BOTTLE

A Jake Moriarity Novel
by
R. G. Ryan

God has marked all of my sorrows;
He has collected all my tears in a bottle
and has recorded each one in His book.

David, King of Israel
ca. 1011 BC

PROLOGUE

Tom Marshall sat unmoving in the hospice room's lone chair, staring at his wife, Helen, as she struggled to draw another breath and wondering if it would be her last. For the past two days he had done little else.

Neither had she.

Breathe in.

Breathe out.

Breathe in.

Breathe out.

The noise of the respirator hypnotic in its regularity.

Her eyes closed, body unmoving.

Breathe in.

Breathe out.

Suddenly the breathing stopped.

He sat bolt upright wondering if this was the end. He counted the seconds: thousand-one, thousand-two, thousand-three, thousand-four...

She started breathing again.

He sat back in the chair feeling inexplicably relieved. But why? Why would he feel relief that she was still breathing? Wouldn't it be better for her—and, yes, for everyone—if her spirit were finally able to escape the crippled body that had become its prison? To finally have an end to the debilitating effects generated by the massive, ischemic stroke that had wreaked such havoc on her once proudly toned body?

Helen.

His beauty.

His bride of thirty-five years.

She was only fifty-six.

Fifty-six!

He still couldn't believe that this had happened to them...to her. He took the opportunity to once again rail at the heavens if for no other reason than informing God, *again*, that at least one of His subjects, "children," if you will, was madder than hell.

She had really been something back at the start of their relationship. The romance had shocked their small circle of friends at Eastern Tennessee Christian University. Even though it had been the latter part of the 20th Century, a mixed-race marriage still made some people uncomfortable. But it was more than that. She had been the prize catch —the most beautiful girl on campus, courted by everyone from the captain of the football team to the graduate student in quantum physics. And yet she had chosen him, a slender black man of average height with dubious prospects as a jazz bassist. People just couldn't understand how their relationship had come to be. It was just so...so...irregular. Between the two of them they had thought nothing of it. They had been in love and that was that.

They married, graduated; Helen accepted a position with *Vereda Creative Management* in Los Angeles and they moved west. Pure fate had arranged that the management company would eventually contract with Aaron Perry, who just happened to need a bass player at the time for his jazz trio. Tom, who by then was a ten-year veteran of the industry, auditioned. Aaron loved his "vibe" and the rest, as they say, is history. His association with Aaron had been financially lucrative, given the man's innate propensity toward generosity, and had provided opportunity to travel the world, with Helen accompanying him regularly, yet another manifestation of Aaron's generous heart.

He chuckled quietly as he recalled the incalculable

number of times Aaron had reminded him, "Tommy, my man, now you know the only reason you're here is because it gives me regular opportunities to convince Helen of the grave error she made in marrying you instead of me." It was all in good fun as Aaron Perry was the most honorable man he had ever known. And when Aaron's ex-wife, Sylvie, had so unceremoniously divorced him, Helen had been instrumental in pulling Aaron out of the emotional quagmire into which the separation had plunged him.

She was good like that. Hell, she was just good.

Even though her job required long hours and his touring schedule took him away from home and out of the country many days per year, when they were together it was magic.

Lovers.

Friends.

Companions.

It wouldn't be long now. He could smell death in the air; could, in fact, sense it, whatever "it" was, hovering just out of sight in the recesses of the room's darkened corners.

He allowed as how, at this point, anyway, he was quite glad they had made the choice early on in their marriage to not have children. Although there were times when the loneliness of his struggle as a caregiver made him long for respite, assistance, anything at all from anyone else that cared as deeply as he. And what about her two brothers and imperious mother? Muttering something about how she wanted to remember Helen as she had been, her mother and brothers had chosen to not make the trip south from Seattle to bid Helen farewell. Requesting to be notified regarding a memorial service and, most importantly, the date for the reading of her will, she had terminated the call abruptly.

How he loathed each and every one of them.

A slight stirring jerked him back into awareness. Glancing at the bed he saw Helen's head turned toward him, her eyes open and mouth working to form words.

Rushing to her side he smoothed the hair away from the alabaster skin of her forehead.

"Hey, baby. I didn't realize you were awake."

Closing her eyes, she made what seemed a supreme effort to form the phrase, "I have something to tell you."

Tom leaned in until his ear was close to Helen's mouth.

"Okay, baby. I'm here. What is it?"

In a barely discernable whisper, one side of her mouth sagging, she said, "Charles, I had to move the key. You...know where it is. Go get it...for God's sake, get it or all will be lost."

Just as he started to correct her mistake and tell her that it was Tom, not Charles—whoever Charles was—standing over her, the breath slowly left her body and Helen Marie Marshall stepped into the eternal stream.

Hovering over her for a few seconds, mainly to make sure that this time she was really gone, his mind began frantically searching mental references for anyone named Charles who could possibly be in their circle of friends, acquaintances and business associates. He came up with nothing.

Raising up to his full height and staring down at Helen's lifeless form, something struck him as being profoundly strange. He wasn't crying nor was he feeling a surge in grief. The woman he had loved for more than half his life had been lost to him the day she had been transported to hospice. As such, his grieving had already been done. At least that's what John, the hospice chaplain had explained to him.

But beyond all that, her final words echoed through his mind: "Charles, I had to move the key. You know where it is. Find it...for God's sake, find it or all will be lost."

What would be lost?

What key?

And who the hell was Charles?

Had something been going on with his wife that he

hadn't known about? His mind quickly grasped at a possible scenario that he just as quickly dismissed only to have it come roaring back immediately and demanding consideration. An affair? Was Charles someone with whom Helen had had a relationship in the past? Could it be that it was current? And this mysterious key. Was it perhaps the key to wherever it was they met regularly? An apartment? A hotel room rented regularly?

Turning in place a full circle his eyes cast about the room as if searching for anything that would help his understanding.

Anything at all.

There was nothing, and no one to talk to.

Turning back to his wife's body he leaned slightly over her, whispering, "Why did you say that to me? Did you even know who I was? Did you care what it would do to me? How could you leave me like..."

And then the tears came.

In torrents.

Shoulders shaking, chest heaving, he collapsed against the bed's rails clinging as a man clings to a lifeline against a raging torrent bent on snatching him away.

Drying his eyes, he suddenly knew what he had to do.

He had to call Jake.

CHAPTER 1

Saturday 8:30 a.m.

I t was one of those classic, southern California coastal mornings. Marine layer above; a light fog hovering just over the water; mysterious images darting in and out of the mist like spectral wraiths; fog horn braying in the distance and Vanessa demonstrating "a killer new move" she had just learned from some world-famous Hollywood choreographer whom I had never heard of, and whose name I promptly forgot as soon as it was spoken in my hearing. Okay, maybe Vanessa being part of the "classic southern California coastal morning" thing was a bit of a stretch, but it was morning, we were on the coast and, well, there you have it.

Michael and Cassie were still in St. Augustine on a vacation/sabbatical that Cassie had basically forced, so Aaron and I were housesitting their place just north of Carlsbad State Beach. Vanessa was home for the weekend from WeHo, or West Hollywood where her dance academy is located; Muriel and Eddie were jogging somewhere; and Aaron was sleeping in.

It's a musician thing.

I must say that the fact that Muriel was walking without a limp, let alone jogging—albeit very slowly—is a testament not only to modern medicine, but also her fiercely relentless spirit. The twelve-inch vertical scar running along the outside of her right thigh stemmed from two surgeries to replace a shattered femur that came as a result of the same horrific accident that put Michael in a wheel-chair where he would remain for the rest of his days.

Vanessa and I were on the expansive deck of Michael and Cassie's beachfront home where I watched in wonder as she put her body through a few moves that, were I to be so foolish as to attempt even one of them, would land me in traction. But I am not a foolish man, which is why she worked out and I sipped a very delicious dark Italian roast coffee.

It's a good arrangement.

"What do you think?" she asked breathlessly, holding on to the final pose.

Being the good, almost adoptive father that I am, I replied, "That was amazing. What was it?"

She relaxed, hands on her hips, staring suspiciously.

"Were you even watching?"

"Watching, and yet not even close to comprehending."

She relaxed her posture and walked over to plop down in the generously cushioned comfort of the chaise lounge next to me.

"This doesn't suck," she pronounced while staring out at the Pacific Ocean.

"No...no, it doesn't," came my rejoinder. "This house is pretty special."

"Right? Even though it's not much bigger than yours and Aaron's, it's like whoever designed it maximized every square inch to take advantage of its location." She paused and then added, "You know, Cassie's condo—well, ex-condo —is like that too."

I gestured toward the water and said, "This is kind of the Holy Grail for real estate, at least on the West Coast. Actually, anything coastal California is like that to varying degrees."

"Seems unfair, somehow, that only a very few and very wealthy people should get to experience this."

"Not true," I replied forcefully. "The state of California owns..." I had to stop and recall what a state official had told me once, "...the land seaward of what is called the mean high tide line."

"What the heck does that mean?"

"Well, it means that the public has access to the wet sand, but not the dry sand, above the tide line."

"Huh?"

"It means that anyone can walk along the beach, as long as the sand is wet beneath your toes," I said with a laugh.

"Then why doesn't the law just say that?"

"Bureaucracy one-oh-one: Never say in one sentence what can be said in three hundred pages of regulations. Anyway, the point being that the beach and the ocean are available to anyone."

I took a long, slow sip of my coffee and noticed that the fog had dissipated to the extent that I could now see that those previously spectral shapes were actually surfers on the water.

"Yeah, I get that," Vanessa replied. "I guess I'm just dealing with some teen angst regarding capitalism, or something."

"Ah-ha. Must be having socialism discussions in the dorm."

"Not in the dorm. In this coffee bar where I hang out with my friends."

"Of course. And what, pray tell, is the prevailing view among these sociologically, politically and economically enlightened sages?"

She stood and began stretching, which, to my untrained eye, looked to be every bit as dangerous to one's physical well being as the contortioned dance moves she had executed earlier.

"It's interesting," she said. "The people who are the most vocally opposed to capitalism are the ones who also seem to enjoy most of its benefits."

"So, by definition, am I to assume that you are referring to rather privileged young people?"

"Rather privileged? Ha!" She stopped stretching and stood with her back against the railing and arms crossed. "Absolutely entitled is more like it."

"I see. And yet they resist the basic core values of capitalism?"

"Completely. It's disgusting. And on the one or two occasions when my BS quotient had reached its limit and I attempted to challenge their points of view, they treated me like I was an idiot."

"I can't imagine that went over very well," I remarked.

She went back to stretching. Ah, to be young.

"This one kid—I mean I don't like saying bad things about people, but, he's...he's just a troll. You know, one of those guys who basically hides behind his computer screen all day and night picking fights with people he can't see and who can't see him?"

"I've heard of the species."

"Well, he's friends with a friend of a friend, who is friends with one of my really good gay friends—another dancer in my class—and this kid, the troll, just showed up one night at our coffee place. And before you know it, we're having this raging discussion about politics and how socialism is the ideology of the future, which I don't believe for one second, but anyway...I notice that he's wearing glasses that had to cost at least a thousand bucks; one of those fancy European watches that are around $10,000—Patek something-something; and that he drove up in a Porsche Panamera—a *Porsche*, can you believe it? And yet he's just throwing down this crap about how the wealthy are ruining our country. So, I said, 'Would it make you feel better if you gave me your car?' He looked at me like I'm crazy and said, 'What are you talking about?' So, I said, 'If you're so concerned about the wealthy ruining the country, give me your car. You're obviously rich and I'm not. It'll help even things out.'"

"What'd he do?"

"He just looked around at the people in our group, called me an ignorant, unenlightened little bitch and then got up and waddled out to his car and drove away into the Hollywood Hills where he lives with mommy and daddy."

That made me laugh.

"And how about the others? Did any of them get the irony?"

"Oh, they were loving every minute of it. I think I became an instant folk hero or something for calling him out because no one else had the guts."

Aaron wandered out onto the deck dressed in sweats and tank top—his version of pajamas—his dread's making him look like that alien in the original *Predator* movie.

After we exchanged morning greetings, he sat down next to me and sighed deeply.

"Just got off the phone with Tommy."

"Marshall?"

"Yeah. Helen passed about an hour ago."

"Ohhh, man. That's rough."

"Who is this?" Vanessa asked, concern coloring her voice.

Aaron said, "Tommy Marshall. My bass player. He was with me at Cassie's wedding, and Helen is—was—his wife. She worked on my management team at Vereda."

I explained, "Helen suffered a massive stroke."

"Yeah, been in hospice for the past ten days or so," Aaron added.

Vanessa said, "Yeah, I remember seeing him at the wedding. What's hospice all about anyway? I mean I've heard the term, but I've never known what it is."

"Well," Aaron answered, "toward the end, patients who suffer from certain diseases are often in so much pain that oral medications just can't keep up with their level of suffering. Hospice offers what they refer to as palliative care, where the patient is given what amounts to a cocktail of pain medication that basically relieves all suffering. It's a similar situation with people who have had strokes."

"But they die?"

"Yeah, they die."

"And they stop trying to cure them?" she asked.

I replied, "For some patients, no cure is available. When that happens, palliative care is a godsend." I was quiet for a moment, making sure my emotions were under control before adding, "I, uh...I put Abby in hospice before she died. It was tough to let go, but at least she wasn't suffering any longer."

We were all quiet for a few moments before Aaron said, "Tommy asked if I could arrange a meeting with you."

"Why?"

"Something Helen said with her dying breath that just devastated him."

"Wonder what that's all about?"

"I don't know, man, but he was really cryptic about it. Almost like he was afraid to tell me."

"Okay," I said, "now I'm intrigued. Sure, I'll meet with him. I have absolutely nothing going on for a few days, so set it up."

"I'll do that. But first, coffee."

"I'll get it for you," Vanessa said as she hurried off toward the kitchen.

As Aaron watched her go he observed, "Seems like our girl is doing well."

"She is. Time and distance work wonders, my friend."

"Yeah, but it's more than that...it's also love and hope."

He was right. And Vanessa had been surrounded by both for more than a year.

Speaking of love, I needed to call Gabi.

CHAPTER 2

I walked back inside the house and into the master bedroom, shut the door behind me for privacy and called Gabi.

She answered on the first ring.

"Hey, handsome," her voiced dripped with honeyed overtones as if having just awakened.

I had invited Gabi to come with me to house sit for the Harvey's—The "Harvey's", a reality that was going to take some getting used to—but she had things going on at work that just wouldn't wait, so she remained in Las Vegas.

I replied, "How's my favorite senior administrative assistant this morning?"

Possessing a very unique set of skills, Gabi was, and had always been, very highly sought after in the corporate world, and the corporate executives she worked for unabashedly acknowledged that their success was largely a result of Gabi's influence.

"Oh," she said around a yawn, "I'm feeling lazy."

"And beautiful?"

"I never feel beautiful when I first wake up."

"Well, you know what they say."

"Okay, I'll bite. What do *they* say?"

"'Even *I* don't wake up looking like Cindy Crawford.'"

She laughed.

"And who said that?"

"Cindy Crawford."

After laughing some more, she quieted before saying,

"The simple truth is, the only time I feel truly beautiful is when I'm with you, tall sir."

Gabriella Marcus and I have been an "item" for several months, much to the delight of everyone in my growing family. Cassie is the only blood relation I have left, but with her marriage the previous year to Michael Harvey—novelist Charleston Hawthorne to his millions of readers—Mike is now official, as is Vanessa Phillips whose adoption will be completed within the next four to six weeks, or so we've been told. Aaron and his girlfriend, Muriel Palmer, are also core members and have been for a long, long time. The most recent addition is Eddie, or Edwina Madison, a young lady who, along with Cassie and Muriel, was at one time trafficked for sex by the recently deceased Paul Morgan. We have all been through so much together, but those are tales for another time.

I said, "Then I probably need to find a way to spend more time with you."

"A notion I wholeheartedly endorse."

And what, precisely, was I suggesting by that statement—certainly not marriage. I was far from being ready for that eventuality. But, what if that was the very thing she was reading into it?

It was a tricky corner I had painted myself into—into which I had painted myself? I never know which is correct.

"Hey," I said, hoping to jar the conversation in a new direction. "Did everything go okay getting Brett, Laurie and Abby settled into my house?"

I was referring to Brett and Laurie Hansen, Vanessa's sister and brother-in-law and her eight-year-old niece, Abby. I had arranged for them to spend a few days at my house while I was gone. Brett and Laurie run a place called, *Mosaic PB: A Center for Sustainable Creativity.* It's an artist's colony, community center and refuge for homeless teens in San Diego's Pacific Beach neighborhood just south of La Jolla.

"Oh, yes. I met them there, gave them the keys and made sure they knew where everything was."

"Thank-you for that."

"Of course. It's what I do, remember? I'm a professional assistant. And if I may say so, Mr. Moriarity, you are more in need of assistance than practically anyone I've ever known."

It was true.

"So, what are you saying, that you want to jump ship and come to work for me?" I prompted.

She was silent long enough for it to be a little uncomfortable.

Finally, she said, "Look, Jake, I know that we're still feeling our way along here in this relationship, but I think this might be a good time to, well, lay some cards on the table, so to speak."

"Okay. You go first."

"I'd be delighted to." She took a deep breath, blew it out and said, "I love you, Jake. I've loved you far longer than you've loved me in return, or at least that's what I've come to believe. And that's okay. But it feels like I'm still driving this relationship, you know? And, well, I don't know if that's a good thing."

I had been a very reluctant participant at the start. Hell, for a long while *after* it had started. If you want to know the truth, being single for close to twenty years had made me very...sovereign. Not solitary, for there had been women throughout that time whose company I had enjoyed immensely. But the sovereignty thing—you know, master of my own fate, ruler of my own domain—had become the driving force behind my decision to remain single.

Until Gabi, that is.

With her arrival in my life I had discovered something I loved more than all of that. Her. I loved her. So, if that was true, then why was I still sitting back and letting her lead?

"Gabi, I completely agree. It's not a good thing."

"Okay...good. I'm glad to hear you say that. But I need something more than that, Jake. I need you. I—boy, this is hard—but...I need *all* of you."

And there it was.

At the heart of everything was my nearly pathological reluctance to give myself completely to anyone except Cassie, who had been my ward since the age of seven.

"For what it's worth," I said, "that's what I want as well. It's just that, well...look, you know my history so I don't need to rehash all that horror and drama. Besides, at some point it ceases to be relevant and merely serves as a form of enablement; an excuse to perpetuate dysfunction."

"Very eloquent."

"I wasn't going for eloquence. I was going for honesty."

"High marks on both counts, then."

"So, how about you get ready, get on a plane and get over here. I...really miss you."

I could sense her thinking it over.

"Hmm..."

When she didn't' say anything else, I said, "Is there anything that goes with 'hmm', or is that all I get?"

Seconds of silence ticked by like someone ratcheting up the tension on an already too tight cable.

"Okay, but on one condition."

"What's that?"

"That I get to be *with* you when I get there—"

"Meaning?"

"Meaning that between now and then you don't get involved in a new case, or something; you leave Agent Polk's mentoring to someone else and just *be* with me."

Agent Polk was a reference to Bridgett Polk who had assisted us in rescuing Father Jack Mahoney's grandson, Bart, from a sex trafficking ring in Portland. She had been temporarily reassigned to the San Diego field office for the specific purpose of shadowing me on everything I did. I thought about Aaron saying that Tommy wanted to meet with me and considered trying to squeeze something in before Gabi arrived, whenever that would be.

Nope! I knew myself well enough that if Tommy presented something enticing, there was no way I'd be able to resist. It's just the way I'm wired.

"Fair enough," I replied. "So, you'll come?"

I could hear rustling in the background and the sound of a door opening.

Then, "Oh, my God. I'm a fright! I don't know if there's enough time in the universe to fix this mess."

Women.

"Well, do what you can and I'll try not to laugh."

"Heeeeeyyy, watch it, buster."

I chuckled, "Call me when you have a viable schedule put together and I'll start checking on flights."

"Okay. And, Jake?"

"Yeah?"

"Thanks for being agreeable. This means the world to me right now."

"Means the world to me that you'd even consider hanging out with a guy like me."

"Stop it. All right...I love you, Jake Moriarity."

"I love you too, Gabi. See you soon."

The call ended, but my mind pressed on in an attempt to further unravel the mental coils that had held me bound for so long.

I figured it was going to take a while.

In the meantime, I had to find this woman a flight.

CHAPTER 3

Tom Marshall sat in his car, hands gripping the steering wheel, staring sightlessly through the windshield. After pulling in to his designated place in the underground parking garage of the Dana Point condo he had shared with the only woman he had ever loved, he simply couldn't make himself open the door and get out.

"Charles?" he said out loud. "Who the hell is Charles?"

It was easily the ninth or tenth time he had uttered the same disturbing question. And even though he had no idea who Charles was, he found that he already harbored a burgeoning hatred for the man. While Tom Marshall was in no way, shape or form a violent man, he was quite certain that were he to meet this phantom face-to-face, a good, old-fashioned ass whuppin' would ensue.

The vibrating of his phone disrupted further ideations of violent scenarios.

It was Aaron.

"Hello?" he answered shakily.

"Tommy..."

Aaron's deeply burnished baritone seemed to vibrate all the way to the core of his being. He loved the man, and the man loved him back.

"Bro..." he began, but was overcome by sobs that shook his shoulders, causing him to drop his head, his free hand pressed against weeping eyes.

"Hey...you just go on now, brother," Aaron said softly.

"Just go on. Let it out. Let it all out. No shame in a man crying."

Tom nodded his head, even though he knew Aaron couldn't see him.

"Take your time," Aaron added. "I ain't going nowhere. I'm here for whatever you need."

Tom finally managed, "Thank-you, Aaron. Means a whole lot right now." Quickly drawing a shirtsleeve across his face, he barked out a humorless laugh. "Funny...well, not funny at all...but, you know, I've been thinking for the past couple of weeks about how good it would have been to have children around me, you know, someone to help carry the load; someone to...hell, I don't know what I'm talking about, Ivory."

Aaron smiled at the nickname. Tom had called him, "Ivory"—in reference to the keys of a piano—since early in their relationship and he, in return, had called his bass player, "Lowdown."

Aaron said, "Sometimes you don't have to know what to say, Low. You just need to talk, you know? Just get it out there before stuff gets trapped down in your soul and begins to fester."

"You got that right. You sure got that right." Tom paused to draw a deep, cleansing breath and then blew it out. "I have to say that I thought her final passing would be easier, 'cause of the severity of the stroke, you know. But, bro, this is rough. Made rougher by what happened at the end."

"This what you wanted to talk to Jake about?" Aaron queried.

"Yeah, I do. It's just the strangest thing."

"Maybe you should tell me about it."

Another deep breath, and then, "I was alone in the room with her, just listening to her breathe. As you know from the last time you visited—when was that, anyway? Last week?"

"I think it was last Thursday or Friday."

"Yeah, anyway, as you know she hasn't been alert since we transported her to hospice. Now, the doctors tell me that hearing is the last thing to go in these cases, so even though her eyes were closed and she couldn't speak, I felt like she could hear me. So, I'd talk to her, sing to her, play some of our recordings for her."

"That's good, Lowdown. That's real good. So, what happened at the end?"

"Well, I was doing something—can't really remember what—when I suddenly noticed that she was staring at me. So, I rush over and start talking to her and it looks like she wants to say something to me. I lean in real close and..." His voice caught as another sob came unbidden. "She...she said, *'Charles, I had to move the key. You know where it is. Find it...for God's sake, find it or all will be lost.'* And then...she died."

"Bro..." Aaron started and then stopped as if unsure of how to even proceed. "Bro, that's—"

"Weird? You have no idea. I mean, hell, Ivory, I don't know who Charles is. Why would she call me that? Was it a dementia thing where she thought she was someone else and I was someone else and didn't really know what she was talking about because I don't really have another explanation and it's been—"

"Hold up, Tommy," Aaron said to slow the rush of words. "You sure you don't know anyone named Charles? Maybe someone she worked with at Vereda?"

"You tell me. Do *you* know anyone by that name at your management agency?"

Aaron thought through the various employees at *Vereda Creative Management* or, "VCM" as it was known in the industry.

"I don't know every single employee, but I know most of them and a good seventy, seventy-five percent are women. And of the men, I'm pretty sure there's no one named Charles. I can find out, though."

"Would you do that?"

"Yeah, as soon as we get off the phone I'll call Viola in HR. In the meantime, you should think through all of your contacts, you know, social media friends—both yours and hers—and see if anyone turns up with that name."

"Yeah...yeah, that's a good idea. Can't believe I didn't think of it."

"Well, you've been a little preoccupied, brother."

"Ain't it the truth," Tom answered rhetorically. "Okay, I'm going to check that stuff out as soon as we hang up."

"Do that, and then let me know if you come up with anything."

"I will, I definitely will. And, Ivory?"

"Yeah?"

"Thanks for being you. You have no idea how much that means to me right now."

Aaron answered, "Aw, it ain't no 'thang, brother. You'd do the same thing—*have* done the same thing for me."

And with that, the call ended.

Tom Marshall sat staring at his reflection in the rear-view mirror and said out loud, "What the hell did you do, Helen?"

CHAPTER 4

When I came onto the deck about twenty minutes later, Aaron and Vanessa were still sitting there, basking in a late morning sun that seemed to be having trouble deciding whether to burn through the marine layer or not.

It was there.

It was gone.

It was there, gone and back again.

I know, first world problems.

"I talked to Tommy while you were on the phone with Gabi," Aaron said.

"And?"

"Well, it's a crazy thing that happened and…it's right down your alley. I think we should set up a meeting with him."

"When?"

"Today would be good."

I shook my head.

"I can't do today *or* tomorrow."

"Because…?"

"Because Gabi's coming over and I promised that I wouldn't get involved in anything new while she was here."

Vanessa sat up and clapped her hands rapidly.

"Oooh, Gabi. I just love her. I miss her."

"She misses you too, kiddo. I didn't tell her that you were down for the weekend, so we'll let it be a surprise for her."

"Sweet! When is she coming?" Vanessa asked.

"That sort of depends on when she can get herself together and I can find a flight."

Aaron said, "So, what do I tell Tommy?"

I thought through a few options. While so engaged, the doorbell rang and Vanessa ran to answer it and came back with Special Agent Bridgett Polk in tow.

"Look who's here," Vanessa announced cheerily.

The two girls had become fast friends during Bridgett's time with us. Partly because Bridgett was staying with Muriel and Eddie and shared a room with Vanessa when she came down on weekends, but also because they just seemed to click.

"'Morning, boss," Bridgett said.

"You don't have to call me boss," I complained for about the thousandth time.

"Okay, boss," she replied with a sassy smile. "What's on the agenda for today?"

Special Agent Bridgett Polk is a tall girl. Probably close to Muriel's five-eleven. And in addition to being smarter than just about everyone I know, including me, she is also tough as nails. According to Assistant Director Zack Hastings—my immediate supervisor at the FBI and close friend—she is "something special." Thus, her presence in our little organization.

Currently, she is about five weeks on the other side of taking a point-blank round in her chest from an AR-15 Bushmaster rifle. Had it not been for the discrete body armor she had on under her clothes, she would have been killed instantly. As it was, she suffered severe bruising of the heart muscle and a cracked sternum.

I said, "Aaron's bass player, Tommy Marshall, just lost his wife. And he has asked us to look into some suspicious elements of her death."

"Oh no. I'm so sorry to hear that, Aaron. Were you close to her as well?"

"I was," he replied. "Helen was part of my management team." Turning his attention back to me, he said, "So what I should tell Tommy about meeting up with him?"

"Well, why don't you go up to Dana Point, meet with him in person, you know, hear the whole story and then you can relate it to me and—"

"Hold it. Whether I talk to him and relay the info back to you, or you talk to him yourself, you're still gonna be involved."

"Not technically," I replied.

"Not technically? Then what do you call it?"

"Semantics," Vanessa answered with a wink.

"It's *not* just semantics," I argued.

Aaron asked, "How is it different?"

"Well, for one thing, *you're* the one talking to him, not me. And for another, I'm not," I added air quotes, "'getting into a case.' And lastly, you're staying under the same roof with me and will be talking to me anyway."

He smiled, shaking his head slowly.

"Damn, bruh. You good...you real good."

I returned his smile and said, "I've been told."

Bridgett rolled her eyes dramatically, saying, "Oh, man. That's a good one. Corny, but good."

"He says that all the time," Aaron explained. "It's kind of his version of that, 'that's what she said' thing that was going around a while back."

"Well, if Gabi's coming," Vanessa said around a long stretch. "Then I guess I should clean myself up, 'cuz I stink like a big dog."

"Wait...wait..." Aaron protested. "So, you saying that because Gabi's coming you're gonna clean up, but if she wasn't you'd just go ahead and rock the stink?"

She nodded vigorously.

"Yep! Pretty much."

"Isn't that a form of discrimination, or something?" he asked.

Vanessa leaned over, kissed Aaron's forehead and said, "Yep!" before bounding off for the bathroom.

As his eyes tracked her progress through the house he intoned, "That little girl is gonna be trouble."

"Already trouble, bro." I waited a beat before saying, "So, you'll go talk to Tommy?"

"Yeah. I mean I need to see the guy anyway. Doesn't much matter that Helen's stroke left her terminal. She's still gone, and *gone* hurts."

"Yeah, it does. So, just see if you can get the basics, and then if it sounds like something I could help out with maybe I can meet up with him sometime on Monday."

He had just started to answer when my phone rang.

It was Gabi.

"That was fast," I said as Aaron and Bridgett moved away to the other end of the deck to give me some privacy.

"Oh, I may not have been quite as nasty as I had first suspicioned."

"What a shock. So, when can you get to the airport? Southwest has flights leaving virtually every hour or so. Takes an hour and ten minutes to get here."

"So," she replied, "it's about ten-fifteen right now. Any idea when their next flight is?"

"As a matter of fact, I have their flight schedule right here." I opened my computer and pulled up the reservations page. "Looks like there's one at one-thirty that will get you in here at two-forty. Want to shoot for that?"

"Sure. I can do that."

"Okay, let me check the availability." I clicked around on the appropriate buttons and found that there was, indeed, space available. "We're in business, speaking of which, I'm going to upgrade you to business select so you can get in the A 1-15 boarding group."

"Is that important?"

I laughed.

"You haven't flown Southwest very much, have you?"

"I haven't flown Southwest at all. So, what's the deal?"

I said, "The deal is you sit anywhere you like, but it's on a first come, first serve basis. There are three boarding groups, A, B and C. The joke at Southwest is that 'C' stands for 'Center', as in, if you're in that group, you're going to most likely be stuck in a center seat with no bin space. But business select will get you in the very first group."

"Interesting," she replied. "I'll just bring a carryon so I can save some time. Now, should I eat before I leave or…"

"I was thinking of hitting that place we like down on the waterfront for a late lunch."

"Coasterra?"

"That's the one."

"Oooh. Sounds fun. Okay. Book it and I'll see you soon."

"Not soon enough."

After the call was done, Aaron said, "Be good to see Gabi. We all love her too, you know."

"Yeah, I know you do, and I appreciate it."

"Well, hell bro, how could anyone *not* love her? She's beautiful, funny, smarter than, basically, all of us put together…"

"And she smells good," Bridgett blurted out and then covered her mouth. "Oops. Sorry boss. Didn't mean to say that. But, it's true.

"Smelling good is definitely a plus," Aaron agreed. "And having had the pleasure of walking in her vapor trail on more than one occasion, I definitely agree."

"What does she wear, anyway?" Bridgett asked.

I said, "She swears it's just a combination of the soap and shampoo she uses, but I'm not sure I totally buy that."

Aaron suggested, "Could be she's just got some sort of natural fragrance going on,"

"Banho Citron Verbena," Vanessa hollered from the kitchen.

"What?" The three of us replied in unison.

She came out onto the deck, her hair still glistening from the shower.

"It's called Banho Citron Verbena."

"And, you know this because..." I prompted.

"Because the last time we were all at her condo she let me try it out when I showered. Amazing. That soap rocks."

Aaron and I stared at each other.

He said, "Who knew?"

Bridgett said, "I've heard of it, but never used it."

"It's not cheap," Vanessa added. "Pretty sure a bar is over twenty bucks, but *so* worth it."

"Well," I replied, "maybe to you. I have a different economy on the smelling good thing."

She raised her eyebrows questioningly.

"See, in my world a man shouldn't necessarily smell good. He just shouldn't smell."

Smiling widely, she said, "Yes. I am totally going to rock that the next time I'm around some of my hipster friends who are addicted to that god-awful body spray stuff they douse themselves with. That stuff should be outlawed. I mean you get within, like, ten feet and you can already smell it. Makes me sneeze."

Aaron leaned toward me and sniffed dramatically.

"Seem to me like you could use a little dousing, bruh. Just saying."

"Crap. I forgot that I have to take a shower before Gabi gets here."

"When's she coming, boss?" Bridgett asked.

"Her plane will be here around two-forty."

Vanessa said, "You've got plenty of time...if you start now."

That last part was added with a wink and a smile.

You should probably know that I am not known for, shall we say, rapid deployment in the mornings or any other time for that matter. There are some things that shouldn't be rushed. Like showers. Drought or no drought, I enjoy a long, hot shower. I'll save water someplace else. Just give me my shower.

I smiled at her joke and then said, "Seriously, Aaron, do a face-to-face with Tommy and see what you can learn."

"All right, man, I'm on it."

"And Vanessa, my darling?"

With a roll of her eyes she answered, "Okay. What is it?"

"Why does it have to be anything?"

"Because you *never* use that tone of voice unless you want something from me."

I could have protested, but she had me.

"All right, you win. So, do you think you and Bridgett could take my car to somewhere appropriate and get some flowers for Gabi on my behalf?"

The two wrinkled up their brows, and pretended to think it over.

"Let's see," Vanessa said. "Do I want to be handed the keys to your Range Rover and have it all to myself for a couple of hours?"

Bridgett added, "Gosh, boss, that's a tough one. We may need some time to think it over."

"You're hilarious," I said, handing Vanessa the keys and two one hundred-dollar bills.

"Two hundred bucks?"

"Get nice flowers."

"Okay. How much of this do you want back?" she asked.

"Just buy the flowers and you guys can get some lunch with whatever is left."

"Lunch? No way," they fist bumped, "we're getting some of that soap Gabi uses and pounding some Ramen. A girl's got to have priorities, you know."

CHAPTER 5

I walked into the bedroom and stood staring at the sparse selection of clothing that I had brought with me from Vegas. It was pathetic. Mainly shorts and tee shirts, with the occasional long-sleeved casual shirt and ripped pair of denim jeans thrown in to break up the monotony. Well, you work with what you've got, right? So, I pulled a white linen, long-sleeved shirt off a hanger and held it up to the light trying to determine whether it needed ironing. It didn't. I mean, hell, it's linen! What's the point of owning linen if you go ironing it every time you wear it? There was a grand total of two pair of denim jeans from which to choose, so I picked the one on the right. Not exactly rocket science, people. I suppose it's fair to say that I ascribe to the late Gilda Radner's school of fashion: *"I base most of my fashion taste on what doesn't itch."*

Amen.

I flipped on the light and entered the bathroom. Did I say, "bathroom?" I apologize. No standard bathroom, this. This was a full-on spa. I'll resist the urge to describe it in detail for fear it will render some so envious that their normally taciturn personalities would begin to manifest in crass materialism.

Or something.

I stared at my reflection and thought about shaving off my beard. Why? Well, let's just say that gray is not one of my favorite colors. At least on me. And my beard was definitely flecked with gray. It's not that I'm against aging, I just thought it would take a little longer than forty-four years. I mean come on. Forty-four and already dealing with gray? But, Gabi was quite fond of my beard—as long as I kept it, as she put it, "a decent length." Which, being interpreted, means that she likes the three or four-days worth of growth look and nothing more.

I decided to leave it for the time being and jumped into the shower.

Honesty compels me to admit that knowing Tommy had an issue, and that I could probably help him, made it nearly impossible to resist calling the man. For one thing, I like Tommy—always have. And for another, I'm good at what I do. No brag, just fact. What could it hurt? Just spend five minutes on the phone, hear what was on his mind, and then go get Gabi.

Simple.

That same pesky honest streak also compels me to admit that "simple" is a word basically foreign, not only to my vocabulary, but also to my experience. The bottom line is that there is no way I could do it without violating my promise to Gabi. And right now, it feels like that is something to which I need to direct my attention.

Michael had one of those ultra-showers with a rain forest spout on top that was nearly a full square yard in size, and jets spaced strategically and vertically up and down and all around the sides of the stall so that, should one choose to do so, one could be completely surrounded in a stinging deluge of water.

I chose.

It was amazing.

I reluctantly left the shower's liquid assault and dried my dripping self off, realizing that all of the old wounds and injuries were not only catching up, but overtaking me. Not that I planned on doing anything about it. I mean what could I do? Violence was part of my profession. Fortunately, and historically, I had been far better at dishing it out than others were in dispensing, thus my continued presence among the living.

But I've got to tell you, it's getting old.

Lord have mercy, it is getting *very* old.

My phone started buzzing.

It was Gabi.

"What are you doing?" she asked lightly.

"Well, at present I am standing buck-nekkid in front of the mirror and taking a stroll down memory lane courtesy of my many scars."

She made a low noise in her throat.

"What does that mean?" I asked.

"Oh, just imagining me standing there with you and being a, you know, tour guide."

"You have a very dirty mind for a Jewish girl."

"Haven't you heard? We're all incorrigible when it comes to such things."

"So, the chances of me corrupting you further are remote?"

"Oh," she said with a laugh, "I think that in the arena of, um, corruption there are always further depths to which one can plummet."

"Lucky me. So, is everything okay?"

She sighed.

"I'm so sorry, Jake, but I'm not going to be able to make it after all."

"Why?" I said forcefully.

Another sigh.

"In my excitement to come see you I totally forgot that I had promised our company CEO that I would help he and his wife throw a big party at their house tonight for some visiting, potential customers, and I just don't think I can bail on them in good conscience."

I remembered her mentioning the party a couple of weeks back.

"Is that the one for those Japanese investors?"

"That's the one."

"Yeah, from what you told me before, it's kind of a big deal."

"No kidding. In the world of venture capitalists—in which, as you know, my boss is a major player—this group from Japan is a real game changer. There are at least two other investment groups that *I* know of who are courting them on this trip to the States. If he can get them onboard, our company will easily triple their investment potential overnight."

"Wow. Well, okay then. I'm disappointed, but it sounds like you really need to be there."

A third sigh.

"You know, sometimes it just sucks to be so...so..."

"Proficient?" I suggested.

"Yes. If I were just your average administrative assistant I could get on that plane with impunity and come see my fella. But, nooooooo! I have to be me."

I laughed and said, "But it's the being you thing that makes the world a better place. At least my small corner thereof."

She put on a faux, and very thick Brooklyn accent.

"Ooooh, you're a smooth talker, you are."

"You sound just like Nana Laura."

Nana Laura was Gabi's grandmother who had been instrumental in her formative years in New York.

Gabi laughed. I loved that laugh and decided I wanted to hear it for the rest of my days.

"I know, right? And you haven't even heard her when she's had a couple glasses of wine."

"I'm looking forward to that. In fact, I've been planning to drive down to Coronado in the next day or two and pay her a visit."

"She will love that." She paused for a few seconds and then said, "You know, she told me just last week that it's a good thing she's the age she is or she'd give me a, 'run for my money', with you."

"And she'd probably have a good shot," I replied.

"Oh, I have no doubt. I wish you could have seen her back in the day."

"I have."

"What do you mean?"

"What I mean is...I can see her essence, her spirit alive in you."

I could hear her choke back a sob.

"Jake...that's...one of the most incredible things anyone has ever said to me. It's just so honoring."

"Well, she's a woman who deserves honor. And so are you."

A fourth sigh.

"Well, damn. Now I'm *really* sad that I'm not going to be able to come. Oh, Jake. How I love you."

"Even though I believe the fact has been well established at this point, I must hasten to say that I enjoy hearing you repeat it. And I love *you*, Gabriella Marcus. I had come to believe that I was incapable of feeling what I feel for you ever again, and yet, well...here we are."

"Here we are."

"Okay," I said, coughing to clear a pesky lump that was dead-set on forming in my throat. "Well, so, have a great time tonight. You're going to blow them away, sweetheart."

She giggled and said, "You know, that Humphrey Bogart impersonation thing you do is just awful, right?"

It was the only impersonation I could do and, awful or not, I rocked it, as they say, like a boss.

I turned it on full force.

"I'm sorry I had to slap you around last night, sweetheart, but when I said no more you got a little crazy."

She laughed loudly.

"You're so bad."

"I know. You bring it out in me."

"Okay. I've got to go," she said. "Call me later?"

"Count on it."

We ended the call. I turned and looked at my still dripping body reflected in the mirror.

Bogart said, "You lucky bastard."

My reflection agreed.

CHAPTER 6

I t was about eleven a.m. when I came back into the kitchen to give Aaron the news about Gabi. I found him out on the deck with Muriel and Eddie. Muriel said, "I hear Gabi is coming for a visit."

I shook my head and replied, "She was, but then remembered promising her boss and his wife that she'd help them host a party for a group of visiting Japanese investors."

"So, she's not coming?" Aaron asked.

"No, she isn't."

"Poo," Eddie said around a pout, "I was really looking forward to seeing her again."

"Me too," Muriel added.

"Couldn't be helped," I replied. "You two have a good run?"

They glanced at each other conspiratorially.

"Well," Muriel said, "let's put it like this, we had really good *intentions*."

"Ah-ha," I replied with a laugh. "You made it as far as the French bakery and took a detour."

Another glance between the two girls before Eddie replied, "I don't think we could technically call it a detour."

"Wait, so that was your destination all along?"

Muriel innocently batted her crazy green eyes.

"Is that wrong of us?"

Aaron said, "And while you two were shamelessly engaged in self-indulgent activity, did you think to bring sustenance for your starving menfolk?"

Eddie giggled, ran into the kitchen and came back with a box containing two chocolate croissants and a couple of cinnamon something or others for Vanessa and Bridgett who were, at present, still at the florist.

"Now *that's* what I'm talkin' about right there," Aaron exclaimed as he bit into the flaky, buttery wonder. "Oh, man. That is—"

"A mouth-gasm?" Muriel suggested.

"While I would never personally use a crass descriptive such as that, sometimes you just gotta go with what works. And, baby, that works."

I asked Aaron, "So, did you set something up with Tommy?"

"I did," Aaron replied around a mouthful of croissant. "He's gonna meet me here at two o'clock or so depending on traffic."

"Good. Now I can be in on the meeting."

Aaron slowly swallowed his bite before saying, "Tommy will be thrilled."

"Well," Muriel said, "we're out of here. Me and Eddie have places to go and stuff to do."

"What about lunch?" Aaron asked.

Muriel widened her eyes and stared.

"Lunch? Wasn't that you who just finished pounding that chocolate croissant in three bites?"

"So?"

"So, there is no way you're still hungry. I mean it's only, like...eleven-fifteen!"

"Now, listen here, little missy. I thought we had already covered this topic in the extensive and often exhaustive discussions regarding our relationship and had come to an understanding about burly men."

She smiled coyly, playing along.

"Remind me."

"Burly men—such as Jake and myself—in order to maintain our burly-ness have to consume quantities of food

TEARS IN A BOTTLE

that are somewhat...uh..."

He appealed to me for help.

"Uh..." I filled in, "somewhat more substantial..."

"Yeah, substantial than what normal non-burly men eat. It is at the core of our nature that we, well..."

I blurted, "Overeat regularly and prolifically."

"Yes, regularly and prolifically—really dude?—in order to maintain the glory that is ourselves. Does that make sense?"

Muriel said, "Eddie? Let's go before it gets any deeper in here."

We all laughed and as they started to leave, Eddie came back and threw her arms around my midsection.

"Hey, what's that for?" I asked.

With her face pressed against my chest, she replied, "For rescuing me and taking care of me. No one has ever cared before, Jake, and I want you to know how much it means to me."

Aaron rumbled, "You part of the family now, Little Bit, and in this family, we take care of our own. Ain't that right, Jake."

"Little Bit" was Aaron's nickname for Eddie—reflective of her diminutive stature.

"It is."

After the girls left I said, "So, about Tommy's predicament. Did you learn anything else?"

"No, because there's basically nothing to learn. I mean, dude, it's just the craziest thing. Imagine being married as long as those two and then with her dying breath, Helen throws down something like that."

I shook my head slowly, pondering just such a scenario.

"Do you think there's a possibility that the stroke, or the drugs they were administering had triggered some form of dementia? I'm asking because Abby's last days were anything but lucid."

"That's definitely something to ask him. But let's say that she *was* experiencing dementia on some level. That's still a very random thing."

I walked over to the railing and leaned against it, staring out to sea.

"I'm not sure I want to bring this up with Tommy just yet, but if we get involved, you know at some point we're going to have to investigate the possibility of her leading a double life."

Aaron grinned hugely.

"Bro, we already involved."

"I suppose we are. Technically, Tommy and Helen have been within our extended family circle."

Aaron stood and moved over to join me at the railing.

"I'm glad to hear you say that, Jake. Family's important."

"Yes, it is. And like you told Eddie, we take care of our own."

"Damn straight!"

After a few moments silence I said, "I'm thinking Harbor Fish for lunch. You in?"

"Man," he replied, drawing out the word. "Am I in? Who you think you talkin' to?"

I laughed and pulled out my phone to call Vanessa and tell her the flowers were no longer required.

She answered on the second ring.

"Hey," she said. "I was just about to call you. What kind of flowers are you looking for? Because there are a lot of options."

"Well, as it turns out, Gabi isn't coming after all."

"She's not?" I could hear the disappointment in her voice.

"No. It's a work thing she couldn't get out of."

"Okay. Since I'm already here, I'm thinking about getting some flowers anyway, you know, to brighten up the house a little."

"That'd be great."

"What are you and Aaron up to?"

"Tommy is coming over around two to brief us on his predicament, but we're going to lunch first."

"Lunch? Where?"

"Harbor Fish on Carlsbad Blvd."

She said, "We'll meet you there. Who needs flowers anyway?"

It made me laugh.

"Okay, see you in a few minutes."

Aaron inquired, "They joining us for lunch?"

"Yeah. Apparently matters concerning hunger trump matters concerning floral feng shui."

"Heard that."

CHAPTER 7

In Portland, Oregon the man with three names and no past sat in a corporately owned coffee shop in the downtown Pearl District. He sipped a dark roast coffee and stared through the windows onto the frenetic pedestrian traffic—young, hip, busy people, all with important things to do and important places to go; lives unsoiled by the sorrow presently washing over his soul like a flume of toxic waste.

Another stray tear eased over the rim of his eyes before freefalling down the surface of his skin and ultimately getting lost within the abundance of his thick, curly beard. How he hated the heinous, red thing. But it was necessary, or so his handlers had told him.

To his immediate family he was Brandon Crawford, "Bran" for short. To those who had set him up in the Witness Security Program, commonly known as WITSEC, he was Wallace Bennington. But to Helen Marshall, he had been, by mutual agreement, Charles Sutton.

Helen.

He couldn't believe she was gone...and with her, the secret. Or was it? Had she said anything before dying? Did her good-guy husband know, or was he just as clueless as he'd always been. And what must that feel like—to be a good guy? He had never known, did not know presently nor was it likely to happen in the foreseeable future. And even though he had done a good thing, *one* good thing, it could never rise to the level of sufficiency to erase the pollution of his past.

"You mind if I sit here?" came a softly voiced query from a young woman with trendy glasses, a black, knit beret and black hoodie.

He stared at her without reply for a good ten seconds.

"I could sit somewhere else, I suppose," she finally said, anticipating a negative answer from him. "It's just that I love looking out the window when I write."

"Oh, no problem. Sure, go ahead. I'm not going to be here much longer anyway," he replied hastily not wishing to cause a scene. *"Never cause a scene,"* his handlers had told him the month before during his initial briefing. That was followed with, *"Never do anything to draw attention to yourself because you never know who might be watching."*

The young woman nodded her thanks and offloaded a bulging backpack onto the narrow ledge of the counter running the length of the window.

"I'm Libby, by the way," she said offhandedly while continuing to settle in for a long haul, or so it appeared to him.

"Uh, nice to meet you, uh, Libby. I'm..." Who? Who was he? He actually didn't know anymore. "I'm Char...uh, Wallace."

"Char-Wallace?" she replied with a laugh. "That's a funny name."

"No. No. Wallace. Just Wallace." He laughed nervously. "Sometimes my tongue doesn't follow my brain very well."

She stopped what she was doing and stared at him directly.

"You know, I know exactly what you mean. It happens to me all the time."

"It does?"

"Yes. In fact, when I was placing my order I couldn't decide between a mocha Frappuccino and a chai latte and it came out something like 'I'll have a frappe-latte please.' Embarrassing."

That made him laugh.

It had been a while.

"Okay, well," he said, "it's good to know that I'm not alone in my affliction."

She sat on the stool and stared at him again—an experience he found to be most unnerving.

Probably something about her eyes. They were light blue almost to the point of being gray and when she looked at him her gaze was unwavering. Add the fact that she was disturbingly pretty—bearing a striking resemblance to the Hollywood actress, Scarlett Johansson—and the effect was profoundly unsettling.

"So, tell me something, Char-Wallace," she said jokingly. "Why are you sitting here at one p.m. on a Saturday just staring out at the people passing by?"

Her directness provoked an involuntary cackle of nervous laughter.

"What am I, well, you know I...I'm...say, isn't that kind of a direct question from someone I only met, what, two minutes ago?"

Libby shrugged her shoulders.

"Maybe, but I don't believe in beating around the bush. I always go after what I want."

He sat up straighter and leaned back slightly.

"What does that mean?"

"Well, it means that I spotted you sitting here when I was standing in line." She smiled. "You probably thought that this was random, right—me asking if I could sit here? Well, it wasn't. I *wanted* to sit by you."

"By me? What on earth for? I'm like...twenty years older than you and—"

"And what? What difference does age make when people are attracted to each other? I mean you're attracted to me, right?"

"Attracted to...I'm...you seem like a nice young lady and all, but—"

"So, why are you sitting here, Char-Wallace?"

By this point he was so completely flummoxed, he had forgotten all about Helen's death and the inescapable quandary into which he had been flung headlong.

"You okay?" Libby said lightly as she removed the beret, shaking loose one of the most luxurious manes of auburn hair he had ever seen.

For the first time it occurred to him that he was being played, something his handlers had also warned him about.

"Listen, Libby? Was that your name? It's been nice chatting with you—surreal, but nice, to quote one of my favorite movies—but I have to be going."

Her eyes widened as her mouth formed a perfect "O" of surprise.

"You can't go yet, you just can't," she said quickly. "I haven't even had a chance to talk to you, which, if I'm being truthful, is why I came over."

"To talk?"

Arranging her lovely backside onto the stool, she answered, "Well, yes. You see, I'm a writer and writers need characters and you, if you don't mind me saying, have 'character' written all over you. As in, there sits a real character."

"And you can tell this, because...?" he prompted, growing less nervous by the second.

"Because it's, well...you just look like a character, okay? Someone I'd like to get to know."

He smiled slyly and said, "So you aren't trying to pick me up?"

She laughed brightly.

"Do you *want* to be picked up, Char-Wallace?"

He joined her laughter.

"I didn't think I did."

"And now?"

"Now, I'm not so sure."

"So, you're telling me there's a chance?"

"Ah, another one of my favorite movies."

She frowned in confusion.

"Dumb and Dumber," he explained. "You know, Jim Carrey? He said that line in the movie."

"A little before my time, I'm afraid."

"What?" he exclaimed. "It was only 1994."

"Yeah, well," she replied, "I would've been four years old. Not exactly going to movies yet."

"So, you're, what, twenty-four?"

"Yep. As of last Wednesday, actually."

She did the direct staring thing again, which he found preposterously off-putting.

"I'll give you this, Libby," he said, "you are quite bold."

"I've heard that before."

"I'm not surprised."

She dropped her head, shaking it slowly and replied, "What's the point of being shy? Shy people don't get anywhere in this world."

"And you think being bold does?"

She grinned.

"I'm talking to you, aren't I?"

"Yes...yes you are," he said around a chuckle. "I still haven't figured out your angle."

"My angle?"

"Yeah, your angle. Everyone's got one; you know, something of an advantage you're trying to gain on another person."

"Oh, I see. You're one of those conspiracy theorists, huh?"

"I don't know if I'd go *that* far, but, okay. I do tend to see subterfuge in a lot of situations."

"And why is that?" she asked.

He was silent while he pondered the question before answering, "I've worked with numbers my whole life—you know, accountant type—and I've seen people do things with money that are unbelievable."

"Like what?"

It was his turn to stare.

Finally, with eyes as cold as stone he replied, "Like Dr. Frankland said to Sherlock Holmes, 'I would love to tell you, but then, of course, I'd have to kill you.'"

CHAPTER 8

We had just gotten back from lunch and were putting away a few groceries we had picked up on the way home when the doorbell rang announcing Tommy's arrival.

"I'll get it," Aaron hollered as he hustled toward the door.

I heard the door open followed by muffled sounds of sobbing—both Aaron and Tommy's.

Aaron came back into the kitchen with his arm around Tommy's shoulders.

"Jake? I didn't think you were going to be here," Tommy said in his deep, Tennessee drawl.

I walked toward him and put my arms around him.

"I'm so sorry, my friend. I know all too well what you're feeling."

He stepped back, nodding his head and wiping tears away with the sleeve of his shirt.

"Yeah, I know you do, brother, and I appreciate the compassion more than you'll ever know."

Vanessa came into the kitchen from the powder room.

"Hi," she said softly. "I'm Vanessa. I'm so sorry for your loss, sir."

"Thank-you. I remember seeing you at Cassie and Mike's wedding."

"Yes, I was there. It's too bad Aaron didn't introduce us," she teased.

"Hey. I was a little pre-occupied," Aaron said in his

defense.

I gestured toward Bridgett.

"Tommy, this is Special Agent Bridgett Polk. She's with the FBI and is working with me for a while."

"Pleased to meet you, sir. And I am so sorry to hear of your loss."

"Thank you," he replied. "FBI, huh? You gonna help us out?"

"Well, from what I hear, Jake is going to help you out, and I'm here to help him."

"So, why you here, Jake?" Tommy asked.

"The simple answer is that my plans changed, so let's just go with that. Why don't we grab some beers and go sit out on the deck? You can tell us your story."

"That sounds good, but you got anything stronger than beer?"

"Do we have anything stronger than beer?" Aaron repeated rhetorically as he walked toward one of the more sophisticated home bars you will ever see. "What'd you have in mind, bro?"

Tommy said, "Got any Jameson?"

"Sure do."

"Good. Make it a double."

"Jake?"

"Oh, the usual."

Tommy chuckled.

"You still drinking that vodka and wine thing, Jake?"

"The 'winetini'? Yes, I am, at least when I'm not downing Long Island's."

He shook his head.

"Don't know how you stand it, but, you know, to each his own."

Since Bridgett and Vanessa offered to stay behind and bring the drinks out when they were ready, I led Tommy out onto the deck and got him settled in one of the overstuffed rattan chairs, sitting down directly across from him.

"Mike's done all right for himself," he stated without rancor or envy as he took in the scope of Michael's home. "The boy has sure done all right."

"Yes, especially given what he's had to deal with over the past year."

The freak automobile accident I referred to earlier had happened eight months ago at the culmination of our conflict with the late Paul Morgan. Aaron had been driving my Range Rover with Muriel in the front and Michael in the right rear passenger seat. A drunk driver traveling at a high rate of speed had t-boned them in an intersection, totaling my car and killing the drunk driver instantly. Aaron's injuries, while painful, had been largely superficial; Muriel, as mentioned, had a titanium rod in her leg; but Michael, due to where he was sitting, had taken the full force of the collision leaving him a paraplegic. Even though his six-foot-seven height has been reduced considerably, his heart makes him one of the largest people I have ever known.

"Yeah, that was straight up brutal. How's he doing anyway?" Tommy asked.

"Well," I said, "to say that recovery has been challenging would be a laughable understatement. Having to face life confined to a wheelchair is bad enough, but he also sustained severe nerve damage to his right hand. And when you're a novelist, you kinda need your hands to do your job."

"But from what Aaron has told me, he's overcome all of that," Tommy replied.

"Yes, he has. He even wrote a novel in record time just to prove that he could still write. *And*...he's most of the way through another."

Vanessa and Bridgett came onto the deck carrying the drinks.

After they passed them out and we were all seated, I said, "Why don't you tell us exactly what transpired toward the end, Tommy? I know it's painful, but if we're going to help you, we need to know everything."

He took a long pull on his double shot of Jameson and began, "Well, as you know, Helen spent the last ten days of her life in a hospice facility. We discussed having in-home care, but her doctor felt that because of the severity of the stroke she would be more comfortable in hospice." He paused to take another drink before continuing, "Yeah, that day, you know, the day when she had the stroke...that was a bad day. One minute we were talking about a trip we, uh, had been planning to the east coast...and then...she was just gone. Staring at me; helplessness in her eyes; trying to speak, but no words would come; trying to move, but paralyzed. And then..."

He drained his glass and held it out toward Vanessa hopefully, saying, "If you don't mind?"

Vanessa took it from his grasp and hurried off toward the kitchen.

"I'm usually not a big drinker," he explained sheepishly.

I said, "Don't worry about it, Tommy. Trust me, I get it."

"Anyway, I was trying to help her get up, and," His eyes teared up, darting back and forth between Aaron, Bridgett and me before he continued, "It was just so sudden. I didn't really comprehend in that moment what had happened. But, I will never forget the look in her eyes."

Vanessa came back with Tommy's drink and handed it to him.

"Thank-you," he said and immediately took a sip. "Basically, I had to ease her back into the chair and listen to her cry and moan until the transport arrived. It was... well, I suppose out of all the terrible things we had to go through during her illness, that was the worst—you know, just watching her be in that much confusion and not be able to do a single, solitary thing that would help."

Vanessa was seated next to Tommy and reached across the divide to grasp his hand. She didn't say anything. She just sat quietly and held his hand.

He continued, "So, after they did everything they could for her in the hospital, they came and took my girl to hospice. I have to say that prior to this experience, I was fairly ignorant of what went on in those facilities. I mean I had heard of hospice, but I didn't understand that after a certain point, your loved one is basically lost to you."

"Why is that, Tommy?" Vanessa asked.

"Give me a minute," he said and took another sip of Jameson. "Even before she was transported, Helen was basically immobile and unable to communicate on any level. So, once the hospice staff took over, they began looking for non-verbal signs of pain. Things like changes in breathing, agitation; changes in all sorts of stuff they monitor. At that point, they gave her what they called palliative doses of medication. Strong stuff, Vanessa. It can almost take a person right into a coma. Not too long after that, Helen entered what they called imminent death protocol, and they stopped feeding her or even giving her any water."

"Why?" she exclaimed. "Isn't that just, I don't know, cruel?"

"It seemed that way to me. It *sure* seemed that way to me. I even had a big fight with the administrator over it. But she and the doctor explained to me that following a stroke on the level of what Helen had suffered, the body's organs begin shutting down and the ingestion of food or water would actually increase her suffering. I understood that intellectually, I guess you could say, but it was torture."

He raised the glass toward his lips, his hand trembling noticeably; stared down at the amber liquid; seemed to think better of it and sat the glass on the side table.

"So," I said, "how long from the time she was admitted to hospice and the onset of the comatose state?"

"Well, she started going out for long stretches almost immediately—you know, times where she would sleep for ten or twelve hours. Then she would wake up and say a few mumbled words." He stopped and sobbed. "She, uh...a couple of those times she...begged me for water." He let his head fall back against the chair's cushion, staring at the sky. "It was so hard. I guess she was basically gone for good about three days into the stay. But I kept talking to her because the hospice doctor said that I should always act as if she was aware of what was going on."

"Yeah," Aaron said. "I remember you telling me that hearing is the last, or one of the last, senses to go."

Tommy nodded his head.

"That's true. And there are some other things related to, well, the dying process that make what happened at the end even more confusing."

"Can you tell us about that?" I asked.

He picked up the glass of Jameson and drained half of it.

"Another thing the doctor stressed—and I witnessed this first hand—is that during the dying process it's very common for people to, I don't know, I suppose a good way to put it is that they confuse reality. I remember Helen raising her head at one point and asking me why I was crying. I wasn't crying. At least not then. But she insisted that I was and I realized that she had been hearing the wind blowing outside. That same day, she looked at me with the strangest expression and said, 'Now, I know most of these nurses who take care of me...but who are you?'

"Another time she looked over toward the lounge chair in the corner, you know, the kind you can sleep in if necessary? There was a floor lamp right next to it and she asked me who was standing over by the chair. I told her no one was there; that it was just a floor lamp, but she wouldn't hear of it. Actually, got very upset with me because I wouldn't tell her who was visiting—accused me of trying to hide something from her."

"So, she was hallucinating?" Bridgett asked.

"Basically, yeah. At one point she even started arguing

with someone and I was the only other person in the room."

I said, "Do you remember anything about that?"

His eyes widened and he replied, "Damn! I do. She was arguing with Charles."

CHAPTER 9

Aaron glanced at me before saying, "And Charles is the name she called you by right before she died, right?"

"Yeah, it was."

I said, "And you're certain that you heard her correctly—that 'Charles' is what she called you?"

"Like I said, most of what she said came out pretty funky—you know, garbled and indistinct—but not this. This was crystal clear. Like I was telling Aaron on the phone, she had been out for two days. Eyes closed; just breathing, no response at all. I was sitting in my usual spot by her bed when I noticed her eyes open and staring at me. So, I hurried over to her side thinking that there was something she wanted to say. Well, there was, only she wasn't talking to me. She was talking to Charles. She said, *'Charles, I had to move the key. You know where it is. Go get it. For God's sake, get it or all will be lost.'* And then she stopped breathing."

We were all silent for a few seconds, just letting that sink in.

"And you're saying that the time previously when it seemed like she was arguing with someone you couldn't see, Charles was the name she was using?" I asked.

"Yeah, I had totally forgotten about that until just now."

"But, you don't know anyone named Charles?"

"No. And since talking to Aaron earlier, I've been wracking my brain trying to come up with someone in our extended circle of friends named Charles, or Charlie and there's no one."

"Okay," I said. "What do you remember about that other incident?"

He removed his hand from Vanessa's with a grateful nod and scratched his chin.

"I'm not sure if any of it will make sense."

"Just try to recall as much as you can," I encouraged.

"Well, as was usually the case, I was sitting by her bed reading one of her favorite books out loud to her. I had probably been reading for fifteen or twenty minutes, when suddenly she started mumbling. Her eyes were closed, but she was definitely talking, so I stood and leaned as close to her face as possible and asked her what she had said. It was like I wasn't there, because she busts out with something like, *'No...no! That won't work, Charles, and you know it won't work,'* like she was having a conversation with someone. I asked her what she meant, but she just said, *'I know you believe in what you're doing, but it's going to hurt a lot of people,'* or something along those lines."

After a few moments of silence, Bridgett asked, "Do you think Charles is a real person, or was this whole thing just a hallucination?"

"That's exactly what I was wondering," I added.

"That's just it," Tommy said. "I have no way of knowing, which is what's been driving me crazy."

I waited for a couple of seconds before saying, "I hate to ask this, Tommy, but it has to be cleared up. Is there any possibility that Helen could have been having an affair? Anything you noticed over, say, the past couple years? Money missing that you couldn't explain; trips she took that seemed out of the ordinary; nights where she stayed late at work; phone calls she would leave the room to answer...things like that?"

He closed his eyes, shaking his head slowly.

"Jake, I...I don't know. I just don't know. I mean, hell,

Aaron plays over a hundred dates a year on average. Add in travel time and such, I'm gone half the year. So, if she had wanted to carry on an affair, there would have been plenty of opportunities where I was gone, sometimes for two or three weeks at a time."

"How about money?"

"Early on in our marriage we decided to keep three accounts. One for the money she made, one for the money I made and a household account that we both contributed to."

I said, "So, she had money in a separate account that you didn't see?"

"Basically. And I had the same thing. Probably not an ideal situation, now that I think about it. But it worked for us."

Aaron asked, "How about phone calls, Low? Did you ever observe anything like what Jake was describing?"

"You mean where her phone would ring and she'd leave the room?"

"Yeah, like that."

He stared upward as if trying to summon a memory.

With a humorless laugh he replied, "It's amazing the things that you just don't pay any heed to when they're happening. But...man! This is just crazy! I'm just now remembering several times—and I'm sure there were more—when we'd be together and her phone would buzz. She'd glance at the screen and say something like, *Looks like things are going sideways at the office again. I need to go put out some fires,'* and then get up and leave the room and be gone for, I don't know, sometimes close to half an hour."

"Did you ever overhear any of those conversations?" I asked.

He screwed his face up in concentration.

"Yeah, I did. What was it...she had gone into the bedroom to talk and I popped in on her after about ten minutes because I needed something out of the closet. I remember the look in her eyes when I came into the room. At the time I didn't think anything of it—actually just wrote it off to me startling her. But as I'm thinking of it right now, it was a look of fear. You know, like fear that I had heard what she had been saying."

"And what had she been saying?"

"Damn," he said softly, drawing the word out, his eyes wide in disbelief. "I heard her say the name *Charles*."

Bridgett asked, "Do you recall the context, sir?"

Tommy shook his head slowly and said, "This was a couple of years ago so..." He closed his eyes for a couple of seconds before continuing, "This isn't anywhere close to exact, but I'm pretty sure it was something like, '*No, Charles! He can never...*' and then she stopped speaking when she saw me."

"Anything else?" Aaron prompted.

"No. And I didn't ask because I thought she was dealing with something at the office. Even her using Charles' name wasn't weird at all because, as you know, Aaron, she dealt with hundreds of random people on a regular basis—men *and* women."

As Aaron nodded his agreement, I said, "Listen, Tommy, the way this works is, I look at the evidence in front of me, beside me and behind me. And I do it without emotion. Facts are facts. As you've been talking a clear fact has begun to emerge. I need to see her phone, Tommy."

He looked startled.

"Why?"

"I need to search through all the incoming and outgoing texts and calls."

"You can do that?"

"FBI, bruh," Aaron said with a grin.

"Oh, yeah. Of course. Sure. I don't have it with me but —"

"Do you mind if Aaron and I follow you home so we can get it?"

TEARS IN A BOTTLE

He stared at me in silence for a few beats before replying, "I think I need to know where you're going with this, Jake."

I took in a long breath and blew it out slowly.

"The way I see it, there are only two possibilities. Number one, *Charles* is, was, a figment of Helen's imagination—a hallucination—driven by the severity of the stroke and the intensity of the medication she was receiving. In which case we should just let it die with her. Number two, he is a real person who was involved with Helen on a level she didn't feel comfortable having you know about. Add the fact that you overheard her apparently talking to this man on the phone and it lends tremendous credence to number two. And since Helen used, literally, her last breath to issue a warning—cryptic though it may be—to this individual makes this something that cannot die with her. It *has* to be investigated."

Tommy looked helplessly at Aaron and then at me.

"What the hell is going on here, Jake?"

"I don't know, Tommy, but with your permission, I'd like to make a serious effort to find out."

He sat without speaking for several seconds, just staring out to sea. Not moving. Barely breathing. Eyes fixed far beyond the blue horizon that had finally made an appearance by virtue of a reluctantly dissipating fog bank.

"Okay," he said finally. "I'm not sure how I'm gonna pay you, but—"

"This one's on me," I replied, interrupting his equivocation.

"And me," Aaron added.

Vanessa reached over and squeezed his arm.

"Me too, Tommy."

He reached down and patted her hand, his head nodding slowly as tears began to form in his eyes.

"I...don't know what to say."

"No need to say anything, Low," Aaron said softly.

"You family."

Wiping away the tears he replied, "That's good, because I got this feelin' that I'm gonna be needin' me some of that before all this is over."

CHAPTER 10

After establishing a loose timeline for getting together again, Tommy stood to go. Hugs were exchanged all around and as Aaron was leading him toward the door I started thinking about how utterly bizarre the whole thing was. I mean who does that? What loving wife, with their dying breath, calls another man's name and issues a cryptic message—a message that hints at an illicit affair? Helen Marshall? One of the kindest, sweetest, most loving and caring women I had ever met? Someone who, by all outward appearances anyway, was consummately in love with her husband?

On the other hand, how well had I actually known her? For that matter, how well did I know Tommy? The answer was, I knew all that I had been allowed to know. Given my relationship with Aaron, I had met and interacted with both of them numerous times over the years. And I liked them both. If you want to know the truth, I liked them a lot. Tommy tended to be more reserved—sedate, one might even say. Aaron said that it was the nature of bass players given the amount of concentration required to be the band's timekeeper. Since Tommy was the only bass player I had ever known on more than a cursory level, I had no basis for comparison. But I trusted Aaron's judgment.

Tommy was intelligent, articulate, literate and self-effacing even though in his own right he was one of the most respected practitioners of his craft in all of jazz. If you wanted to "go deep," as Aaron was fond of saying, Tommy was your guy. Sitting down with Tommy around a fire pit, with a fine cigar and glass of cognac firmly in hand, was a recipe for reasoned discourse, typically on topics regarding the devolution of the species, the death of journalism, corruption of political systems or similar, weighty matters. But it was an interaction reserved only for a select few and I was fortunate to count myself among that august assemblage.

Helen, on the other hand, was an extrovert. Not in the classic life-of-the-party-I-have-to-be-the-center-of-attention way. She was simply engaging. Irresistibly so. She drew you into the conversation, because when you were in her presence, you knew that you had all of her.

No distractions.

No looking over your shoulder to see who else was available to talk to.

No checking her phone in mid-sentence.

No body language to suggest that she was growing weary of the conversation.

None of that.

When she spoke with you, it was one-on-one, eyeball-to-eyeball; a stare so direct that it almost made you uncomfortable, as if she were peering into your soul.

But it wasn't flirtatious. Not even remotely. Her kind face, understated in its elegant beauty, would, at times, reflect such compassion for what you shared that it made you wonder if you shouldn't offer a fee at the conclusion of the colloquy. There was a reason why she was called "St. Helen" at Aaron's management agency.

And now, she was gone, leaving behind a potentially libelous legacy.

I walked through the house, hollered that I was going for a drive and got into my new Range Rover—a replacement for the one tragically ruined in the wreck eight months ago.

I didn't really know where I was going, just that I had to go. It happens to me infrequently, this need to drive, but when it does, it's very strong.

Like now.

I headed south on PCH—that's Pacific Coast Highway for those of you unfamiliar with coastal California—thinking that a leisurely drive along the shoreline would be mindless enough that I could direct energy toward thinking instead of driving. I got as far as Cardiff before I realized the folly of that line of reasoning. In short, the traffic was at a standstill due to a massive accident on I-5 southbound that had people exiting off the freeway at Birmingham Avenue hoping for an easier time of it along the coast. Apparently, for anyone going south you had to have an abundance of patience and/or time. It was one out of two for me. I had the time. I just didn't have the patience.

At least not today.

Okay, not on *any* day.

If you want to know the truth, patience has never been one of my strong points.

So, I rode out the traffic jam as far as Solana Beach and pulled off into the Cedros Avenue Design District, one of my favorite places to hang in San Diego County.

Cedros Avenue is home to the legendary Belly-Up Tavern, a six-hundred seat, intimate concert venue where I had seen some pretty amazing artists over the years, including Red Hot Chili Peppers, John Mayer, a very young—and largely unknown at the time—Sheryl Crow, and Joe Walsh, to name a few. It remained my absolute favorite place on the planet for live music. Aside from that, though, Cedros is just a very pleasant place to while away a few hours.

I parked my car in front of a design store specializing in rare woods and antiquities and just started walking. Luckily, pedestrian traffic was light so I had the sidewalks largely to myself.

My phone started vibrating and playing, "She," the theme song from the movie, *Notting Hill.*

It was Cassie.

"Hey, little girl."

"Hey yourself, Uncle. What are you doing?"

"Oh, just walking down Cedros Avenue in Solana Beach."

"Ohhhhh, I'm so jealous," she said with conviction. "You know I love it there."

"Well, when you get back, we'll drive down and go to that antique store you like so much."

"That would be awesome."

"This is most likely a rhetorical question, but are you enjoying St. Augustine?"

"Oh, you know, as much as one can enjoy pristine beaches, perfect weather and tons of history."

I laughed and asked, "So, when are you guys going to be back?"

"Well," she replied, drawing the word out. "That's one of the reasons I'm calling."

I didn't like the tone of her voice, so I asked, "Okay, let's have it. What's going on?"

"It's Michael. He's..." Her voice caught. "Well, I don't think he's doing all that great."

I said, "Why? Something physical? Emotional? What?"

She sighed deeply and replied, "I don't think he's being honest with me about the way he's feeling."

"Okay, can you elaborate on that a bit?"

"I'll try. He's losing weight. And it's not like he had all that much left to lose after his surgery, rehab and then jumping right in to writing that novel—a novel that I now hate with all my soul."

"Why? It's a best-seller."

"Because of what it cost him to do it."

I said, "I know what you mean. He hit it pretty hard."

"You have no idea. And keep in mind that while *that* was going on he had to recover from his injuries and learn how to be a paraplegic—basically be a completely different person than he was before the wreck."

"How is he doing emotionally?"

"You mean, is he depressed?"

"Yes."

She was silent for a few seconds before replying, "He is, but it's more than that. It's the unguarded moments when he thinks I'm not looking at him and I catch him just sitting and staring. I think you'd call it a thousand-yard stare or something like that. And other times the expression on his face is like…like…oh, I don't know. It's like he's fighting something internally—pain, or something—and not telling me about it. It makes me wonder if he's healed properly, or has developed an infection; maybe even blood clots. They warned us about that possibility, you know."

I said, "Yeah, I do know. So, what are you going to do?"

Another sigh.

"We are kind of open-ended here with the vacation rental house and travel arrangements, so we can come home any time we want." She paused for a couple of seconds and then said, "I think I'm going to see if I can get him to go back early and see his doctor."

"Well, if he's as bad off as you are describing, that's probably a good idea."

"Oh, he is. I was actually sugar-coating it quite a bit."

"Wow, Cass. Do you need me to do anything?"

And more sighing.

"Just be prepared to back me up if necessary."

"And knowing Michael as I do, it will probably be necessary."

I heard her sob softly and imagined her wiping away tears. It broke my heart.

"Uncle, I'm scared for him. I think this is way, way serious and I don't know what to do."

"Listen, for now, just get him on a plane, get him home and let's get him examined. It's pointless to torture yourself with a bunch of what-ifs when nothing is known for sure. If I need to talk to him, or even fly out there and accompany you guys home, let me know and I'll be on the first flight out."

She sobbed a little more and then said, "Knowing that you always have my back makes me feel so loved."

"Well, you are and always have been."

"I love you, Uncle."

"Love you more."

Suddenly I didn't feel like walking any more. What I *did* feel like doing was calling Aaron, apologizing profusely and telling him that I wouldn't be able to help Tommy with his conundrum after all; that I was leaving immediately on the next plane for St. Augustine, Florida to help my niece with whatever she required of me.

That's what I wanted to do.

But I didn't, because as much as my heart compelled me to rush to Cassie's aid, it wasn't completely clear what was even going on with Michael. Maybe he was just going through a rough patch. Hell, I've been through many recovery and rehab programs due to injury and had plenty of bad days, depressing days, days when I didn't think I would survive. Besides, the last thing in the world Mr. and Mrs. Michael Harvey needed was a meddling uncle charging into something that may not require outside assistance. It was something I was going to have to learn moving forward.

On the other hand, *quite* clear was the fact that Helen Marshall had been keeping secrets from her husband. And I needed to find out what they were.

Quickly.

CHAPTER 11

The man Helen Marshall had known as Charles stared at Libby as if attempting to determine what to do next. Was she merely a distraction, or a complication? Only one way to find out.

She was still laughing at his Sherlock Holmes joke and said, "No, seriously, what kind of things have you seen people do with money? I mean are we talking embezzling here? Hiding money from the mob? The government? Stealing it from family members? What?"

He had already said too much. Why did he do it? Why had he even mentioned that he'd been an accountant, especially when his handlers had specifically forbidden him to ever mention that part of his past to anyone? And especially not to a funky, pretty, twenty-four-year-old hipster girl he'd known for all of fifteen minutes.

"Look, I kinda wasn't kidding about the having to kill you thing. I should never have told you about my past— about *anything* from my past."

"Why?" she asked, her inquisitive eyes widening. "Are you a secret agent or something? Oh, wait, I know. You're in witness protection."

At the mention of the term, his heart constricted in his chest and he nearly fell off the stool. He caught himself and glanced quickly around the room to see if there was anyone paying too much attention to the two of them.

It appeared to be all clear.

"Holy cow," she exclaimed. "Are you okay?"

"Why did you ask me that?" he said, piercing her with a fierce gaze.

"Which part?"

"The part about being in witness protection." He forced a laugh while trying to regain his composure. "No one is really in that, right? It's all made up, isn't it?"

"I don't know, Char-Wallace. From what I hear there are more people than we would ever realize." She glanced around the room. "In fact, I bet there are people right in this room who are living entirely new lives thanks to Uncle Sam."

This had now officially blundered into the realm of too close for comfort.

How did she know?

Had he given himself away, or was she merely a bright, intuitive girl who had an inordinately quick and active intellect?

"So, you're a writer, huh?" he asked hoping to change the subject.

"Uh, yeah, I am," she replied, turning her attention back to him. "I guess I should say that I am an aspiring writer. Haven't had anything published, but I do have a manuscript that is nearly finished."

"Fiction?" he queried.

She nodded her head slowly while taking a long sip of her drink.

"Yeah. I really enjoy writing about things that happened in the sixties."

"I've always heard that you should write about what you know. How could you possibly know anything about the sixties?"

"Helloooooo," she replied, holding up her phone. "Internet. You can literally find anything about anything on there. In fact, every single bit of research I did for this novel was done through Google and Wikipedia."

"Wow. Reliable," he teased.

"Okay. I know, I know. You can't believe everything you read."

"So, what's the novel about?"

She scooted around on the stool so she was facing him.

"Well, see, it's about this girl who hitchhikes across the US from Maine to California so she can be a part of that whole Haight-Ashbury thing that was going on in San Francisco in the late sixties."

"Ah, yes, the summer of love. Sex, drugs and rock 'n roll."

"Hey, don't knock it if you haven't tried it."

He was silent while he took a long drink of coffee and then said, "Yeah, well, I tried just about everything there was to try when I was younger."

"And?" she prompted.

He burst out laughing, "It was great! I loved every minute of it."

"Every minute of what? The sex? The drugs? The rock?"

"All of it. I wasn't there at Haight-Ashbury, of course. That was about ten years before my time. But when I got to Stanford to do my MBA—"

"You went to Stanford? So did I."

"No kidding? That is unbelievably random."

"Right? So, you were saying?"

"Yeah, so, when I got to Stanford things were still pretty happening."

She leaned in close and whispered, "I bet you were wild when you were younger. You just look like you were a wild one."

He laughed.

"Well, I had my moments."

"So, tell me, Char-Wallace, what's a wild man like you doing in accounting. It doesn't suit you."

He stared out the window shaking his head slowly, not believing where the conversation had gone.

"Yeah, about that. Forget that I ever said anything about being an accountant. There are people who...well, it's just best if you forget it."

Libby's eyes grew wide with disbelief.

"Oh my God! It's true, isn't it? You're—"

"Shhh," he said sharply. "Listen, Libby, you seem like a nice girl; like someone who has a good life in front of them. You're pretty, smart, funny. You need to get up and get away from me right now and never look back. You see, you're right about me—I *am* a character." His eyes drifted toward the street as he continued, "Just playing a part in a play that I didn't want to be in—and don't even understand—but now I have to stick it out until, you know, until the final curtain. Corny, but trust me, when it comes down you don't want it to fall on you."

She stared at him for a few beats without expression before saying, "Hoyt Axton."

"What?" he asked in confusion.

"That line you just said. It was almost a Hoyt Axton song. 'When it all comes down I hope it doesn't land on you.'"

"Libby! I'm not kidding."

"Look, Char-Wallace, or whatever your real name is. How about we stop bullshitting each other here and talk seriously."

"I *am* talking seriously. This is nothing you want to be involved in. You need to trust me on this."

He was momentarily distracted by a tall muscular man, with a short beard and hair to match, who had stopped on the sidewalk about six feet away from where he and Libby sat. He wasn't staring. In fact, his gaze had come to rest first on Libby and then on him and then moved on. But in that brief appraisal, they had locked eyes. And in that moment, something trembled inside of him. It was the oddest sensation, as if some form of energy transference had occurred. And then the man had moved on without a backward glance.

"And how do you know that I don't want to be involved?" she asked. "Maybe it's *just* the thing I'm looking for. Maybe I need a little something to spice up my writing career."

"Spice up your writing career?" He was so exasperated by this point that he could barely speak. He continued in a pronounced whisper, "These people will kill you. Do you understand what I'm saying? Why am I even telling you this? This is the real world I'm talking about here. The world you apparently live in is one of make believe."

She scooted the stool closer and stared deeply into his bloodshot eyes.

"I'll make you a deal. I'll help you get out of whatever it is you've gotten yourself into, and in exchange, you give me the rights to your story."

He stared at her in disbelief.

"You just don't get it, do you? You come strolling in here, sit down by me and because, what, you're cute and young and have a great body—"

"Ah-ha," she said. "So you noticed. Good. That's good."

"Is everything a joke to you," he replied in frustration. "My point being that you can't just bull your way into someone's life by simply being bold."

She smiled.

It was a very nice smile.

"It's working pretty good so far. I've been talking to you for about twenty-five minutes and I already know that you're somehow involved in something bad enough that you had to be entered into WitSec."

"Keep your voice down," he said in an even more exaggerated whisper. "You don't know that. You can't *possibly* know that!"

"Sure I do. You just told me."

He started to say something in reply, but nothing came to mind so he simply sat and shook his head in disbelief at what had transpired over the past few minutes.

"So, how about it, Char-Wallace? Do we have a deal?"

"Stop calling me that. My name is..." he couldn't believe that he had just about told her his real name. "It's Charles."

"Now there's a surprise," she said sarcastically. "Never would've figured that one out on my own."

Glancing around quickly he said, "Can we go somewhere besides here and talk?"

She winked at him dramatically.

"Trying to get me to take you back to my place so you can have your way with me, huh Charles?"

"No, no, no. Nothing like that. I'm old enough to be your father."

"You are not. Besides, I kinda dig older guys. But, to answer your question—and I'm being totally serious here—yeah, we can actually go to my loft. It's, like, five blocks; Southwest Washington and Twelfth, sort of."

"You have a loft?"

She shrugged.

"Rich dad. What can I say?"

He considered it for a few seconds and finally said, "Okay. Let's go."

As he stood to go she grabbed his arm and stared seriously into his eyes.

"Just so we're clear, I'm not expecting sex from you."

"You're crazy. You're absolutely crazy."

"Yeah, I get that a lot."

CHAPTER 12

By the time I got back to Michael and Cassie's house in Carlsbad it was pushing four p.m. and I was still so distracted by Cassie's call that I was finding it difficult, if not altogether impossible, to concentrate on Tommy's dilemma.

Vanessa was in the kitchen, mixing up some ground beef per Aaron's instructions while he and Bridgett lounged in front of a flat screen TV that was bigger than the screens I had seen at several local multiplexes.

"Hamburgers on the barbecue tonight?" I asked rhetorically.

"Yeah, man," he replied. "Got the girl learning the family recipe."

"Start 'em young, huh?"

Vanessa hollered, "What next, Aaron?"

He replied, "Take that bacon you fried and chop it up into pieces no bigger than about a quarter of an inch."

"Okay."

The "family recipe" in question was something Aaron and I had stumbled upon one evening when left to our own devices. We had ground beef; bacon; one whole, sweet onion; black pepper and Himalayan Sea Salt, all of which was combined and formed into patties. After that, it was slathered with Sweet Baby Ray's barbecue sauce—with a splash of Jack Daniels—and grilled to perfection. It made for legendary burgers.

I'm totally serious.

Ask anyone.

"Now what?" Vanessa asked.

Aaron said, "Take the bacon, the diced onions and start working it into the ground beef."

"You mean, like, with my hands?" she replied in horror.

"Of course with your hands."

"So, I have to touch the raw meat?"

Aaron sighed, "Girl, how you think hamburger patties get made? Fairies come through in the night and pound them out?"

"It's just so...gross," Vanessa said disgustedly.

With a roll of his eyes, Aaron extricated himself from the lounger and tramped into the kitchen and immediately washed his hands.

"Okay, I'mma do this one time to show you, but if you gonna be in *this* family, you got to learn how to make these burgers."

"But, touching raw meat," Vanessa grimaced, "I mean...ew."

He had just started mixing the ingredients into the meat when his phone rang.

"Jake, do me a solid and see who that is. My phone's right there on the table by the chair and my hands are all nasty and stuff."

I picked up the phone and checked the caller ID.

It was Tommy. I put the phone on speaker.

"Tommy it's Jake. Aaron is a bit occupied at present."

"Jake, great. You're the one I wanted to talk to anyway. I've got Helen's phone. I went ahead and checked the calls —incoming *and* outgoing; texts, emails and her list of contacts."

"And?"

"No texts to anyone named Charles; no calls to or from anyone of that name and no emails."

"How about the contacts list?" I asked as I walked into

Michael's office to continue the call.

"Nothing."

"Okay. I'll call Zack Hastings, the FBI's Assistant Director in Charge of the western United States and get approval to have his team run some forensics. You'd be amazed at what they can recover in the form of deleted texts and emails."

He paused and then said, "I know we have to move forward on this, Jake, but I'm not sure I really want to know."

His was a valid concern. I mean who would want to know that his recently deceased wife had been having an affair and that the last thing to pass her lips was her lover's name?

"I get that, but at the same time you can't realistically expect to go through the rest of your life with a mystery like this hanging over you and never knowing the truth."

"I know, I know," he replied wearily. "Okay, so how do you want to do this?"

"Like I said, I'll call Zack and then Bridgett and I will drive up tomorrow and get the phone from you. Then it's just a matter of waiting to see what the forensics guys come up with. In the meantime, Aaron can start checking with people at VCM. I find it hard to believe that there isn't someone there who saw something, or overheard something. And what about that key she mentioned? Any idea what that was about?"

"Bro, I don't have one clue. Wish I did 'cause that seems like it'd be critical to helping sort out what's going on."

I thought for a second and then suggested, "Why don't you look through her closet—I'm assuming she had her own?"

"Oh yeah, yeah, she did. And it is full, bruh."

"Okay, if you can deal with it emotionally, look through all her clothes that had pockets. Look inside her shoes. Look in drawers, rolled up sweaters, underwear, pants, socks, old shoe boxes, clutches and purses—"

"Behind brims of hats," Bridgett suggested.

"Yeah, stuff like that. It's amazing how much stuff I've seen people hide in places you'd never even think of as being a hiding place."

"Okay, I can do that. If nothing turns up there, any other suggestions?"

Bridgett said, "Files are always a great place to look as well, sir."

I added, "Also, search her car, under floor mats, in the cracks of the seats, trunk, glove box, center console. Even check under the wheel wells to see if there is one of those magnetic key containers. This is going to sound funny, but look in the freezer as well."

"Damn. That's a lot. I'd better get busy. So, what time tomorrow?"

I said, "Ten, ten-thirty."

"All right. And thanks again, Jake."

"My pleasure Tommy. And you'll get through this."

After disconnecting the call, I thought about my last statement to him. It had rolled so confidently off my tongue. But if you want to know the truth, based on my own experience in dealing with profound loss, "getting through" took years, if it ever happened at all.

"Tommy okay?" Aaron queried as I walked back into the kitchen.

"Yeah. He actually wanted to talk to me anyway."

"So, what's up?"

I sat down directly across from him on one of the stools that lined the overly large kitchen island. Vanessa stood by his side staring at the meat, her face an odd mixture of disgust and fascination.

"Well," I said, "he checked her phone out."

"Let me guess," Aaron mused, "nothing there."

"You're right. So, I'm going to call Zack in a minute and see if he can get his forensic guys on it."

"Those dudes are scary when it comes to finding stuff

that isn't there."

"Indeed. Bridgett and I also gave him a long, laundry list of places to look for that mysterious key."

Vanessa said, "That's just the weirdest thing. It's like something you'd write a book about or something."

"Hey, maybe I'll suggest that to Michael."

As I returned to the office to reach out to Zack Hastings, my thoughts were immediately drawn to Cassie's call and the desperation I had heard in her voice.

Throughout her life, Cassie had never been given to fragile emotions, nor had she ever been prone to overstating the facts. She's the strongest person I know. She had to be in order to have survived being trafficked for sex by the late Paul Morgan. Through that ordeal, and subsequent kidnapping by the monster, she had grown a hard-as-nails resolve that, to my knowledge, nothing could shatter. As a result, I trusted her instincts. If she said something was going sideways with Michael, then it was worthy of serious consideration.

In fact, it was more than that.

It was actionable.

I was scared for my niece.

CHAPTER 13

J ake Moriarity, how you doing, my friend?" Zack's sincere greeting seeped through my phone's earpiece like a balmy breeze. "How's it going with Agent Polk?"

I know that movies and TV shows tend to portray FBI personnel as being unfeeling, narcissistic automatons with a yard of lumber up their asses, but the men and women I'd had the pleasure of working with were just normal, hard working people who were passionate about bringing bad guys to justice. Are there some bad apples out there? Of course. But tell me one place on the planet where that couldn't be said about virtually any organization.

"Hey, Zack," I said in reply. "I'm doing well and Bridgett is so good it's almost scary."

He laughed, saying, "I told you she was really something. So, you and Gabi still a thing?"

"A thing? What the hell does that even mean?"

"You know, now that you ask me, I'm not sure I even know. It's just something my kids say all the time and I guess I've picked it up from them."

"Well, to answer your question...yes, we are most definitely still a thing."

"That's good to hear. I like her. I like her a lot."

"Yeah, me too. So, listen, I just caught this case and I need some forensic help."

"Okay," he said. "Shoot."

"You know Aaron's trio?"

"Love it!"

"Well, his bass player, Tommy Marshall, just lost his wife. She had a massive stroke about ten days ago that resulted in her being admitted to hospice."

"Oh, man. Sorry to hear about that."

"Yeah, it was rough. Tommy called me and Aaron because of what Helen said to him literally with her final breath."

"Go on," he prompted.

"She had been comatose, but suddenly she woke up. Tommy goes over to the bedside because he notices her trying to say something, but when he bends down to hear, she says something like—hang on, I have it written down—okay, she says, *'Charles, I had to move the key. You know where it is. Go get it. For God's sake, get it or all will be lost.'* And then she died."

"Wow! Who is Charles?"

"Tommy doesn't know. He's can't identify a single person in their circle of friends and acquaintances who goes by that name. Same thing with the people Helen worked with at the talent agency."

"That had to be hard for a guy to hear."

"It was devastating on many levels."

He said, "So, how can I help?"

"Well, I had him check her text messages, email messages and list of contacts but he didn't come up with anything. So, I figured if your forensic guys could dig into it maybe they'd be able to retrieve something that could be helpful."

"I'm sure they could, but we don't really deal in domestic stuff, Jake. And the way you've presented it, that's exactly what this sounds like. How am I supposed to justify accessing bureau resources?"

A question I had pondered at length before calling.

"I guess the best answer I can come up with is that there's something really weird going on—something far beyond a simple domestic issue. I know these people, Zack, and infidelity isn't really something either one of them seem capable of."

"Fair enough, but you and I both know of cases where everything was cool on the outside, but underneath the smooth and shiny veneer, deplorable things were going on."

"I know, but that isn't what was happening here."

"Would you be saying that if you weren't a family friend?" he asked.

I hesitated briefly and then replied, "It's not about friendship. It's a feeling I have about this that just won't go away."

"That's what I wanted to hear. If you're feeling it, then that's good enough for me. Bring the phone up and I'll turn my guys loose on it. Who knows, there may be a phantom bad guy out there that we'll uncover and all be heroes."

"I'd be satisfied with just giving my friend some peace of mind."

"No reason we can't have both. See you tomorrow."

After disconnecting the call, I swiveled Michael's chair around to take advantage of the ceiling-to-floor windows that provided an unobstructed panorama of the blue Pacific. Leaning back, I stared at the line of surfers waiting outside for the next killer swell and thought about the aforementioned feeling, attempting to put it into words.

Based on her last statement to Tommy, plus what he had overheard when he walked in and surprised her on the phone, I was ready to bet my life that this wasn't about an affair. It just didn't fit. But if it wasn't that, then what? My "feeling" was shoving me toward a scenario wherein Helen had gotten herself involved in something that posed a potential threat to her husband and with her final breath was attempting to protect the man she loved. It was who she was and exactly the kind of self-sacrificing thing she would do.

But who in bloody hell was Charles? What was his role

in my developing hypothesis? Furthermore, how had Helen Marshall gotten tangled up in a situation so volatile as to cause genuine concern for Tommy's safety?

If this wasn't about sex—and I was quite certain that it wasn't—then it had to either be about money or murder, and the two typically went hand-in-hand. It didn't feel like murder, although it could eventually lead to that. So, I had to focus on all of the ways money could potentially be involved.

For the sake of moving my thinking forward, I decided to create an arbitrary profile of "Charles." Granted, it would no doubt be far from accurate, but I had to start somewhere. I opened a drawer in Michael's desk and pulled out a legal pad and wrote, "*CHARLES*" at the top of the page in block letters. Then I started writing down everything that came to mind.

He would be five and five to Helen's age—that is, either five years younger or five years older. As I pondered that prospect, I started sensing that they were in all likelihood the same age. So I wrote, "*53.*"

Since I had decided on money as being central to the conundrum, I made him an accountant. Why? I don't know. It just fit. But how were Helen and Charles related? Helen had her own checking account, so it required no leap of logic to assume that she also had her own savings and investment portfolios, something I would confirm with Tommy. I know of very few people who are into investment portfolios who passively put money aside month after month, year after year without getting involved with a stockbroker or investment counselor.

I crossed out accountant and replaced it with, "*investment counselor.*"

So, Charles is a fifty-three-year-old investment counselor with whom Helen consulted regarding her investment portfolio. Nothing wrong with that. I even had one of my own. Maybe...

My mind suddenly blew up with a whole new scenario. Don't ask me to explain how it happened, but I suddenly saw Charles as someone Helen had known previously. High school friends? Sweethearts? College?

I started scribbling things down on a piece of paper as fast as I could write.

High school sweethearts.

Separate ways following graduation.

Lost touch for a number of years.

They both get married.

Helen starts looking for investment counselor.

Charles...somehow ends up working in LA.

Helen finds him randomly.

Fond reunion...Charles is...divorced...still has feelings for Helen.

Helen is committed to Tommy, but retains soft spot for old flame.

I sat back and stared at my list, thinking through each item critically to see if it still felt like it fit.

I came forward quickly and wrote...

Charles is not his real name.

Why? Don't know.

He tells her to trust him with her investments—has big deals working.

Double...no...TRIPLE her investments.

She trusts him.

Somehow he's dirty. Has to be.

Gets in trouble...but, how?

I sat back again to ponder the possibilities. Was he really dirty in the classic sense of being a con artist, or, in his zeal to do well for his clients, did he involve their money in something that turned out to be less than integral?

I scribbled...

Con artist. Has to be.

Maybe that was what broke up their romance in high school. Helen was a straight shooter, or at least that was the impression I, and everyone else in our circle of friends, had of her.

I wrote...

High school romance reveals a dark side to Charles.

Helen can't handle it—terminates the relationship.

But then, if she knew him previously as being basically dishonest, why would she trust him with her investments? Maybe he had reformed. Maybe somewhere in his heart his lingering fondness for Helen made him want to do well so he could prove that he had really changed. And maybe...

I turned the page and started scribbling again.

Maybe some of the people he had worked with before put the squeeze on him.

Mob types? Extremists? Terrorists? Human trafficking?

Stroke induced?

I needed to talk to Tommy.

CHAPTER 14

4:30 p.m.

I know the place is a mess, but I'm a writer. What'd you expect?" Libby said with a laugh as she walked Charles through the door and into her loft.

He whistled softly as he glanced around the spacious unit.

"Man. You could fit *two* of my apartments in here."

"It's not really as big as it looks. It's just the way it's configured with all the open space, you know." She tossed her backpack on the dining table and hollered over her shoulder, "I'll be back in a sec," before disappearing behind a partial wall he assumed divided her bedroom from the rest of the area.

Walking over to the large front windows, he gazed down on the busy street scene three stories below as a question assailed his conscious mind like a medieval battering ram assaulting a fortified keep: *What the hell are you doing? You're going to get both of you killed, you moron. Get out! Turn around and just start walking and don't look back.*

"Do you need to use the restroom?" Libby asked as she strolled back into the open space.

He turned to look in her direction. She had changed out of her hoodie and now wore a loose fitting, cotton pullover sporting an elaborate tie-dyed design, like something you'd see at a Grateful Dead concert.

"Uh, no. I'm good. That shirt looks good on you. The colors really set off your eyes."

Her eyebrows raised.

"Wait, you're alone in a pretty, young girl's loft and you're talking about her eyes?"

Charles grinned and shrugged as he replied, "Old school, I guess. Could never bring myself to comment on a woman's, uh...you know."

"What, you can't even say the word? They're boobs, Charles. It's okay to say it."

He laughed uncomfortably.

"Okay then. If it makes you feel better, you have perfectly lovely, uh—"

"Oh, I was just messing with you," she said, laughing lightly. "So, here we are. We've already established that you're not interested in sex—weird, but to each his own. So...why *are* you here?"

He glanced around the room and spotted a sofa with an adjacent overstuffed chair.

"Can we sit down?"

"Of course. Take your pick."

He chose the chair, sinking into its cushioned comfort while he watched her crawl dramatically down the length of the sofa and finally curl her legs under her, propping an elbow on the arm and cupping her chin.

"You look as if you're afraid I'm going to jump on you and start tearing your clothes off, Charlie," Libby said with a wink and a salacious smile.

"Are you still messing with me, Libby, or are you genuinely, like, one of those nympho-what's-its."

"Nymphomaniac? Hardly. You're safe with me, Charlie boy. I'm just trying to figure you out, you know, press a few buttons and see if you're really who I think you are or just another horny, middle-aged guy looking for a good time."

"And...who do you think I am?"

"Oooh," she purred. "I don't know. Let's see. Man of mystery? Tragic figure beset by life's cruel machinations? Guy on the run?"

"Machinations? Really?"

"Hey," she jerked both thumbs toward herself. "Writer."

"Well," he began and then paused as if collecting his thoughts. "Umm...all of the above?"

"Okay. Should I be taking notes?"

"No," he replied quickly and forcefully. "No notes. In fact, when we're done here, you're going to forget all about me."

She laughed.

"Fat chance of that happening, Charlie. So, tell me your story."

He leaned his head back, closed his weary eyes and felt the tears building, feeling helpless to thwart their inevitable overflow.

He felt a presence by his feet and looked down to see Libby curled up with her hands resting on his knees.

"Hey," she said. "Hey, Charlie. It'll be okay. Fate put us together. I'm with you and you can trust me."

"Can I, Libby? Can I trust you? Can I trust anyone?"

"Well," she replied with a small smile. "Only one way to find out. Just tell me what's going on."

She seemed so sincere that he couldn't stop himself.

So, he told her.

Told her everything.

Even the part about WitSec; and Helen; and the box; and the key, that he didn't have; and that people were going to die—horribly—if he didn't find the damn key.

When he was finished, Libby stood and walked over to stand staring out of her window.

"Wow, Charlie. That's some story. I don't think on my best day I could craft a plot that intricate."

"I didn't plan any of it, Libby. You have to believe me.

I mean why would I willingly do something that would put people I love and care about in that kind of danger?"

"Well, the obvious answer is that you wouldn't. But, if your story is true, then the people who are after you will also be after your friends."

He leaned forward so suddenly that it caused Libby to jerk involuntarily.

"These are bad people, Libby. They make the mob look like choirboys. Do you understand that? And WitSec can't protect me. No one can protect me."

CHAPTER 15

When Tommy answered my call I said, "Tommy, it's Jake. Listen, do you know the name of the investment counselor Helen used?"

"Investment counselor?"

"Yeah, like, the investment firm she used? Or, better yet, the one you guys used together?"

"I'm not sure she used one, Jake. Then again, I'm not sure she didn't."

"Can you check through her personal files for me? It's really important, Tommy. I'll be glad to stay on the line while you check."

"Sure. Anything you need."

I could hear him start moving through the house.

After a thirty second period of silence, during which I heard drawers opening and closing, papers being shuffled and Tommy muttering to himself, he finally said, "Jake, I'm not seeing anything. Sorry."

"It's okay. Is there anywhere else you can think of where she may have kept personal files?"

He let out a long breath of air.

"You know—and I kinda feel bad about admitting this —but, we had one of those tracking things on our phones. You know, where you can see where someone is when they're away from you?"

"Yeah, I have that set up with everyone in my family, including Gabi."

TEARS IN A BOTTLE

"Okay, so you know what I'm talking about. So, anyway, there was this one time a while back—well, further than a while, more like a year or maybe two. Anyway, I wanted to know where she was, so I opened the program and saw that she was at a bank in Lake Forest."

"And I presume that was unusual?"

"Well, yeah," he said. "We don't bank in Lake Forest. Neither one of us. All of our banking—and we use three different banks—is done right here in Dana Point."

"Could she have been there on business for the talent agency?"

"I don't know. To my knowledge the talent agency does all of its banking in downtown LA."

"Okay," I replied. "Did you ever ask her about it?"

"No...I didn't. I mean how do you bring something like that up without sounding like you're a jealous, paranoid husband, or something? I know, I know, that's stupid, but it's what I was feeling at the time." He paused, sighed deeply and then continued, "Look, Jake, Helen's dead and this doesn't really matter anymore, but, well...at the time, we weren't getting along very well."

"Can you be more specific, Tommy?"

"Yeah, so, man, this makes me feel so small."

I could sense his struggle and chose to remain silent figuring that he'd eventually get around to whatever it was that was on his mind.

"Helen sat me down saying something about how in the spirit of openness, there was something that had happened that I needed to know about. So, she told me that a guy she'd dated in high school was living in Orange County. A guy that she had been very much in love with and probably would've ended up marrying had he not been so manipulative and controlling."

Bells started going off.

"This is getting interesting, Tommy. Tell me everything."

"I will. His name is Brandon Crawford, but she called him Bran. She told me she had randomly run into him—"

"Where?" I said suddenly cutting him off.

"Oh, uh, he worked..." Tommy stopped talking and then swore loudly. "He worked for a venture capital firm. How do you like that?"

"Huh. Gabi works for a venture capital firm. Do you remember the name?"

"It was...uh...come on. Uh...something about Saturn, no. It was Latin. That's it. Hang on."

I heard the sounds of rummaging through the contents of a drawer.

"Here it is. I wrote it down because of the way I was feeling at the time. Didn't want to forget where the boy worked in case I needed to lump him up a little."

"I totally understand. So, what's the name?"

"Aurea Saturni Investments."

I asked him to spell it and then said, "Any idea what it means?"

"Well, my high school Latin is a bit rusty, but I looked it up online and I think it means, like, 'golden chance', or something like that." He barked out an ironic laugh, and then continued, "As I'm standing here holding this piece of paper with that name scribbled on it, I can't begin to tell you why this guy, Brandon, or Bran, or whatever, made me so jealous. But it was bad—it was real bad, bro. And I know that my mistrust really hurt Helen. I could see it in her eyes."

"Jealously is often hurtful."

"You sure got that right. Well, anyway, that's what drove me to check up on Helen a little more than—okay, a *lot* more than usual. But the bank I spotted her at wasn't anywhere near where the dude worked. His office was closer to Newport Center."

"So, Aurea Saturni Investments in Newport Center. That's a great lead. And how about the bank where you spotted her?"

He said quickly, "I have absolutely no idea. I know that it wasn't a national brand, like B of A, or Chase or anything like that."

"How about a location?"

He sighed before replying, "The only thing I remember is that it was in Lake Forest. Keep in mind that this was all very traumatic for me—the stalking thing. My mind just wasn't right. Hell, Jake, I was even having trouble remembering the chord progression of some of Aaron's songs. Songs I'd played hundreds of times."

"That's all right, Tommy. We'll figure this out. So, I guess that's all I need for now. I'll see you tomorrow morning."

"Thanks, bro. And, Jake?"

"Yeah?"

"Listen...don't tell Aaron about this. You know, about the trouble between Helen and me. I don't want her memory to suffer because of my jealousy."

"Absolutely. See you tomorrow."

The call disconnected and I sat staring at my list, feeling a bit dizzy by how close I had been on much of my speculation. I started putting check marks by the items that were close, or in some cases spot on:

High school sweethearts. Check.

Separate ways following graduation. Check.

Lost touch for a number of years. Check.

They both get married. Didn't know about that one yet, so I put a question mark by it.

Helen starts looking for investment counselor. Check.

Charles...I don't know...somehow ends up working in LA in the investment industry. Check.

Helen finds him randomly. Check.

Fond reunion...Charles is...divorced...still has feelings for Helen. Not enough information, so that one got a question mark as well.

Helen is committed to Tommy, but retains soft spot for old flame. A check with a question mark.

Charles is not his real name. Check with, *real name Brandon Crawford* added.

I scanned through the rest of the list, skipping over most of it until I came to:

High school romance reveals a dark side to Charles.

Helen can't handle it—terminates the relationship.

Those two got double checks.

Okay, so what did I have except further confirmation that my intuition is truly scary at times? I needed to talk to Brandon Crawford, check out the venture capital firm where he worked, and I needed to find the bank in Lake Forest that Helen visited.

Of course, none of that was going to happen after—I checked my watch—five p.m. on a Saturday afternoon.

CHAPTER 16

L ibby stared at Charles for a few seconds in silence, attempting to process what she had just been told.

His had been a fantastic story, compelling in its complexity.

Following college, Charles had started out as an accountant; did well and managed to get hired by a small investment brokerage in Orange County, California. While in their employ his old, deceitful and manipulative ways caused him to attempt to form a low-level ponzi scheme. Of course, his employer found out about it and fired him on the spot.

After sitting out for a couple of years—during which time he supported himself by preparing tax returns—he found a venture capital firm willing to take a chance on him. Starting on the proverbial bottom rung of the ladder, over a period of ten years he worked himself back into respect and prominence.

Eventually, he got promoted.

As acknowledgement of his hard work, Charles was handed a client that, unbeknownst to anyone, was the grandson of a man rumored to be a kingpin in the Russian mob.

The grandson, after testing the waters for a few months, invested a hundred thousand dollars. Because Charles was so good at what he did, the return on that investment was substantial. The next time the grandson approached him it was to ask what would happen if he invested a larger amount—say, a million. The amount terrified Charles, but, feeling that the market was ripe for someone who was willing to take a chance—and given that his investment firm specialized in high risk investments—he told the guy that he wouldn't let him down.

And he didn't.

The investment returned twenty-eight percent.

The client was very happy. So happy in fact, that the next investment was twenty million.

Charles, as it turned out, had just heard of a venture capital opportunity that could return up to fifty percent, but it was extremely high risk. He told the grandson about it; the grandson, flush with confidence from his previous successes told him to go for it.

He did.

It worked.

The grandson was ecstatic.

It was as if everything Charles touched turned to gold.

In the meantime, Helen, Charles' old high school flame, chose his firm on the recommendation of the owner of the talent agency where she worked. As fate would have it, Charles was assigned to her portfolio. They have a reunion; decide to start over with a clean slate; and, on the sly, Charles begins working her money into every transaction he made on behalf of the Russian.

By now, he's feeling as if he can do no wrong.

The grandson came back and wanted to know how Charles would feel about investing one hundred million quietly. Off the books, as in, no one could ever know the source of the money.

He should have said no. He should have figured that this had trouble written all over it. But he didn't. The risk-to-reward potential was too great to ignore. So, he did it and padded the grandson's investment with fifty thousand dollars of Helen's money. It was a completely unethical thing to do without consulting her, but if it worked out, she would more than double her money. It was the least he could do for his old flame.

And then one balmy, spring evening two men and one woman from Homeland Security showed up at his house.

Seated around the dining room table in his smallish condo, they told him that his client, the grandson, had been under DHS scrutiny for over a year and a half due to his involvement in funding human trafficking for the Russian mob.

The process was demonically brilliant in its conception and execution. Ads for casting calls would be placed through social media and online forums throughout the Ukraine for "exceptional young women of rare beauty and adventuresome spirits." The hook was a "limited time offer" for acting or modeling opportunities in the United States. The ad directed applicants to a bogus agency for an initial interview. If the initial interview "went well", they would be driven to a "studio" for a test photo session, or script reading, after which they would be returned to the agency. Except, the only thing awaiting them at the studio were men who would rape them, drug them—and keep them drugged; torture them into submission and eventually transport them to the docks where they would be loaded like cattle into shipping containers.

Once onboard the ship, they were told that they had been sold into slavery and would never see their families again. Before that shock could wear off, the rapes and torture would begin at the hands of their captors, the captain and ship's crew, and continue throughout the four to five-week journey to New York. While minimal food and water were provided, constant doses of heroin would be administered resulting in profound addiction by the end of the voyage. Upon arrival in New York, they were farmed out to a network of underground brothels where they would spend the rest of their days satisfying the greed of the Russian mobsters and the lust of their insatiable clientele.

On average, they would be dead by the age of twenty-one.

Additionally, the mob would routinely kidnap young girls—some as young as ten to twelve years old—to satisfy the ever-growing demand for younger and younger girls by wealthy men in the Middle East and global pedophile networks.

After that long sad tale, the Homeland Security agents indicated that should they wish to do so, they would have no problem charging Charles with a wide array of felonies, any one of which would result in serious prison time. But, there was no need for that, *if* he would agree to help bring the grandson and the entire trafficking network to justice.

Of course, because Russian mobsters take a dim view of people they deem duplicitous, he would have to be placed in the Federal Witness Protection program when it was all over. That, or suffer a torturous demise at the Russian mob's cruel and bloody hands.

What could he do? He *had* to cooperate. So, he did. He gave them everything in exchange for protection and immunity.

Almost everything.

The FED's wouldn't care that Helen Marshall was totally ignorant of the circumstances that had generated the massive increase in her portfolio. It was all dirty money to them and, therefore, would be subject to seizure, *if* they found out about it. And Charles was determined that that would never happen. But the only way they'd never find out was if he brought Helen in on the details.

And so, he did.

However, Helen, being possessed of a good and compassionate heart, cared far less about the potential for losing her investments than she did about the plight of young girls. She insisted that Charles find all the information he could about the next shipment. Fortunately, the Russian grandson, while possessed of intense cruelty and vast financial resources, was also possessed of an inflated ego and a need to feel important. And so it was that over drinks—that included consuming nearly a pint of vodka—the grandson started bragging. In the process, he revealed that a ship was on its way and would dock in New York harbor in three weeks. The girls from that ship would be transported to Los Angeles in the back of a big rig. Once in LA, they would be trafficked for sex resulting in massive quantities of cash for him and his grandfather's mob family.

That had been exactly one month ago.

And now, the girls were in LA.

He knew where they were.

Helen had known where they were, as well as knowing the location of the safe-deposit box containing the offshore account information.

And that's why she had to die.

After the FED's had picked Charles up, the Russian mob had broken into Helen's condo in the middle of the night and injected a lethal dose of methyl iodide into her favorite wine—a wine that her husband refused to drink. Poisoning from methyl iodide exactly mimics the symptoms of massive stroke.

She drank the wine.

She died.

Prior to all that, however, Helen had secured a safe-deposit box into which Charles placed six USB drives. The drives contained the codes for the offshore accounts containing the bulk of the traffickers' money. And only he and Helen knew of its existence.

Or so he had believed.

But, the Russian mob knew, and they were coming for him.

Libby thought through Charles' story. He was in a horrible situation.

His beloved friend was dead.

The FED's would soon be after him for breaking cover.

The Russian mob wanted him because he had their money.

And Libby? Well, while she found the thought marginally disgusting and morally disturbing, as soon as she finessed the location of the safe-deposit box out of him...she would kill him.

CHAPTER 17

We were sitting on the deck, watching the sunset and savoring every last, succulent bite of our burgers that had been grilled to absolute perfection courtesy of a well-rehearsed effort between Aaron and myself.

Here's the way it worked: I grilled and he told me when to flip the meat.

Teamwork, baby.

I had just finished filling everyone in on what I had learned from my conversation with Tommy when my phone vibrated.

It was Gabi.

"Hey. I thought you were working."

"I am," she said. "Just taking a quick break before the big shots arrive. So, how was your day?"

"Well, it got real interesting," I replied while walking to the far end of the deck. "You remember meeting Tommy Marshall?"

"Aaron's bass player, right?"

"Yeah. Well, his wife died yesterday after suffering a severe stroke."

"Oh, I'm so sorry to hear that. I never met her, but Aaron spoke very highly of her."

I said, "She was an amazing person. Well, with her dying breath she said something to Tommy that has sent his world into a tailspin. I'm not going to go into all the details, but it's something that I've got a feeling about."

"You talking about your famous intuition?" she asked with a chuckle.

"That's exactly what I'm talking about. So, since you aren't coming over I agreed to look into it."

"Go get 'em, tiger," she said sincerely.

"I've already started. So, listen, part of it involves a guy who works, or worked, for a venture capital firm over here in Newport Beach. Aurea Saturni Investments. You ever heard of them?"

"Aurea Saturni? Who hasn't!"

"Really?" I replied, drawing the word out. "What can you tell me about them."

She huffed, "Nothing good. Those guys are notoriously slimy."

"How slimy?"

"Slimy enough that the SEC has them on speed-dial."

"Interesting."

"The owner, Benson Harald, has been called before investigative committees more times than I've gotten pedicures. And that's really saying something."

"So," I said, "if they're so slimy, why and how are they still in business?"

"Because nothing has ever stuck. It's like some politicians you read about that get accused of things, are brought before a Senate Committee, or something, and then walk away unscathed. And because of people like Mr. Harald, those who are honest and above board—like my boss, Martin Pierce—have to suffer through needless scrutiny. So, basically we, along with everyone else in the industry, loathe them."

"Don't hold back, Gabi. You can go ahead and tell me how you really feel."

She laughed and replied, "I *do* get a little intense at times, don't I?"

"I like it. So, if someone was working for Aurea Saturni, would that mean that they were dirty as well?"

"Not necessarily. They hire good people. The problem is, good people can go bad very quickly depending on the strength of their character."

"How so?"

"Well, for instance: let's say that you have a client with a substantial venture capital portfolio. Your boss tips you off to an *opportunity*..." (I could hear the air quotes in her vocal inflection) "...that could generate substantial returns for the employee, the client *and* the firm. But it has to be handled discretely, which is basically code for off the books. As the broker, you stand to make, oh say, a twenty-thousand-dollar commission. It's not right. You know it's not right, but because your boss instigated it and you want to please your boss and do well for your client, you go for it anyway."

I said, "It's almost always about money, isn't it?"

"Money and power." She was silent for a few seconds before adding, "I sometimes wonder, in the history of the world, how many innocent people have lost their lives because of those two things?"

"I'm sure the numbers would be staggering."

She said suddenly, "Jake, I've got to go. The guests are arriving. Promise that you'll tell me everything about what you're working on. I might be able to help."

"You can count on it. I love you."

She giggled.

"You already told me that."

"Ah, yes, but that was hours ago. I was just reminding you in case you'd forgotten."

A long sigh, and then, "You are such a sweet man, Jake Moriarity. And I promise I won't tell anyone."

"Better not. It'd ruin my reputation. Can you imagine me facing down a bad guy and he says, 'Oy! I got no worries. It's Moriarity. He's a real sweetie-pie.'"

She laughed and said, "I'm hanging up now. Bye. Oh, and I love you too."

I walked back along the length of the deck to rejoin the others.

Muriel asked, "Was that Gabi?"

"Yeah, it was."

"I'm so bummed that she couldn't come over."

Aaron said, "She okay?"

"She is. Just wondering how my day went."

"You tell her about the new case?" he asked.

"Just the basics. Funny thing though, she knows about that venture capital firm where the mysterious Charles worked."

"You mean Brandon," Bridgett corrected.

"Yes. Apparently, that firm has weathered numerous SEC investigations."

"What's SEC?" Eddie asked.

"Securities and Exchange Commission. They're kind of a watchdog agency in the world of investing. Brokers, dealers, investment advisors, et cetera, all fall under their authority."

Aaron added, "They basically protect investors from, shall we say, less than integral financial counselors."

"Wow," she replied. "Who knew?"

"Yeah," I said. "As it turns out, working with large sums of money often brings out the worst in people."

Vanessa added quickly, "I know a little about that stuff first hand from my former brother-in-law. It seemed—and I think this was proven out—that there was nothing he and Harry 'O wouldn't do if it meant making money. Even if they had to ruin lives and even kill people to do it."

I watched as her eyes ran away inside of herself for a moment, and then she was back, as if she had started to take a step down a hall of memory and at the last second drew back forcefully. She found my eyes and nodded her head curtly as if to acknowledge that she was okay.

"So, how we gonna proceed?" Aaron asked.

"We'll go up to Tommy's tomorrow morning, get

Helen's phone and take it to Zack."

"Oh, so he's okay with Zack's guys checking it out?"

"I forgot to tell you. Yeah, he is. Even though it seems at this point to be more closely related to a domestic issue, he trusts my, well, instincts."

"Spidey Sense," the three girls said in unison.

CHAPTER 18

Y ou want some wine, or maybe something stronger?" Libby asked as she opened the doors to her liquor cabinet.

"Stronger. Definitely stronger," Charles answered shakily.

"Okay, I've got, let's see, vodka, gin, Remy Martin cognac, Jack..."

"Can you make a Greyhound?"

"Like, with grapefruit juice and vodka?"

"Like that," he answered.

She turned to face him.

"Okay, I can do that. Provided that you tell me the truth."

His eyes widened dramatically as he answered, "I *did* tell you the truth."

"But not all of it. I mean, come on."

"What part don't you think is true?"

"Oh," she answered, "let's start with your name. We both know that your name isn't Charles."

He stared at her trying to determine what she was playing at.

"Brandon," he said finally. "Brandon Crawford."

She walked toward him with her hand outstretched.

"Nice to meet you, Brandon. Libby Longstreet."

He laughed.

"Libby Longstreet? *Now* who's not being truthful."

"Okay, you got me. Elizabeth."

As they shook hands he said, "Okay. Fair enough. Nice to meet you, Ms. Longstreet. And, can you please call me Charles?"

"Okay, but why?"

"It's...well, Helen and I came up with the name and, honestly, I like it better than Brandon. I've always hated that name."

She stood in front of him not speaking, just looking intently into his eyes.

"What?" he asked after a few uncomfortable seconds.

She shrugged her shoulders and said matter-of-factly, "Okay, Charles it is," as she turned back toward the cabinet. "One Greyhound coming up."

"And make it a double."

"You got it." She started busying herself making the drink and then asked, "So, this safe-deposit box that has all the damning evidence..."

"I didn't say it was damning."

"Then, what is it?"

He took a breath to answer and then stopped.

"Well, that's just the thing. I can't tell you. I can't tell anybody."

"Why not?" she asked. "You've told me everything else, which, for the record, was very strange."

"I know. I know. And I have no idea why I did it. I guess I was just, you know, like a pressure cooker or something and I was ready to blow."

"Yeah, I get that. But if the stuff about the safe-deposit box is still generating pressure, so to speak, wouldn't it be better to get that off your chest as well?"

For the first time she noticed a wariness about him, as if he were starting to put some things together. She decided she had to back off for now. Play the line like a good fly fisherman—just the way her pig of a father had taught her to do when soliciting information from people.

"Look," she said while pouring the ingredients into a

martini shaker. "It doesn't matter one way or another to me. I'm just trying to be helpful."

He seemed to relax a bit.

"Okay. I see that. You just have no idea how uptight this whole thing has made me."

Handing him his drink, she replied, "Associating with the Russian mob can definitely have that effect."

He downed half of it in one swallow.

"Oh, man, that's really good. Maybe even the best Greyhound I've ever had."

"Thanks. One tries."

"One succeeds," he affirmed while taking another sip. "You know, I never used to like the taste of strong liquor."

"But now?" she prompted.

"Now I find that I can't get through most days without it."

"About that."

"Yeah?"

"Is the witness protection thing really *that* stressful that you have to drink all the time just to survive emotionally?"

"Listen, you don't know these people. The Russian mob is notorious for their cruelty. I mean these are the guys who invented shoving their enemies in steel barrels and pouring lye all over them while they're still alive and then sealing the top shut and leaving them to die."

"So, it's true? All that cruelty and violence?"

He nodded vigorously.

"Without question. I even saw some of it."

Libby sat on the sofa and motioned Charles to return to the chair.

"Tell me about it."

"Well," he said hesitantly. "This guy who worked with me—I mean I had to tell someone, right? And," he paused to take another drink, "and I told Andy. This was even before the Fed's got involved. I told him what was going on and the money that was flying around along with the kind of profit that could be realized. Well, Andy was always a greedy bastard, so he wanted in, which was fine with me because I had come to the point where I didn't want to be all alone in something that big. So, Andy starts helping me on a *very* small scale.

"The problem was, Andy had a big mouth."

"Had?"

"Wait for it." He took another drink. "Always did. And the more he drank, the bigger his mouth got. We went out for drinks one night after work. It was late. Probably like, nine-thirty or ten. After we'd been there for an hour or so, he picks these two girls up who were sitting at the next table—invites them to join us. They agree and he orders drinks for everyone; says he can afford it because of the big deal *he* is about to close. Can you beat it? That *he* is about to close? He had nothing to do with it! It was *my* deal. I just wanted him there for support." He drained the last of his Greyhound. "Umm, can I have another?"

"Sure," Libby said as she took his glass and walked over to the bar. "So, what happened?"

"Well, he pounds two more shots of tequila, and all of a sudden just blurts out that we are working with the Russian mob and that we're all going to be rich."

"Wow. What did those girls do?"

He hung his head, shaking it slowly from side to side.

"Those young, fresh faced, innocent looking girls were actually tailing us on behalf of the Russians."

"Oops," she replied while handing him his drink.

"It was a little more than that. They invited us to come back to their place. I mean, hell, I was horny—Andy was *always* horny—they were beautiful, and, honestly, we were all about three sheets to the wind. So, we went with them."

"In their car?"

"Yeah," he replied sadly. "That's where everything

really went to shit. The one girl—can't remember her name or even what she looked like except that she was blonde —but, they drove us to this abandoned lot somewhere in East LA; parked; told both of us to get out; and then this blonde girl pulled out a knife and slowly...uh...very slowly just...cut Andy to ribbons. And I'm not exaggerating. He was bleeding everywhere."

"Where were you while all of this carving was going on?"

"The driver held a gun on me and told me that I'd be okay as long as I watched everything that was happening without turning my eyes away."

"So, obviously you complied or you wouldn't be here."

"Yeah," he said softly, with a quiet sob. "I did. I didn't know a human body had that much blood in it."

"Andy died?"

He nodded, "Slowly. Horribly. And when that girl was done, she spit on his dead body and we drove away with a promise from her to do even worse to me if I ever said anything about it to anyone."

"And you didn't believe her?"

"Of course, I believed her. I had just watched her butcher a man."

"But, now you're telling this to me?"

"Yes, Libby...I am. And I still don't know why."

"Is it because I am young, pretty, have a killer body and am demonstrably pure of spirit?" she said lightly.

"That's it. Has to be," he replied with a smile. He glanced at his watch. "You know, I really should get going. It's getting late and—"

"Nonsense. You're already too drunk to go anywhere and by the time you finish your story you're going to be out cold. Stay here tonight. I have an extra toothbrush you can use."

Charles blinked a few times, thinking it over.

"Are you sure it's okay? You're not worried about having a strange man in your place?"

"Please," she said dismissively. "If I had been worried about you, I never would've invited you up here in the first place."

"Well, okay." He paused and then added, "Besides... honestly? I don't really have anywhere else to go."

"Then it's settled," she said with a curt nod of her pretty head. "Now, about the safe-deposit box."

He drained the last of his second drink and held the glass toward her hopefully.

Libby stared at the glass and said, "I'll make you a deal. I will keep you supplied with Greyhounds if—and this is a big *if*—you tell me the whole story."

He seemed to think it over and then replied, "Okay. Deal."

As she turned to mix the drink she said, "But even if you get liquored up I promise not to take advantage of you in the middle of the night."

"Will you just stop."

As she poured the vodka and grapefruit juice into the shaker, she mentally relived killing Andy and marveled that Charles hadn't recognized her.

Then again, it *had* been night, he had been *very* drunk and her overdone makeup, long blonde wig and revealing sweater had been an effective disguise.

She wondered if she would kill Charles in the same manner when the time came. She thought not. She was actually growing to like Charles in the same way a predator likes their prey right before delivering the killing blow.

CHAPTER 19

8:00 a.m.

Why are the streets always wet in the movies?

You can file that question under, "stuff that I think about in the middle of the night when I can't sleep."

And last night had been long on pondering and short on slumber.

Sunday morning.

And contrary to Lionel Ritchie's classic song, there was nothing "easy" about it.

I was tired. "Dog tired" as they say.

Definitely moving slow.

"How slow?" you ask. Slower than hotel Wi-Fi. Which is to say, pretty darned.

Part of my somnolent paucity was due to Gabi calling me at eleven p.m. to tell me all about her boss's party, how successful it had been and that the Japanese investors were ready to sign an agreement. Of course, her boss—rightly so— had credited her with, "sealing the deal," as he had put it. We had talked about that and other things relating to investment counseling until almost twelve forty-five, at which time I had doused the lights and laid my weary head on the pillow with the intention of falling quickly and blissfully into the arms of blessed oblivion.

I didn't "fall" into anything. My overactive mind drug

me down a well-worn path of thought.

It was all about Cassie.

Wasn't it always?

I don't really know what to say other than, well, she is my world. I couldn't love her any more if she were my biological daughter. So, anything that hurt her, hurt me.

And she was hurting. Big time. But, as was almost always true with my beloved niece, she hid her pain well. If Cassie, Muriel or Eddie, the main girls in Paul Morgan's illicit Seattle escort service, showed any pain, it merely stoked the flames of his sadistic fire and he would do whatever he could to make the pain worse. But by remaining stoic and not showing any emotion whatsoever, he would eventually tire of the game and move on to something else.

This thing with Michael, though, was a new kind of pain. It was pain begotten of pain. Michael was in bad shape, or at least that was what I surmised from Cassie's description. And his pain caused her pain.

I think it's because of the tears. You know...the wet streets. All those forlorn, timeworn and world-weary, quietly desperate people just sitting, waiting for the dawn. After midnight, that's when the tears start to fall and then drop by soul wringing drop they run together until the whole world is saturated in a mist of sorrow.

No wonder the streets are wet.

Sadly, Cassie's tears are part of that universal torrent. And there is nothing I can do about it. I have to tell you, I don't like it. If you want to know the truth, I hate it.

In my first year as a seminary student one of my professors had us write an essay on a psalm written around 1011 BC by David, King of Israel. The Biblical David was, apparently, a man well acquainted with sorrow. In this particular psalm he talked about God saving all our tears in a bottle. Well, if that's true, then the bottle with Cassie's name on it must be nearly full. Which begs the question: why is it necessary for her to continue to weep? Hasn't she had enough sorrow in her life? I'm mad as hell about it and frequently vent my anger toward, well, now that's a topic of some dispute. As I may or may not have mentioned before, I have issues with the Deity. I know he's there. He knows I'm here. But, near as I can tell, the "goodness" his followers love to talk about and sing about somehow doesn't apply to me. So, I vent my anger in his direction, wherever the hell that is, fully realizing that I am most likely talking to the ceiling.

But at least I'm talking and not holding it inside.

Aaron thinks I have a bad attitude. Hell, *I* think I have a bad attitude! But, given what I've had to endure throughout my life, I feel it's justified. I mean how can you watch your wife die slowly, horribly, from pancreatic cancer and be okay with it? I'm not. Never have been. Just as I'm not okay with Cassie suffering any more than she already has.

I threw some clothes on and passed on taking a shower. Glancing at my reflection in the bathroom mirror—or "mirrors" in the case of Michael's bathroom—it occurred to me that it was for moments like this that I wore my hair in a buzz cut and tolerated a full beard. Speeded things up immensely.

When I walked into the kitchen, Aaron was already there waiting and pouring a cup of coffee for me in a travel mug. It was Aaron waiting and not Bridgett. We had determined the night before that it'd be better if Aaron accompanied me and she stay behind with the girls, who already had a day filled with "girl stuff" planned. She had been disappointed, but since "girl stuff" was a rarity in the life of a female FBI agent, decided to give it a try.

"Morning sunshine," Aaron said in his impossibly low voice.

"How'd you sleep?" I mumbled around a yawn.

"Based on that response, I'm thinkin', better than you."

I shook my head to clear away the cobwebs as I gratefully accepted the proffered cup of coffee.

"Is it that obvious?"

"Uh, yeah. You got that unmistakable patina of fatigue that typically comes from a combination of insomnia enhanced by stress and worry. Let me guess. Cassie?"

I nodded.

"Isn't it always?"

"Look, bro, barring life-threatening circumstances, Cassie and Michael need to deal with things on their own as a married couple." He paused and then added, "When Sylvie and I were first married, her momma 'bout did us in by bein' all up in our business all the time about every little thing that came up between us. I'm not suggesting that you're anything like her, but—"

"Point made, point taken," I replied, cutting him off. "And I know you're right, but I've always been a problem solver for Cassie."

"Yeah, you have. And you've been a good one. But, unless she officially invites you to intervene, she needs to deal with this on her own. And even then, I'd be very wary if I was you."

It wasn't until we were in my Range Rover and headed toward Dana Point that I finally responded.

"I hear what you're saying."

He wrinkled his brow in confusion.

"What I'm saying about what?"

"You know, about Cassie and Michael and how I just need to stop worrying and allow them space to deal with whatever is going on in their own time and in their own way."

"Oh, yeah. That. Okay, so what have you been thinking?"

"Well, that."

"That, what?"

I turned my head to glance at him.

"Are you kidding me right now?"

His eyes widened as he said, "In order to be kidding

you about something I'd have to have a clue about what we were discussing. And, obviously I don't."

"You said I only needed to get involved if Cassie specifically requested me to, and even then to be wary."

"Oh," he replied. "Then why didn't you just say that?"

"What?"

He threw his hands up in the air, one of which was holding on to a travel mug full of coffee. Had it not been equipped with a spill-proof top, my car would have been doused.

"You messin' with me now, bro. I know when you're messin' with me."

He had me.

"Okay, but, seriously, thanks for the advice."

He shifted his eyes toward me as he replied, "You're welcome...I think."

CHAPTER 20

Sunday morning

L ibby walked into the kitchen and glanced at the clock in the microwave.

9:30 a.m.

Charles was still snoring softly on the sofa.

She padded over and stood staring at him, wondering again if she could actually go through with killing him. She had never gotten emotionally involved with a victim before and certainly didn't intend to start now. And yet, there was something about the guy.

Before he had literally passed out the night before, and as he was working his way slowly through his third Greyhound, she had reminded him that she had kept her end of the bargain—providing him with bottomless Greyhounds—and that it was now time for him to keep his.

Wiping his mouth clumsily with the sleeve of his shirt, Charles had sat the drink down and leaned back in the chair, his eyes narrowed to slits as he regarded her.

"Yeah, about that. I know that's what I said I would do."

"But?" she'd prompted.

"But now, I'm not sure I really want to involve you any more than I already have. Like I said, you don't know these people—what they're capable of."

Sitting on the end of the couch closest to the chair, she girlishly tucked her feet up underneath her body, a well-practiced move she had used many times before to put men at ease.

"Look, Charles, I get all that. But I just want to help and I can't help you if I don't know everything that's involved."

"But that's just it, Libby," Charles had protested. "You already know too much. I mean if these people somehow found out that you were involved, well...I don't really want to think about what might happen to you."

"Well, it's not like I can force you to tell me. So..."

Charles drained the last of his drink; stared at the empty glass and started to ask for another before changing his mind and setting it carefully onto the end table.

"Even if I told you about the safe deposit box, there's nothing that can be done about it."

"And why's that?" she asked.

"Because, I don't have the key."

"Okay, who does?"

Charles sighed deeply, throwing his hands out to the side and then letting them flop against the arms of the chair.

"That's just it. I don't know for sure."

"Who had it last? Helen?"

"Yeah," he replied, "she did."

"But now, Helen is dead."

Charles had nodded slowly as tears began to course down his cheeks.

"I loved her, you know. I never stopped loving her. She was just one of those girls that are easy to love. Hell, everyone loved her. But none more than me. If I hadn't been such a jerk, we could've been married and then none of this would've happened."

After waiting for his emotion to subside, Libby reiterated, "So, Helen was the last one to have the key."

"Right."

"Do you think her husband—what was his name?"

"Tommy."

"Do you think Tommy would know where the key is?"

He shook his head vigorously.

"No. No way. Tommy didn't even know that Helen had invested money with me, at least not at first."

"But, they were married. How could he not know?"

"Separate accounts. Couples do that all the time—especially situations where each spouse contributes significantly to the household income. As in the case with Tommy and Helen, she had her own account and he had his own account. Then there was a joint account for household expenses, utilities, et cetera. But she was adamant that Tommy not know any details about her investments."

"Why?"

"Well, I'm sure it had as much to do with me being the investment counselor as anything else."

"So, Tommy knew you?"

"Oh, hell no! He didn't know anything about me or even that I existed until right before Helen, you know, had the, uh...stroke."

"And how'd that go over?"

"Not good. They had one of those tracking features on their cell phones where you can see where the other person is at all times."

"Creepy, but, go on."

"Yeah, so, anyway, one day Tommy just happened to see that she was at a bank he didn't recognize. It was where she kept the safe-deposit box."

"What bank?"

He had stared sleepily at her, struggling to keep his eyes open.

"What? Oh, yeah. The bank. I...have...you know, I think I'm about to pass out."

And with that, his head had fallen back onto the headrest and he was sound asleep.

She had considered waking him and extracting the information through more forceful means, but drunks made very poor interrogation subjects. So, she had hauled him over to the sofa, thrown a blanket over him and gone to bed.

She suddenly noticed that he was staring up at her, his mouth screwed up as if he had just tasted the worst thing ever.

"Good morning," she said lightly. "How did you sleep?"

He sat up shakily, rubbing his temples.

"Oh, man. It's been a long time since I passed out from drinking." He paused and then asked, "I did pass out, right?"

"Oh, yeah. And as far as I know you haven't moved for the past ten hours or so."

"Excuse me," he muttered and walked quickly and unsteadily toward the bathroom.

She popped a pod into the coffee maker and when Charles returned handed him a steaming cup of dark, Italian roast.

"Thank-you very much," he muttered while taking a long sip. "That's quite possibly the best coffee I've ever tasted."

After getting a cup for herself, she directed him toward the stools along one side of the small, kitchen island.

"Okay now, a deal's a deal. Last night you promised me that you'd finish telling me your story. Of course, that was before you passed out."

"Right, I did, didn't I? Okay, where was I?"

"You had just gotten to the part where Helen's husband had spotted her at a bank, but you didn't seem to know what bank it was."

"Yeah. I still don't. It was her idea to keep that information from me. So, anyway, Tommy spotted her there, asked her about it, and she told him all about me and that she had invested some of her retirement savings with the firm where I worked."

"Was he jealous?"

Charles widened his eyes and nodded slowly, saying, "Oh, yeah. Very. So much so, she told me that moving forward we were really going to have to keep our dealings on the down-low."

"But, wasn't that sort of fraudulent on her part?"

"That's not the way I saw it. It was more like her trying to protect him in case things went sideways."

"And it sounds like things definitely went sideways."

"You have no idea."

"Okay, so, Tommy knows about you, but he doesn't know about the safe-deposit box."

"Right."

"But, do you think the key could be at their place?"

"Well, that's probably a logical assumption."

"What if we just flew down there to—where did she live?"

"Dana Point, but I—"

"What if we just flew down there to Dana Point and told him, I don't know, something about the safe-deposit box and it containing something of yours that she was keeping for you and that you desperately needed it? We convince him that it's urgent and get him to accompany us to the bank. If he's next of kin, they *have* to grant him access, especially if he has the key. You do know his address, right?"

"Yeah. He lives in a condo development called *Golden Lantern Villas* in Dana Point. I'll have to look up the exact number."

"So, what do you say?"

"But, what if he doesn't have the key? What if he has no idea about the key?"

"Well, then we'll have to improvise."

"You keep saying *we* like you're involved in this."

Smiling sweetly, Libby batted her eyes and said, "But I *am* involved, Char-Wallace."

He stared at her in silence before standing suddenly.

"I really need to use the bathroom again."

Jerking her head toward the opposite end of the loft she replied, "You know where it is."

When he was out of sight, she quickly dug her cell phone out of her pants and texted: *Golden Lantern Villas. Dana Point.*

CHAPTER 21

10:00 a.m.

S o, how we gonna do this?" Aaron asked as I merged onto Interstate 5 northbound.

"I'm thinking that when we get to Tommy's place, maybe I'll pick up Helen's phone and leave you with him while I run it up to Zack's office."

"Got no problem with that. Be good to have some hang-time with Lowdown. Maybe I'll take him to lunch in Laguna Beach at that Mexican restaurant up there on the bluff; you know, see if I can provide a little distraction."

"That's a great idea, Aaron. I'm pretty sure it'll take me a while to get up to LA and back."

"Yeeeeaaaah man. Between the traffic and talking to Zack you probably won't be back to Dana Point until two or three."

"Sounds about right."

"So, what's really going on here, Jake?"

"I don't know, Aaron. But I'll tell you what's *not* going on—there's no possible way this has anything to do with Helen being unfaithful to Tommy. My sense is that she got caught up in something that got away from her and at the end was—with her last breath—trying to protect the man she loved."

Aaron seemed to ponder that before saying, "Yeah. I'm down with that. Because the Helen that I knew was ridiculously loyal to her man."

"Right, so whatever is going on has to do with money, investments and…"

And what? Well, that was the question.

"You gonna finish that sentence?" Aaron asked.

"Yeah, I am. I think it has to do with Charles, aka Brandon, getting Helen mixed up in an investment that went sideways and, I'm not sure about this but, I think it has something to do with one of those off the books things that Gabi was talking about. High risk, high return. But the money was dirty—maybe even laundered."

"So, you thinking that there are bad people behind all this?"

I nodded my head slowly, still trying to work through the thoughts that had begun assailing my mind like a scorched-earth, air-to-ground onslaught from Uncle Sam's Air Force.

"*Very* bad people, my friend. The baddest."

"Badder than the mob?"

"Much worse. Think, Russians."

"Damn," he breathed as we drove on in silence.

We traveled the thirty-two miles from Carlsbad to Dana Point without one slowdown and pulled in to Tommy's condo development around eleven-fifteen. While driving through the aboveground visitor's parking area, I noticed a black, Chevy Tahoe that was doing the same thing.

"Check that," I said and pointed to the SUV.

"Looks like we got company."

After a while you become very adept at spotting adversaries. It's either that or die. Plain and simple. Unsavory types, such as the people Aaron and I have dealt with on a monotonously regular basis for a decade, are of a type. There's just something about them that is unmistakable. The posture; the body type; body movement; set of the eyes and even the way they dress and the types of sunglasses they wear.

The two gentlemen inside the Tahoe were that type.

And I was dead certain that they were here looking for Tommy.

And that they intended him ill will.

"Call Tommy. Tell him to get into an interior room and if he has firearms to get one locked and loaded."

"Roger that," Aaron replied as he tapped Tommy's number stored in his phone's favorites.

As he talked urgently to Tommy, I tried to formulate a plan on the fly that would, at once, both discourage the bad guys from moving forward with whatever intention had brought them here as well as keep the confrontation as low-key as possible.

Yeah...there was no way.

So, I parked, got out and started walking nonchalantly toward where they were cruising through the parking area. As they drove slowly toward me, their heads pinioning around on their necks searching for a place to park, I smiled, waved and indicated that I wished to speak to them.

As the driver brought the SUV to a stop, I got a better look, which only confirmed my suspicions. He was a swarthy man of some size with eyebrows that formed a nearly unbroken line across his forehead. His head was shaved, but he wore a full, very bushy beard. The passenger's head was also shaved, only he was fair skinned, smaller and craftier in appearance.

I could see extensive tattooing extending up their necks and even onto the backs of their heads.

They stopped the SUV and rolled down the window.

Big mistake.

I said, "I was wondering if you could help me find my friend's condo. I don't live here and this is my first time visiting."

The driver looked at me.

He looked at the passenger.

They both looked at me.

The driver was just about to say something in re-

R.G. RYAN

sponse when I shoved my Sig Sauer P229 .357 in his face.

"I hope you two understand English, because if you don't, then I'll just have to shoot both of you in the head and leave your bodies for the local authorities and Homeland Security to sort out."

"Who are you?" the passenger asked in a thick, Russian accent.

"That's a fair question," I replied. "But a better question would be, *what* am I. I don't mind answering that one. I'm pissed off, that's *what* I am! And do you want to know why? I thought you did. I'm pissed off because you're here to bother my friend Tommy."

At the mention of his name, both of their eyes widened.

Gotcha!

"We don't know nothing about no one by that name," said the driver, whose eyes kept involuntarily shifting downward toward my pistol.

"Nice try, asshole. Horrible syntax, but nice try." I leveled the Sig at the passenger. "With your left hand, take your gun out and toss it out the window as far as you can throw it."

He shifted his gaze to the driver, but since the driver was preoccupied with huge diameter of the Sig's barrel, he did as he was instructed.

"Now, my grammatically challenged friend," I said to the driver, "with your left hand on the barrel, hand me your weapon. But keep in mind that at this point you are not humans to me. You are merely problems. And my job is to make problems go away."

I sensed, rather than saw, Aaron moving up on the opposite side of the vehicle with his weapon drawn.

"Who are you guys, anyway?" the passenger asked Aaron.

"We're no one to be trifled with."

He grinned.

"I love that movie. Princess Bride, yeah? With the giant and—"

"Shut up," Aaron barked.

I glanced around the area and then jerked the driver's door open.

"Get out."

"Hey...Terminator. I lov—"

Aaron hollered, "Dude, if you keep talking, I will be forced to shoot your dumb ass. Now shut it."

Aaron was, apparently, a bit short on patience.

"Now you—movie lover—you're next."

As the passenger carefully exited the vehicle, I said, "Here's what's going to happen. "We're all going to go visit our friend. Now I know what you're thinking."

The passenger's eyes brightened and he began, "Dirty Harry—ouch!"

Faster than my eye could follow, Aaron had backhanded him on the end of his nose, causing the man's eyes to fill with tears.

"Like I was saying, I know what you're thinking. You're thinking that you are very tough. But you aren't as tough as we are."

The passenger had stopped smiling and was now glaring in my direction with what I imagined as being evil intent.

He said, "You don't know who you are messing with," and then followed it with several deprecating comments in Russian having something to do with unfortunate and demeaning uses of a goat's anatomy.

"Aaron," I hollered across the hood. "How many guys have said those very words to us over the years?"

"About the goat, or the other?"

"The other."

He pretended to think it over.

"Oh, now let's see, probably right around...oh...everyone we've ever busted."

I nudged the driver in the side with the Sig.

"Get going and keep your hands where I can see them."

We walked through the parking lot without incident —a situation I credited to the residents all parking in the underground garage and little traffic on a Sunday morning —and had just gotten into the elevator when, for reasons known only to himself, the passenger decided to try something brave.

CHAPTER 22

As the elevator doors closed, the driver spun suddenly to his right and attempted to knock the Sig out of my hand, which would have been far more successful had my right hand still been holding the pistol. But it wasn't. Experience has taught me much, and one of the greatest lessons I have learned is that bad guys are not necessarily perceptive or inventive guys. Since he had seen the gun in my right hand when we entered the elevator, his assumption was that it would still be there when he attempted his ill-advised heroics. Having anticipated just such a move on his part, and since I can shoot just as well with either hand, I had transferred the pistol to my left hand while his back was still turned.

He chopped down hard toward where he believed the gun to be, but I was already moving to counter the blow. I leaned back from his motion so he got nothing but air and then clubbed him with an overhand right that connected just to the right side of his nose, breaking it cleanly. He screamed and brought his hands up, applying pressure and attempting to mitigate the pain and stem the immediate flow of blood.

While all this was going on, I saw Aaron in the periphery of my vision encircle the passenger's neck with one of his oversized hands and lock in on a nerve meridian, sending the man into temporary paralysis.

I said, "You only get one stupid move card, and you just played it. The consequences become very severe from this point forward. Nod your heads if you understand what I'm saying."

They both nodded quickly.

The elevator arrived at Tommy's floor and the doors opened to reveal three young women in beach cover-ups standing there, hands filled with umbrellas, coolers and a couple of beach bags. They saw the man's bloody face and their mouths dropped open in immediate shock.

I said quickly, "He tripped and went head-first into one of the curbs out in the parking lot. We're trying to get him inside and get this cleaned up. So, please excuse us."

I said it so quickly, and it sounded so convincing that they not only moved out of the way but expressed sympathy and even asked if there was anything they could do to help.

I had managed to shove my gun up underneath the man's shirt, pressing it tightly into his left side while holding onto his right arm so it looked like I was helping him walk. Aaron had merely put his gun hand into the pouch at the front of his hoodie, leaving his hand around the passenger's neck in such a way that you couldn't tell if it was palsywalsy, intimate or intimidating.

We stepped off the elevator as the three beauties entered, chattering in concerned tones until the doors closed.

I said, "Okay, move it," and we walked quickly down the hall toward Tommy's unit.

Aaron knocked in what seemed to be a prearranged pattern and the door opened.

Tommy's mouth dropped open.

"What's going down, Ivory?"

"Got us some visitors here. They gonna tell us stuff."

The passenger said through clenched teeth, "I tell you nothing!"

Aaron and I both chuckled.

"Yeah," I replied, "that's what they all say."

With a fierce gaze, he replied, "I have endured interrogation and have never cracked. You will get nothing from me."

I turned to Tommy.

"You have a couple of chairs you don't mind getting messed up?"

He stared at me without answering for a few seconds before replying, "Uh, yeah...okay...chairs. Hang on."

He hurried out of the room and came back with two metal folding chairs.

"Will this work?"

"Perfect. You have a couple of extension cords as well?"

"Oh, maybe one or two."

"Ah," the smaller of the two Russians smirked. "You try to shock us with electricity, huh? It will not work. We are tough."

Tommy came back with a box containing what appeared to be every size of extension cord known to mankind.

"How's this?" he asked with a grin.

"I'm pretty sure that'll work."

Aaron shoved the passenger into a chair and proceeded to tie each ankle to one of the chair's legs; then his hands together and then to one of the cross braces on the bottom. He then did the same with the driver whose nose was still seeping blood.

Tommy said, "Who are these people, Jake?"

"I have a pretty good idea, but we're going to find out for sure."

"Does this have something to do with what Helen said?"

"Possibly."

The driver lolled his head to one side, staring intensely at me with his mouth hanging open to accommodate breathing.

"I could have beaten you if you didn't sucker punch

me."

"No," I replied, "a sucker punch is when someone isn't expecting to be hit. Since you initiated an aggressive move it is ludicrous and disingenuous to assume that you didn't expect, and dare I say, plan on being punched. So, your argument is, therefore, without merit."

While he attempted to decipher what I had just said, I turned to the passenger and asked, "So, why are you here?"

He sneered, "Because your friend made me come."

I pretended to laugh.

"You're a funny guy—"

"So, you'll kill me last?" he said, completing my sentence.

"Very good. No, that's not what I was going to say. Aaron?"

Aaron stepped forward and placed his index finger on a spot at the left side of the man's neck right where it joins the shoulder and began to press. The man's mouth dropped open in a silent scream and he began to jerk slightly, involuntarily.

As Aaron released, I said, "That was level one out of many. Now, we'll try this again. Why are you here?"

The man craned his neck toward the right as if attempting to alleviate residual pain.

"I have nothing to say to you."

"Oh, you will.

The guy spat—or, more accurately, tried to spit, as he seemed to be sorely lacking in saliva.

I decided to take a break and call Zack.

CHAPTER 23

Russians, huh?" Zack said bitterly.

"Yeah," I replied. "And based on the tats I could see, I am almost certain they're vory."

"Vory v-Zakone—Russian mafia. So, you saw the tats?"

"I didn't take their shirts off, but I saw a tat of Jesus on the back of one guy's neck and the steeples from St. Basil's on the other guy's chest where his shirt had popped a few buttons."

"You're probably right, then." He paused and then suggested, "If they're vory, I don't have to remind you who they're connected to."

"Orlov," I said distastefully.

It was reference to Vasily Orlov, the Godfather of the Russian mob in the Western United States. A man I had beaten soundly in Portland, Oregon some five weeks previously, taking down a significant segment of his human trafficking empire in the process—the man who had vowed to kill me by any means necessary and at any cost.

"But," I asked "his vendetta against me notwithstanding, why would a couple of Orlov's guys be here in Tommy's condo development?"

"Are you sure they were looking for Tommy?"

"It's a virtual certainty."

Zack was silent for a few moments and then said, "That makes no sense whatsoever."

"Why?"

"Because in Southern California, Orlov's interests are

primarily human trafficking."

"That's what I thought," I said. "So, think creatively with me. First of all, what would that look like here?"

"Trafficking?" He paused for a moment before continuing, "Well, it would look like one of two things: either they keep a stable of girls in a house somewhere in the area and pimp them out as high-class call girls, or they sell them outright to the highest bidder. Forget everything you've ever known about hookers. These girls haven't gone into the business because they were hard up, or drug addicts—although they are almost certainly addicted now. They are all young and exceptionally beautiful; the kind of girls you see in movies and fashion magazines."

My mind was going crazy with memories.

And none of them were good.

"So, kind of like what happened to Cassie, Muriel and Eddie up in Seattle?"

"That's exactly what I'm talking about."

"Damn, that's bleak."

"Exactly. But, that's reality. As you know, it's what we deal with all day, every day. And it's getting worse. Recent statistics indicate that there are somewhere around eight hundred thousand young women every year that are sold into sexual slavery where they endure months, if not years of torture before being rescued. Or, dying."

"It just breaks my heart every time I think about it."

"I know. But even more heartbreaking are the families who voluntarily choose to sell one or more of their daughters to these traffickers."

I said, "I've never understood how could someone do that."

"Jake, my friend, my experience has been that if you introduce enough desperation, or enough greed into a person's life, they will do almost anything for the right price."

"But, selling your own daughters?"

"Happens every day somewhere in the world,

brother."

I said, "So, let's say that this is exactly what we are dealing with here. How could any of that possibly be related to Tommy and Helen Marshall?"

"I have absolutely no idea. I assume that you are going to conduct some form of interrogation?"

"The thought had crossed my mind."

He chuckled, saying, "I have no doubt. So, here's what I want to know: What did Helen Marshall do to warrant the presence of Vasily Orlov's vory on her husband's doorstep?"

"Exactly. And, who is this mysterious Charles guy and what is that stuff with the key all about?

Zack said, "And, by extension, where does Orlov house the girls and when will a new shipment be arriving?"

"Not asking for much, are you?"

"Well, hey," he replied, "this *is* the Russian mob. These guys are the most heartless and cruel people I've ever met outside of Mano Roja."

"That's really saying something. Mano Roja are the worst."

"So, if Helen was somehow involved..." he paused and then added, "Jake, do you think Tommy would sign off on an autopsy?"

"Maybe. Why?"

"Let me think out loud for a minute. If Orlov is, indeed, involved and if he found out that Helen was mixed up in whatever is going on, it is totally consistent with his MO to somehow have gotten to her and administered something that induced a stroke if for no other reason than to send a message to Charles."

"How would that even be possible?" I said.

"Oh, there are a lot of ways to induce a stroke. The trick is to do it in such a way that it doesn't arouse suspicion."

The world suddenly felt as if it were tilting—things spinning completely out of balance. The fact that my sweet friend may have been killed just because she was an unknowing and unwilling participant in the Russian mob's human trafficking enterprise produced a blind rage. If you want to know the truth, I felt an immediate and intense need to induce pain. And, as it turned out, I had a couple of people in mind to serve as the recipients.

"Zack, I'm going to have to call you back in a little bit."

"Okay. But let me know about the autopsy thing."

"For sure."

I terminated the call and walked back into the other room.

Quickly.

And without breaking stride, I caught the movie-loving passenger under the chin, tipping the chair over backward and straddling his chest.

Bending down until my face was inches from his I hollered, "I am going to begin asking questions and you will answer truthfully and immediately or you will suffer unpleasantness on a level your pathetic mind is incapable of perceiving."

He stared at me in silence, his eyes blinking rapidly.

Then, he shrugged and said, "Okay."

As Aaron helped me raise his chair into its original position, he asked, "So, just like that? You're willing to talk?"

The man shrugged again.

"Western living has made me soft. Besides, I have girl —she is one of ours. I love her. We have chance for life here in America. But, my bosses—terrible people. Hearts of stone. They will torture me to death if I try to take Nastasiya away. So, here is deal with you. I tell you things and you help me get Nastasiya away from my bosses. Deal?"

I glanced at Aaron, who shrugged and said, "That'll work."

I asked, "And how about your friend?"

He glanced at the driver, who had either passed out or

fallen asleep.

"He does what I tell him."

"Okay then. We have a deal."

Tommy said, "Can somebody please tell a brother what in *the* hell is going on?"

CHAPTER 24

12:00 noon

Libby watched Charles as he walked slowly into the great room, unconsciously wiping his hands on the front of his shirt as if to remove excess moisture. He was a pathetic figure, really. A haphazardly dressed middle-aged man whose thinning, reddish hair was an obvious stranger to a stylist's scissors. Eyes the color of dirty rainwater peeked out from behind glasses that hadn't been in style for a good long while. The narrow shoulders that topped a short, slender frame seemed bowed under the weight of woe he carried.

In short, there was nothing special about him.

And yet, she found to her utter surprise and chagrin, that he had managed to stir something in her soul. Pity? Compassion? Since neither was an emotion she was accustomed to feeling, she couldn't say. But, there was something there. Would it interfere with her mission to eliminate him? To terminate him "with extreme prejudice", as characters in movies were fond of saying? She thought not, for above everything else, Libby—or, Oksana, as her mother had named her—was a professional. Consummately so. Emotions had never hindered her in the past, nor would she allow it to happen now.

"You doing okay, Charlie boy?" she asked brightly as he resumed his seat.

"I don't know how to answer that, Libby. On the one

hand, it feels so good to have someone to talk to about my situation. But the reality is, I fear I have ruined your life; that you will be, like me, forced to spend the rest of your days looking over your shoulder and around every corner."

"Oh, I wouldn't worry about that, Charlie. You won't spend the rest of your life doing that."

He glanced up at her.

"You sound very confident."

"That's me," she replied with a wink and a smile. "I am nothing if not."

He was silent for a few seconds before saying, "So... about going to Southern Cal."

"Yes?"

"Well, I actually think it's a good idea."

"Really?" she feigned surprise. "And what brought you to that little revelation?"

"Well," he began, and then paused to pick up his martini glass and swirl the remnants of the last Greyhound. "Until I find that key and regain control of those USB sticks, I have no shot at any kind of life."

"So, you want me to arrange for us to fly down there?"

He sighed deeply.

"If only it were that simple. I can't fly anywhere without the FED's being all over me. They can track me anywhere."

"Not on a private plane," Libby replied.

"What do you mean?"

"If you knew someone with, let's say, a corporate jet, you could just drive to the airport, get onboard and take off without having to disclose your identity or even file a flight plan."

"How is that possible?"

"Well, it's because the TSA figures that if you are flying your own private jet, they already know who you are and treat it as if you were driving passengers in your private automobile."

Charles stood and strolled to the window.

"Wait...so, you're saying that if I knew someone with a private jet, we could just go to, what, an executive airport or whatever, get on the plane and take off without having to undergo a security check or tell the tower, or whatever, where we're going?"

"Pretty much," she replied. "The only thing that would complicate things is if you were chipped, or had an ankle thing that allowed the FED's to track your movements."

"Nah, they do that with my phone."

"Okay, so, if you took the battery out of your phone, it'll be disabled and they can't track you."

Charles sat heavily into the chair.

"But this is a pointless discussion, because it's predicated on me knowing someone with a private jet. And I don't."

"Well, maybe *you* don't."

"What are you saying?"

"Remember when I told you my dad was rich?"

"Yeah."

"Well, he has a Learjet at Atlantic Aviation out at PDX."

"Really?" Charles replied, stretching out the word. "Okay, but what makes you think he'd let us use it? I mean isn't that ridiculously expensive?"

"Not gonna lie, it is definitely expensive. But we can use it."

"How can you be so sure?"

"I'm an only child and he indulges me. In fact, he'll let me do just about anything I want to do. Well, except kill people. He obviously wouldn't let me do that."

Charles waited a few seconds before asking, "Why would you do this for me? I mean you don't even know me."

"I know you better than you think I do, Charlie."

"What's that supposed to mean?"

She said, "It means that I *get* you—that I understand what you're going through, and, well…I just feel like I'm supposed to help out."

He sat in silence, nodding his head slowly as if thinking the situation through.

"Okay. Let's do this."

She stood and clapped her hands together.

"Great. So, I need to make a couple of calls to get the plane prepped and ready to go. And I should probably throw a few necessaries into an overnight bag. How about you? You need to go back to your place and pick some stuff up?"

"No," he replied quickly. "I'm not going anywhere near my apartment."

"Ahhhh, so the FED's don't know where you are right now?"

"Not exactly."

She grinned knowingly and said, "You already disabled your phone, didn't you?"

"I, uh, looked on YouTube and saw how to do it."

"Very smart, Charlie boy."

He blew out a long breath of air.

"I can't believe I'm even considering this let alone doing it."

"What else are you going to do? You can't just sit around and wait for the Russians to find you, right?"

He stood and walked over to stare out the window again.

"I know, but, honestly? I feel like I'm going to die. Like no matter what I do the end result is that I'm going to die—and that it won't be pretty."

Libby came up behind him and encircled his waist with her arms, laying her head against his back.

"Stick with me, Charlie-boy. I won't let the bad old Russians get you."

Turning slowly around, he held her at arm's length.

"Promise?"

She nodded and pecked him on the cheek.

"Yeah. They'll have to get through me to get to you."

Laughing nervously, he said, "You must be very tough, then."

With a wink she replied, "Oh, you have no idea."

CHAPTER 25

The Russian bad guys were still tied to their respective chairs, but the passenger—whose name, as it turned out, was Iosif—was feeling talkative now that he knew there was a chance that we would help Nastasiya, his girlfriend. On the other hand, Spartak, the driver, had yet to utter anything other than his original complaint of having been sucker punched, and continued to cast dark looks in my direction. I figured that if given half a chance he would try to cause trouble.

After confirming that Iosif and his vengeful friend did, indeed, work for the Russian mafia, Iosif said, "I could speak better with hands untied and water to drink."

"I'm sure you could. But that's not gonna happen just yet."

He shrugged.

"Okay. What can I tell you?"

Tommy hollered, "You can tell me what the hell you have to do with my wife."

"I don't know nothing about your wife. I only know we were told to come here and get something you have."

"I don't have shit," Tommy replied heatedly.

Iosif grinned. It was not a pleasant sight.

"You have key."

Tommy cast helpless eyes on me.

"That damn key again. I don't have any damn key!"

I asked, "What is the key for, Iosif?"

"Is for box."

"What kind of box?" Aaron said.

He grinned again.

"No, no. For that, you let me go."

Aaron looked a question at me. I nodded and he untied Iosif's hands.

Iosif said, "Much better. Okay. What was question?"

I replied, "What kind of box?"

"The kind in banks."

"Safe-deposit box?"

"Sure."

I glanced at Tommy and asked, "Do you think that's what Helen was doing that day you tracked her movement on your phone—opening a safe-deposit box?"

"How the hell am I supposed to know?" he replied in frustration. "I suppose she could have been, but, why?"

I turned to face Iosif.

"What was in the box?"

Still rubbing his wrists as if to get circulation restored, he replied, "Don't know. She said to just get key and wait for her."

"She? Who are you talking about?"

"Oksana."

"Okay," I said. "Who is Oksana and what does she have to do with this?"

"Oksana Orlov. She is boss."

Aaron and I exchanged glances.

"Boss of what," Aaron asked.

"Boss of finding box."

"That make any sense to you, Jake?"

"None whatsoever. The Russian mob is a boys' club. So, Iosif, is Oksana related to Vasily?"

His eyes widened as if in sudden understanding.

"Ah, now I see. You are Moriarity?"

"What of it?"

He replied with a grin, "You are not Orlov's favorite person. He would very much like to kill you. You know, because of Portland."

"Right," I said. "I am well aware of that. But answer my question. Is Oksana related to Vasily?"

"Is daughter," Iosif replied. "Oksana is...important."

"Why?"

"She is assassin."

"Now, hold on a damn minute," Tommy shouted. "Are you saying that a female, Russian assassin and my wife had something in common? That's the stupidest damn thing I've ever heard."

It was a fair assessment, at least from Tommy's perspective. The mere suggestion that sweet, kind-hearted Helen Marshall would even walk on the same side of the street as Russian mobsters was ludicrous, let alone being partnered with them in some level of criminal activity. But, as outrageous as it seemed, I couldn't dwell on that. I had to shift gears and try to find something that made sense.

I asked, "Who is Charles, Iosif?"

"Charles? I don't know no Charles."

Tommy blurted out, "Did you know my wife, Helen?"

"No," he replied simply.

"So..." I began before pausing to consider my thoughts "...the only reason you came here today is that Oksana gave you this address and said that the key to the safe-deposit box was here. Is that correct?"

Iosif nodded slowly, "Is correct."

"And you've never seen this man," I pointed to Tommy. "Or his wife, Helen before? And you have never heard of or met Charles?"

"Is also correct."

My phone started buzzing.

It was Zack.

I answered and stepped into the other room to talk.

"Please tell me you've got something," I said.

"Yes," he affirmed, "I do. We were able to pull up hundreds of texts and emails between Helen and this Charles guy. There were also close to a hundred calls placed between them over the past nine months or so."

"And?" I prompted.

"Charles did, in fact, work for that venture capital firm. From what we have been able to gather, the nature of Charles' relationship with Helen was pretty complicated."

"Can you elaborate on that?"

"Well," he said, "they were old friends—high school sweethearts, actually—"

"Which I had already figured out."

"Right, but it doesn't appear that Charles ever got over the breakup. The tone of some of the texts was pretty intimate."

"Intimate, how?" I asked.

"Like—hang on. Okay, I'm going to read an exact quote to you: *I never stopped loving you, Helen. It was hard enough losing you, but then when I finally figured out that the only reason you left me was because I pushed you away, well, that was pure torture.*

"Interesting. And how did she reply? Was the sentiment reciprocal?"

"Not even close. I mean she was polite, but she never went beyond that; never led him on or even encouraged him. But that's not what I wanted to tell you."

"Okay," I replied. "Let's hear it."

"In a nutshell, this guy at his core is just a bad dude. Always looking for angles and get-rich-quick schemes and not seeming to care who he hurts in the process. He started investing a client's money, hang on, uh…Konstantin Morozov is the guy's name."

"That's a new one. What's his relationship to Orlov?"

"I'm not sure yet, but apparently, his grandfather is a major player in the Russian mafia and this Konstantin guy is a major player in the vory's human trafficking operation here in LA. Anyway, Charles starts investing Morozov's money and doing very well for his client. So well that Morozov keeps bringing him bigger and bigger amounts to

invest culminating in a one hundred million dollar investment that Charles does completely off the books producing
an unbelievable return."

"Fascinating. But how does this involve Helen?"

"I'm getting to that. At some point, Charles decided to
take Helen's money and piggyback it with Morozov's. And
according to the texts and emails we've been able to dredge
up, it was done one hundred percent without her knowledge."

"But at some point, she found out?" I asked.

"She found out because he told her. It seems that
Charles had one sliver of conscience left. He had gone into
this arrangement with Morozov thinking that the guy was
laundering money or something like that—acceptable in
his mind. But when he learned that the profits he was generating on his client's behalf were being used in human
trafficking—"

"His conscience kicks in?"

"Exactly. He tells Helen about the entire scheme."

"At which point, he signed her death warrant," I mumbled under my breath.

"Not just yet. She was still under the radar as far as the
Russians were concerned. Where it started getting compli-
cated is when Charles decided to basically steal some of the
Russian's profits."

I said, "Let me guess, he shifted the money to offshore accounts and kept all the access codes; put the codes
on some form of storage device—probably a USB stick; and
then had Helen open a safe-deposit box and had her keep the
key."

Zack was silent for a few seconds.

"How do you do that?"

"What?"

"Just randomly pull stuff out of thin air like that?"

I chuckled, "How close was I?"

"Spot on. And that's what's scary. What you missed,

though, is the involvement of Homeland Security in recruiting Charles as a material witness against the mobsters. His testimony resulted in Morozov being convicted."

"That's good."

"Yes, but it also necessitated Charles being placed in WitSec."

So, not only had Charles gotten Helen involved with Russian mobsters, but he was now in WitSec? This case was getting weirder by the second.

CHAPTER 26

I said, "If Morozov was convicted on the basis of Charles' testimony, then how did Charles and Helen keep the money a secret from the FED's?"

"The details are a little sketchy," Zack replied, "but from the texts and emails I've seen between Charles and Helen, they are the only ones who knew about the stash."

"Hang on, when did the WitSec thing go down?"

"According to the WitSec database, a little over a month ago."

I pinched the bridge of my nose between my right thumb and forefinger in an ineffectual attempt to stave off an emergent headache.

"Zack, I can't even begin to explain to you how confused I am right now."

"Yeah," he agreed. "It's as confusing as hell. But the more texts and emails we read, the more sense it makes."

"I have a question," I said. "Did you say that Helen set up the safe-deposit box and was the only one who had the key?"

"Yes, that's correct."

"That makes no sense."

"Why?"

"Because, if this Charles guy is the money grubbing, manipulative, greedy bastard that I think he is, wouldn't he want to have full access to those funds? I mean just because someone is placed in WitSec doesn't mean they stay there. And especially when they have access to, what...millions of dollars?"

I heard Zack rustling through some papers.

"Make that roughly, twenty-seven million."

The sum was staggering.

"Wait a second. You're telling me that Charles and Helen Marshall had direct and unfettered access to twenty-seven million dollars?"

"Well," Zack replied, "having not seen the actual ledger sheets or offshore financial reports—because in order to do that we'd have to know the exact location of the account, and we don't—I can't be certain. But according to the correspondence between them, that figure is pretty close."

What the hell was going on here?

"Okay, set that aside for a moment. Is there any indication as to what they were going to do with all that money?"

"Actually, there is." He shuffled some more papers. "All right, here we go. Apparently, Charles had gotten ahold of some critical information regarding not only a new shipment of girls that are coming into LA sometime within the next seven days via a big-rig—that, by the way, they hoped to somehow intercept—but there is also an anti-human trafficking organization they planned to help by setting up a trust fund."

Things were starting to fall into place.

I said, "So, Helen wasn't having an affair with an old flame; she was helping her old flame attempt to do one right thing in his misspent life?"

"That's what we're seeing from the correspondence," he explained.

"But we still don't know who had the safe-deposit key."

"Wrong. Reading through the texts and emails there are several references to the mysterious key, but they are decidedly non-specific except in the irrefutable inference that Helen is the only one who knew where it was." Zack was silent for a few seconds before adding, "Jake, I don't like telling you this, but I have to. The Russians found out who Helen was; tracked her down; tried to get the information about the key from her, and then administered something that induced a stroke. I'd bet my career on it."

That was a lot to swallow even if Helen hadn't been my friend.

"I can't even begin to tell you how surreal this all seems. What should I tell Tommy?"

"Well," Zack said, "I've always found the truth to be helpful."

"I was afraid you were going to say that."

"I know. It sucks, but what else are you gonna do?"

I sighed and resumed pinching the bridge of my nose.

"Any suggestions on what should happen next?" I asked.

"Actually, I've been thinking about that. So, Charles isn't his real name.

"Yeah. Tommy told us."

Zack explained, "His birth name is Brandon Crawford. His WitSec ID is under Wallace Bennington, but, for reasons unknown at this time, he and Helen agreed that he'd go by Charles Sutton. We have a solid idea of who Charles is as well as how Helen Marshall got involved in this. We also know what the key is for and why it's so important. What we don't know is where Orlov houses the girls or anything about the arrival of that new shipment. And it would be helpful to know where the damn key is."

"All right," I said. "I'm pretty sure our bad guys will be forthcoming with the information regarding the girls. But the key is another matter altogether." I suddenly had a thought. "Zack, where is Charles right now?"

There was a pause followed by a copulative-referencing expletive.

"Let me see what I can find out from the Marshalls' Service."

"Please do that. In the meantime, I'll see what else I

can learn from Tweedledum and Tweedledee."

CHAPTER 27

3:00 p.m.

T he Learjet had been airborne for a little more than ten minutes and Charles was staring through the window at the ever-diminishing Portland skyline below. Once it had been agreed that they fly to Los Angeles, Libby had turned into a whirling dervish of activity.

Calls were made in rapid-fire order.

Many calls.

In fact, she was still on the phone.

And he was terrified. Terrified because of what he had just heard. Even though he knew it couldn't be true—and was more than likely a figment of his frayed nerves and over-active imagination—he could almost swear that he had just overheard her speaking in Russian. Having spent the past year in the constant company of Russian nationals, he had developed an ear for the language.

Libby terminated the call and turned to face him.

"Everything okay?" he asked anxiously.

"Perfect. I arranged to have a car and driver from my dad's company meet us at the John Wayne Airport Executive terminal."

"Wow. That's very generous."

"Like I said, I'm spoiled," she replied with a sly smile.

"Libby, I have to ask you something."

"Okay. Shoot."

"When you were just talking on the phone I couldn't help but overhear and—this is going to sound crazy—but I could swear I heard you speaking in Russian."

She laughed as if that was the funniest thing she'd ever heard.

"I get that a lot."

"Get what?" he replied in confusion.

"I guess I should have told you. My dad is Ukrainian. It was actually my first language. My dad is old country all the way—still insists that when I speak to him, I speak in the mother tongue as he calls it."

"Interesting," Charles said. "It sounded just like what the Russian guys spoke to each other."

"Understandable. Most people can't tell the difference between the two languages."

"So, what *is* the difference?"

"Well, I could give you a complicated answer, but basically just think about the differences between English spoken in some parts of Great Briton—like a Liverpool accent or heavy Scottish accent—and English spoken in the United States."

"So, same language but different dialect?"

"Well, it's more complicated than that. In fact, if you grew up speaking Ukrainian, you can easily understand Russian. But if you grew up speaking Russian, it would be difficult to understand Ukrainian."

"Kind of like a native Portuguese speaker can understand a native Spanish speaker, but not vice-versa?"

Libby nodded her head.

"Yes. That's almost exactly what it is like."

It all sounded so plausible, and yet there was something that had transitioned once they had boarded the plane; something in her demeanor that Charles found very troubling. While he couldn't exactly put his finger on it, he was fairly certain it had to do with the deference everyone paid to Libby. It was more than her being completely in charge, which she most decidedly was. It was almost as if she were feared. The bubbly, hipster persona he had found so attractive back at the coffee shop and at her loft was not the persona she displayed to the flight crew and limo driver. Maybe it was because she was the daughter of a very wealthy, powerful man and she was used to treating her father's employees—and they, her—in a certain way.

"I can't believe how fast this plane gained altitude," he remarked absently to distract himself from things he really didn't want to consider.

"Yeah, it's pretty amazing, isn't it?"

"I was watching a commercial airliner on another strip taking off about the same time we were, and we just left it in the dust."

She giggled girlishly.

"It's funny, I have flown on this plane so many times that I sometimes forget how cool it is. I suppose I should, what's that old saying, stop and smell the roses a little more?"

Libby glanced down at her phone and noticed that the last two texts to Iosif had gone unanswered. That was unusual. Of all her associates, he was the most communicative. If he wasn't responding, that couldn't be good.

Saying, "Excuse me," to Charles, she stood and walked to the back of the plane and called Iosif's cell.

It rang a few times and then went to voicemail.

In all her years of working with the man, that had never happened before. Stepping into the restroom, she shut the door behind her, closed the lid on the commode and sat down to gather her thoughts. What did it mean? Maybe he was already at the condo and was engaged in a search or interrogation. She dismissed that possibility quickly. Even if he were occupied, he would answer a call from her. But, what if he had lost his phone or left it behind in his vehicle? There was no way that would happen. He knew full well the consequences of not being available when summoned.

Before drawing any final conclusions, she decided to place one more call. After all, he had never failed her before. He deserved that much consideration.

She called him again and waited.

One ring.

Two rings.

Then, "Hello, Oksana."

It was a deep, male voice. Definitely not Iosif. But, who then?

A sudden jolt of alarm prompted her to inquire quickly, "Who is this?"

The man laughed quietly.

"That is a very appropriate question, Oksana. And in answer let me just tell you, that as of this moment you are done. Your organization is done. Everything you have valued or held dear is now gone."

"I don't know who Oksana is. My name is Libby and I have no idea what you are talking about. Can you please tell me what's going on?" she said, feigning ignorance and trying to buy time.

The man's voice suddenly took on a razor's edge.

"Look, little girl. I'm not in the mood to play games. One of my best friends is dead because of you and your stupid Russian goons. I have two of them in my custody and I will soon have you in my custody. And when I do, you are going to tell me things."

The man's tone troubled her. She was unaccustomed to people addressing her with anything less than respect and fear. She found that she didn't like it.

"Who is this, anyway? I think I need to call the police and—"

"Jake Moriarity."

It couldn't be. While she had never encountered the man personally, his legend in the global underground seemed to grow exponentially year after year. In short, no one had ever beaten him. And…he had beaten her father.

"Jake Moriarity," she said, dropping all pretenses. "I have heard much about you. I was wondering if I would ever have the honor of going up against you."

"Yeah? Well, I've never heard of you, so you mean less to me than a piece of dog shit stuck to my shoe—just something to be scraped off."

"I think, sir, you will find me a bit more challenging to deal with than that."

"Everyone always says that," he replied. "Including your father. And yet…I'm still here."

"Well, speaking of dogs, what's that old saying? Every dog has its day? Perhaps this is going to be yours."

She could hear him sigh.

"I can hear the engine noise in the background, which means that you are on a jet—most likely private—and, I'm guessing, headed into Los Angeles. Probably coming in to the John Wayne Executive Airport within the next couple of hours. The FBI will have agents on the ground awaiting your arrival. So, you are effectively trapped. I suppose you could divert to another airport. If you're in a Lear you definitely have the range. But it won't take us long to find your flight plan and begin tracking your movements. Like I said… trapped. Oh, and if you're expecting Charles to tell you anything more about the key than he already has, forget it! He doesn't know anything. But I do."

Libby had heard of the man's nearly psychic abilities when it came to figuring out key elements of cases, but to experience it firsthand was almost breathtaking.

"I hear you used to be a seminarian, Moriarity."

"That's true. So?"

"Perhaps you will remember the Scripture that says, pride goes before destruction and a haughty spirit before a fall."

"Don't mistake confidence for pride. My confidence is based on a track record of which you are undoubtedly aware. Like my very southern mother used to say, no brag... just fact."

"Touché. So, you have never been beaten and I have never been caught. We shall see who prevails, won't we?"

"Yes, we shall. And it will happen very soon."

"Don't count on it," she replied with sudden anger as she stabbed the button to terminate the call, threw the door to the restroom open and stalked angrily down the aisle.

Charles turned at her approach and said, "Is everything o—"

With a high-pitched yell, she knocked him out and stood trembling with anger.

Moriarity.

She really didn't need this right now.

CHAPTER 28

Well," I said, staring at Iosif's phone, "I'm thinking your girl, Oksana, is less than pleased with me right now."

Aaron asked, "What'd she have to say?"

"At first she was evasive, claiming to be someone named Libby."

"Is one of her characters," Iosif muttered.

"Characters?"

"Sure. She has characters for different purposes."

"You mean disguises."

He shrugged and replied, "Characters, disguises. Is all same. There are many."

"Anyway," I continued, "as soon as I said my name, she dropped the act."

"She is bad person," Iosif said with a noticeable shudder. "Has killed many people."

"So, she's what," Aaron inquired, "a contract killer for the Russian mafia?"

"I do not know this term."

"What he means," I explained, "is that the Russian mafia pays her to kill people."

"Ah. Is so. She makes much money in killing." He paused before adding soberly, "Oksana, she enjoys killing."

I said, "I have to call Zack," and stepped out of the room once again.

He picked up on the third ring.

"Jake, I was just about to call you."

"Good, but I have, as they say, some breaking news for you."

"Okay."

"There is a woman whose name is Oksana Orlov. Vasily's daughter. She's an assassin for the Russian mafia and is on a private jet with Charles Sutton. I'm almost certain they're headed for the executive terminal at John Wayne. We need to have agents on the ground waiting for her, but we also need to be tracking her movements in case she redirects the flight."

"So, do you have the N-Number of the aircraft, or what kind it is, point of departure? Anything?" he asked.

"Sadly, no. But I believe it took off from the Portland, Oregon area."

"Right. That's not much to go on, but I'll scramble an intercept team to John Wayne and get to work on identifying the aircraft. Do you at least have an ETA?"

I glanced at my watch.

"Maybe in an hour?"

Zack said, "We'll definitely be there ahead of that. Now, what I needed to tell you is that we uncovered what I believe is a coded text message that passed between Charles and Helen the day before her stroke."

"Interesting. Why do you think it's in code?"

"Well...you'd have to see it in context with their other communications, but simply put, you know how you and Aaron communicate with each other; the words you use; the cadence, et cetera?"

"Sure."

He said, "What if all of a sudden in your communication it was like two different people talking instead of the two of you."

"Okay. I get it. So, what was the message?"

He shuffled through some more papers and then said, "Here we go. Helen wrote, *'And I saw an angel come down from heaven.'* And then Charles writes, *'Having the key of the bottomless pit.'* Then Helen says, *'And a great chain in his hand.'* That's really strange phraseology."

"They were quoting the Bible," I replied. "Revelation twenty, verse one."

"Did you just pull that out of your butt?"

"Hey...seminarian, remember?"

"Oh, yeah. So, what do you think it means?"

I blew out a long breath of air.

"The reference to the key is pretty obvious."

"I got that. But what about the bottomless pit and great chain stuff?"

"No clue. But it's unquestionably pertinent or else they wouldn't have included those quotes."

Zack said, "Listen, I've gotta go. My guys are hollering at me about something. Call me back if you come up with anything."

"Absolutely."

"Oh, I almost forgot to tell you, but the Marshall's Service has no idea where Charles is. Apparently, he disabled his phone, which means that he is in the wind."

"I kind of figured as much. All right, Zack, I'll talk to you later."

As I disconnected the call the first thing that came to my mind was, did Helen use that Biblical reference because she figured that at some point I'd be involved? Or was it completely random? I leaned toward the former as Helen had never been a particularly religious person and for that matter, neither was Tommy. On the other hand, both of them knew my background.

Walking into the other room I pulled Tommy into the kitchen and asked, "Do you have any idea why Helen would have quoted a Scripture verse back and forth with Charles?"

He scrunched up his eyes and replied, "A what?"

"Scripture. You know, a Bible verse."

"No, I don't. Why?"

"Well, the FBI found a text exchange between Helen

and Tommy the day before she had the stroke, and—"

"So, it's true?" Tommy said. "Helen and Charles were in communication?"

"Yes. But it wasn't at all romantic, Tommy. Trust me on this. They were actually trying to do a good thing."

He covered his face with his hands, sighed and wept softly for a few seconds.

"Oh, man. That's good to know. That sure is good to know."

I pressed on.

"Back to this Scripture thing, the day before she had the stroke Helen and Charles texted lines from Revelation twenty, verse one back and forth. Does that ring any bells?"

He was shaking his head violently back and forth.

"Nah, man. We weren't church people. I mean we're not atheists or anything. We believe in God, I guess—well, believed in Helen's case. But I'm pretty sure the last time either one of us was in church was for a funeral or wedding, or something like that."

A thought suddenly bulled its way into my consciousness like an NFL fullback driving for the goal line.

"Do you have any family heirlooms? Like, maybe, an old family Bible? Anything like that?"

His eyes widened.

"As a matter of fact, we do. There's an old Bible Helen inherited from her grandmother."

"I need to see that Bible. I need to see it right now."

CHAPTER 29

Following Tommy through the living room I said to Aaron, "Keep an eye on these guys. We may be on to something."

"Roger that," he replied. "What's going on?"

"Zack thinks he may have uncovered a coded text between Helen and Charles that contains a clue as to where this mysterious key might be. And I think I may have just figured out where to look."

"Get on with it, then. I'm okay here. These guys aren't going anywhere."

When I got into the master bedroom, I could hear Tommy tossing things around inside the walk-in closet and muttering to himself.

"You find it?" I asked.

"Not yet. But I know it's in here somewhere."

I stood in the doorway and watched him. He was standing on a stepladder, pulling boxes off of shelves, peering inside each one and then dropping them onto the floor.

"Anything I can do to help?"

He replied, "Well, as you can see, we aren't the most organized people in the world—weren't the most...damn, Jake." He paused as another wave of emotion overtook him. "I guess it's just gonna take a minute to get used to referring to things in the past tense, huh?"

I stepped into the closet and leaned back against the built-in chest of drawers.

"The only thing I can say, Tommy, is that life has dealt

you a serious blow. It'd be great if there was training on how to deal with it properly, but there isn't. It just comes at you like a freight train; plows over you, and leaves you staggering around wondering what just happened. And it's especially true when things happen suddenly, as in your situation. At least for me, I had a few months to prepare my heart, you know, to engage in some pre-grieving, so to speak."

"You got that right, Jake. You sure got that right. I mean one day we was having dinner up at Las Brisas in Laguna, and the next day I was calling 911 to come and get her." He sobbed for a few seconds, wiped his eyes and then said, "Thank-you for being here, brother. It's good to have someone to talk to who knows exactly what I'm going through."

"I'm honored to help, Tommy." After a pause I suggested, "Do you think Helen would have moved the Bible from where it had been stored?"

He snapped his fingers.

"You know what, that's a great question, because it isn't where she always kept it. Hang on."

He hopped off the ladder and hurried past me into the bedroom where he immediately went to a nightstand on what I assumed had been Helen's side of the bed. Once there he pulled open a drawer, whooped and pulled out a battered, old leather-bound book.

"Right here all the time."

He held the book up for me to see as a smile of triumph lit up his face.

I took the Bible from his hands, sat down on the bed and carefully opened it to the book of Revelation. Licking my fingers, I thumbed through the pages until I came to chapter twenty.

"Well, whadda ya' know," Tommy said quietly.

A thin, sliver key was wedged tightly in the crease where the pages joined the spine. I shut the book without retrieving the key and stared at it from all directions.

"Unless you knew what you were looking for, you'd never know it was there."

Tommy added, "And wedged in there like that, it'd be almost impossible to dislodge."

"You're right."

I opened the Bible up and tried to pull the key out using only my fingers. After three attempts, it finally came free.

"Well," I said, "we've got the key. Now we need to know where the safe-deposit box is."

Tommy asked, "Do you think keys like that are, what's the word, proprietary to certain banks?"

"That's a really good question. And the answer is, I don't know. But I'm pretty sure my guys at the FBI do."

I dialed Zack's number and he answered immediately.

"Jake, you got something?"

"Yeah. I'm holding the key."

"What? Where did you find it?"

"It was in a family heirloom Bible, wedged in the spine at Revelation chapter twenty."

"That's brilliant," he said. "Now we need to know where the box is."

"Right. So, are safe-deposit boxes proprietary to individual banks, or are the boxes produced in bulk by various manufacturers and the keys proprietary to the manufacturer?"

"That's way outside my area of expertise, but I'm almost certain that it's the latter."

"So, I guess the place to start is find out who made this key and what banks in the Lake Forest area use the safe-deposit box system from that particular manufacturer."

Zack asked, "Is there a name on the key?"

"Uh, hang on, I hadn't quite gotten that far." I peered at the key; turned it over; peered at it again. "Hmm...besides a number, not a single identifying mark that I can see."

"Nothing?"

"Not unless the shape itself is proprietary."

"Actually, I wouldn't be surprised if it was. Take a picture of it and text it to me. I'll have my guys get on it."

"All right. Talk to you soon."

I snapped a quick photo of the key and texted it to Zack. When Tommy and I walked back into the living room I found Spartak straining against his bonds as if attempting to break free.

I gestured toward him and said, "He doesn't seriously believe he can get free, does he?"

Aaron chuckled.

"I told him it was stupid, but the boy keeps trying."

"Let him. In the meantime," I whispered to Aaron, "we've got the key."

"What?"

"Yeah. Found it in an old family Bible."

"Given the Scripture reference, that's almost hiding in plain sight."

I walked over to stand in front of the two vory.

"Iosif, do you have any idea where the safe-deposit box is located?"

He shook his head slowly and replied, "No. Is why we come today. Oksana say find from husband."

Spartak jerked violently and held his hands up in front of him with a triumphant smile on his less than handsome face.

Aaron clapped slowly, sarcastically.

"Now what you gonna do, big boy?"

He glanced down at his feet and then at me before standing suddenly and lunging in my direction with a ferocious yell. At least I'm sure he intended it to sound ferocious. As it was, it sounded more like a cat in the throes of labor pains. I'm not sure what he expected to accomplish, but the only thing he succeeded in doing was getting his feet hopelessly tangled in the legs of the chair, which sent him careening face-first into a sturdy coffee table. It was fortunate for Spartak that the edges of the table were rounded or else in addition to being rendered immediately unconscious, he would have received severe facial lacerations. His head bounced off the table's edge and he collapsed into an ungainly heap at my feet where he lay unmoving.

Iosif shrugged and said, "What do you Americans say? Is not sharpest knife in drawer?"

CHAPTER 30

3:30 p.m.

Charles woke up in pain and totally confused as to what had just happened to him. When he tried to move he found that his hands and feet had been zip-tied and that movement was impossible.

"Libby! What...what's going on?"

"Shut-up, Charlie. Just shut-up and let me think," she replied heatedly as she paced up and down the aisle.

"But, you hit me. Why did you do that?"

She stopped pacing and stood facing him, hands on hips.

"Look, I'm sorry about that. But, in a way it's good because now I no longer have to maintain the pretense."

"Pretense?" he replied. "What—"

Without speaking, she reached up, pulled off a wig and shook out her hair. Long, blonde hair. And when she removed her glasses, Charles' heart lurched in his chest.

"You..." he breathed.

"Yes, Charlie," she said sweetly. "It's me."

"But—"

"I know, I know. I fooled you, didn't I? But, it's what I do—I fool people. That's what makes me so good at my job."

"But you killed—"

"Andy? Yes, yes I did. And I enjoyed every second of it. Oh, I know, I'm disgusting." She started ticking the adjectives off on her fingers, "Also heartless, cruel, demonic, evil.

The list goes on and on."

She leaned toward him so suddenly, that he jerked back involuntarily striking his head painfully against the Learjet's bulkhead.

"And you know what, Charlie?" she asked rhetorically. "I am all of that and more."

"Are you going to kill me too?" he stammered.

She wrinkled her brow and said, "Honestly, I haven't decided yet. The only thing I know for sure is that I won't do it until you tell me what I need to know."

"And, what do you need to know?"

"Oh, come on, Charlie. I need to know where the key is for the safe-deposit box as well as the box's location."

He shook his head slowly.

"I have a pretty good idea where the key is, but don't know the location of the box. Only Helen knew that. We did it that way on purpose."

"Oksana," she said without preamble and apparently apropos of nothing.

"What?"

"Oksana. It's my name. I figured since we were dispensing with all pretense that you should know my real name."

He simply stared at her without speaking, the sweat beginning to bead on his forehead.

Giving her head a curt nod, as if having come to a decision, she said, "Okay. I know what we're going to do."

"Do? About what?"

"Oh, didn't I tell you? Things have gotten complicated in the last few minutes and we are being forced to change our plans."

"Complicated? How?"

She ignored his question and picked up a phone that was cradled in a pocket sewn into the back of the seat in front of her. After rattling off instructions in the same Ukrainian language he had heard her using before, she hung up and he felt the jet beginning a slow turn to their left.

She finally replied, "Let's just say that a new player has emerged who—if his reputation is to be believed—could pose a significant obstacle to me completing my assignment."

A smile spread slowly over Charles' face.

"Why are you smiling?" Oksana asked.

"Jake Moriarity," he replied confidently.

Oksana recoiled as if she had just been slapped.

"What do you know about Jake Moriarity?"

With a boldness he'd never felt before, Charles heard himself suggesting, "Cut these restraints off and maybe we'll talk."

Faster than he could follow, a knife was suddenly in her hand and being held within a half-inch of his right eye.

"You are in no position to be bargaining for anything, Charlie boy."

Stifling an inner tremor, he replied, "Oh, I think you're wrong. I think I'm in a very positive position."

"Yeah? Well, how about if I just start cutting body-parts away. Would you feel positive then?"

"You're not going to do that."

She moved the knife closer until it was touching the corner of his eye.

"People have attempted to test me before, Charlie boy. It never worked out well for them."

Struggling to control his breathing he said, "Cut me loose and I will tell you everything I know."

Oksana hesitated, but only slightly. Moving quickly, she cut away the zip-tie around his hands, scoring a deep, half-inch long cut at the base of his thumb in the process.

"That's just so you know that I'm serious," she remarked as she tossed him a linen napkin that he immediately pressed against the wound to stifle the blood flow. "Now, tell me what you know about Jake Moriarity."

"He's a family friend."

"Your family?"

"No. A friend of Helen and her husband. Tommy—that's her husband—plays bass in Aaron Perry's jazz trio."

"Aaron Perry is a very famous guy. But I still don't see —"

"He's also Jake Moriarity's best friend."

"Okay," she replied, nodding her head slowly. "So..."

"So, before Helen died—was killed, I guess would be more accurate—did you do that, by the way?"

"What, kill Helen Marshall? No. Not my style. I like to do things up close and personal."

He nodded his head and continued, "Before Helen died, she told me that if things started going sideways, that I should get in touch with Tommy and have him contact Jake Moriarity, because Jake would know what to do. I had no idea who the guy was, but after she filled me in, I could understand why she made the suggestion."

"And, did you?" Oksana inquired. "You know, get in touch with her husband?"

"No! Everything was happening so quickly that I never even had a chance. And then, of course, you showed up yesterday morning at the coffee shop—"

"And seduced you with my charms," she added, completing his sentence.

"It wasn't like that."

"Oh, please, Charlie. You were hot for me and you know it." Grinning salaciously, she prompted, "Come on, admit it."

He stared at her, not wanting to admit it, but she was right.

"Okay. I, well, you're beautiful and have a killer body and...I responded on a completely, horny middle-aged guy level. And I hate myself for it."

"I knew it. So, the key. Where is it?"

"Well, I can't be sure, but we set up a, I suppose you'd call it a code so we'd know where it would be in case something happened that..."

He stopped speaking as emotion suddenly overwhelmed him.

"Hey," Oksana said sharply. "I know you're sad, grieving for your lost lover and blah, blah, blah—"

"She wasn't my lover," he shouted suddenly.

"Okay, okay, Charlie. Take it easy. We just don't have time for emotion right now. Finish your story. Where is the key?"

Charles breathed out a long sigh in an attempt to dissipate a bit of the emotion he was feeling.

"It's in an old Bible—a family heirloom from Helen's grandmother."

"Okay, and where is this Bible?"

"At their condo in Dana Point."

"Did her husband know about the Bible?"

Charles said, "Well, other than obviously knowing that it was in her possession, no. He had no idea about her hiding the key there."

"Hmm," she mused. "So even if my guys hadn't gotten themselves taken out by Moriarity, it's doubtful they could have ever found the key."

"There is absolutely no way. And, besides, having the key wouldn't do you any good if you didn't know where the safe-deposit box was."

"And you don't know where it is?"

"No," he replied forcefully.

Sliding into the seat by him, she suddenly returned the knife to its previous position next to his eye.

"I like you, Charlie," she said with a long sigh. "But I'm afraid I need to make sure you don't know where the box is. I'm sure you understand."

And then the real nightmare began.

CHAPTER 31

I walked back into Tommy's living room after another long conversation with Zack.

Aaron asked, "So what'd he have to say?"

"Well," I replied, "we won't be completely sure until we see the key actually open the box, but Zack's fairly certain that he knows the manufacturer as well as what banks use their safe-deposit systems."

"So, what bank are we looking at?"

"Well, there are a number of banks in southern California who use Pacific Western Vault Systems, but he's liking one in Lake Forest called *Tenshi Community Bank.* "

"That because of me seeing her in Lake Forest when I was tracking her phone?" Tommy asked.

"It's one reason. But get this—the word *tenshi* is Japanese for angel."

"*And I saw an angel come down from heaven,*" Tommy mused.

Aaron said, "Kind of a long shot, if you ask me, but we need a place to start and that's as good as any."

"I agree. Zack's going to make a few calls and see if he can arrange for us to try the key tomorrow morning. In the meantime, he's going to have a couple of agents come by and take the bad guys off our hands."

"What about that Learjet?"

"Oh, I almost forgot to tell you, they found a Learjet that took off from Atlantic Aviation at PDX right around the time I was talking to Oksana."

"So, we can track their movements and be waiting for

them when they land?" Aaron asked.

"Not exactly. We don't know where they're headed. In fact, we have no idea of the Lear's present location."

"Why not?"

"Because—and this is all stuff I learned from Zack—since 2013 the FAA has allowed certain owners of private jets to block their tail numbers from view. The FAA calls it the 'ASDI block', or Aircraft Situation Display to Industry data feed. The bottom line is that unless you have the tail number, that plane is just another random blip in the sky."

"But, what about a flight plan?" Tommy inquired.

"In good weather, and unless a flight is crossing controlled airspace, filing a flight plan is optional. Actually, if they are flying below a certain altitude the flight plan is optional, controlled airspace or not."

"What?"

"My reaction exactly. Zack said that flight plans are basically just so people will know where you were headed in case an emergency comes up and you crash or have to make a sudden landing. Now, at a towered airport, you will need clearance for taxiing and takeoff, but once you're airborne you can go anywhere you want."

Both Aaron and Tommy seemed to be having a hard time processing what I'd just shared.

"So, let me get this straight," Aaron said after a few seconds silence. "The Learjet that took off from Portland only had to get clearance for takeoff and didn't have to tell the tower where they were headed or even alert the tower at their final destination that they were on their way?"

"Yep."

Tommy sat heavily in one of the overstuffed chairs.

"You make it sound like people can just fire up their private damn jets and fly around the country and be totally invisible if they want to."

"Overly simplified, but yeah, basically."

Aaron said, "Now that I think about it, when we fly

to our gigs on private jets, Tommy, nobody knows where we goin'. It's something management sets up with the pro-moters."

"Yeah, I get that," Tommy replied. "But after 9/11 it seems pretty funky that anybody can just fly anywhere they want to without the FAA, or whoever, knowing what's up."

I said, "Apparently, there are towered airports and non-towered airports in the US. The non-towered airports are as open as any freeway system. In other words, any air-craft is free to land and take off at will based on whether the airspace and runway is clear."

"No questions asked?" Tommy inquired.

"No questions asked. The towered airports are desig-nated either Bravo or Charlie. The Bravo airports—such as LAX or San Diego Lindberg Field—run their towers twenty-four-seven. The Charlie airports—like John Wayne, Bur-bank, et cetera—close their towers at eleven p.m. Any air-craft wishing to land after eleven is free to do so."

Aaron mused, "And lacking a tail number or flight plan, trying to find that Learjet by radar alone would be—"

"Virtually impossible," I interjected, completing his sentence.

"Which is why we have absolutely no idea where Oksana intends to land."

"Well, that's not entirely true."

"It's not?" Tommy asked.

"We're fairly certain that if Charles is with her—and he almost certainly is, unless she's killed him—they are headed for Dana Point. Remember, Charles put the Revelation rid-dle together with Helen. And my guess is that Oksana can be very persuasive when applying advanced interrogation techniques."

"Yeah, what better place to torture information out of someone than at thirty-thousand feet," Aaron said with disgust.

"Right. And from what Zack told me about Charles,

he doesn't strike me as being the brave, hit-me-with-your-best-shot kind of guy. I'm thinking that he would fold pretty quickly under interrogation."

"And if he did," Aaron concluded, "then you're right, she's headed right for us."

"Any idea how long it would take a private jet to fly from Portland to the LA area?" Tommy asked.

"One hour, fifty minutes," Iosif hollered from across the room. When we stared questioningly at him, he added, "Have flown with Oksana many times."

Aaron checked his watch.

"Four-twenty p.m. Which would put them roughly within half an hour of landing somewhere."

"Not necessarily," I suggested as a thought presented itself clearly in my imagination. "If I were in her position, I would find a smallish airport somewhere in route—possibly in the Bay Area—where I could land, refuel and hang out for a few hours before continuing the flight into..." I paused and then continued, "She's going to wait until after eleven and land at a *Charlie* airport."

"Are those the airports whose towers close at eleven?" Tommy queried.

"Yes."

Aaron asked, "Anything come to mind as a frontrunner for that?"

"Actually, it does. If my destination was, ultimately, Dana Point, I'd probably go to Palomar."

"In Carlsbad?"

"That's the one," I said. "It's small, very little traffic and only about an hour's drive to Dana Point."

Aaron grinned, "You feel strongly about this?"

I thought about that. If this was more than a notion, then after Zack's agents picked up the two vory, we should stash Tommy somewhere safe and be at the airport waiting for Oksana's arrival. On the other hand, if it was just one idea among several alternatives...

"Yeah," I concluded, "I do. So, once Zack's guys have our new best friends over there under wraps, I want to take Tommy back to Carlsbad and have him spend the night with Bridgett and the girls."

Aaron nodded his head slowly.

"Be good for Bridgett to have something to do, and Tommy would be totally safe."

"With women?" Tommy asked incredulously.

"Not just any women," Aaron replied with a wink. "Warrior women, my man. Warrior women."

CHAPTER 32

Zack's men arrived about five o'clock and relieved us of the burden of having to watch Iosif and his gray matter challenged friend, Spartak —who, unbelievably, was still insisting that he would beat me in a "fair fight" as he was led away in cuffs and leg restraints. Before they left, I reiterated my promise to Iosif that I would do everything I could to keep Nastasiya safe.

It was a promise I intended to keep.

Tommy was packing a few essentials for the trip and Aaron was filling Muriel in on our plans when my phone rang.

It was Cassie.

"Hey, little girl."

"Hey, Uncle," she replied around a sob.

"What's going on, Cass?"

"I'm, uh...I'm in the ER with Michael."

"The ER? What happened?"

"When I told you yesterday that Michael just wasn't right, I didn't tell you everything."

"Okay, and?" I prompted.

"And, well, I told you about the anxiety and depression, and that I thought he was dealing with pain."

"Go on."

"He's been complaining about migraine level headaches. And he sweats. Like, a lot. Finally, a couple of hours ago he was just sitting in his chair, panting as if he couldn't breathe and basically crying because the pain in his head was so bad."

"And that's what made you bring him in?"

"It's what made me call 911," she replied.

I said, "Have they made any initial diagnoses?"

"They aren't completely certain yet, but, because Michael's spinal cord injury occurred at T6, autonomic dysreflexia is the prevailing consensus."

"You're going to have to explain that to me."

"I don't know the technical aspects, just that it's a condition not uncommon to paraplegia victims. Some of the symptoms include everything Michael has been experiencing, well, ever since we've been on this trip anyway. Extreme hypertension is also part of it. I mean when the triage nurse admitted him, his BP was two-hundred over one-forty-five."

"That's ridiculously high! What are they going to do for him?"

She sobbed quietly for a few seconds before replying, "I don't know. They're not telling me anything and I'm just…sitting out here in the waiting room by myself, slowly losing my mind. I'm just, so alone, Uncle."

Her revelation was like a spike through my heart.

"Have you called Michael's parents? His publicist?"

"No. I didn't call his publicist because the hospital staff hasn't figured out who Michael is yet, and I don't want to have to deal with the media. But it's only a matter of time." After a brief pause, she continued, "I haven't called his mom and dad because I wanted to talk to you first. I don't know what to do, Uncle."

My mind was suddenly sundered; torn between doing whatever I had to do in order to help my niece navigate the rough waters whose inky depths threatened to swallow her whole, and maintaining the integrity of my investigation. My mind said that Cassie was a big girl and totally capable of figuring out what was best for her husband. My heart said to drop everything and go be the rock I had always been for her.

For some inexplicable reason, in my head I started hearing The Clash bellowing, *"Should I stay or should I go, now?"*

It was problematic.

If you want to know the truth, it was a conundrum. Plain and simple.

I said, "What do you want me to do, Cass?"

She was silent for a few moments before asking, "Is there even a slight possibility that you could come and be with me? You know, just help me get through this?"

And there it was.

My "child" asking for her father's comfort and protection. What the hell was I supposed to do with that? Especially since it was *exactly* what I wanted to do.

"I want to, little girl. You know I do."

"But..."

"There's no *but*, really. I just have a few logistical things to work out, not the least of which is finding a flight."

"And?"

She knew me so well.

"Okay, I'm right in the middle of a case involving Russian mafia and human trafficking."

"Human trafficking? You mean like—"

"Young girls, Cass. Some as young as twelve."

Given Cassie's background, it was a subject that hit close to the bone.

She said, "Well, I can't, in good conscience, call you away from that. I'll, uh, be—"

"I'm going to send Muriel right now and I will be on the first flight I can get tomorrow."

"But—"

"No discussion. It's what we're going to do. Okay?"

The sobs had returned.

"Okay, uncle. Yeah, that'll be good if Mur's here."

"So, listen, I should hang up and start getting things organized, but you call me if, you know, something goes sideways with Michael's condition. Do you feel like he's at least stabilized?"

"Yeah, I mean, I guess. Like I said, they haven't told me much. They're actually kind of surly, if I'm being honest."

"Who?"

"All of them. The doctors, nurses, you name it."

That really ticked me off.

"Find whoever is in charge and let me talk to them."

"I don't—"

"Just find the person in charge. I'll wait."

A girlish giggle escaped.

"What are you going to do, Uncle?"

I lapsed into my Humphrey Bogart impression, "Do? Why, I'm gonna slap some sense into their heads, sweetheart."

"Ugh! That impression is actually getting worse. Hang on..."

I heard her calling to someone, and then a muffled conversation ensued before an impatient, gruff female voice came on the phone.

"I don't care who you are, I don't have time—"

"What is your name?" I said sternly.

"My name is Edith Wooley," she replied indignantly. "I am the—"

"I don't need to know your position. My name is Jake Moriarity and I'm with the FBI."

She was suddenly flustered.

"The FBI? But—"

"I need you to be quiet and listen for a moment. Can you do that for me, Edith?"

"Well, certainly."

"The young lady standing next to you is my niece. The gentleman in your care—her husband—is Charleston Hawthorne."

"Charleston—"

"I'm sure you've heard of him."

"Who hasn't?"

"Right. Now, I know you and your staff are busy and most likely stretched to the limit. And while I'm certain you don't really base your level of care on a patient's celebrity status or lack thereof, it has come to my attention that you are not being particularly attentive or even courteous to my niece. So, I need you to do me a favor."

"Well, I will certainly try, sir."

"Great. You have a tremendous opportunity that has been handed to you. America's greatest living novelist is in your care. The media are on their way. You and your staff are about to be under a national spotlight. If I were in your position—and quite frankly, I'm glad I'm not—I would be doing everything humanly possible to make sure your hospital and staff are providing Charleston Hawthorne with the best care available on the East Coast."

"We *do* provide the best care on the—"

"I'm sure you do. You just need to start providing it to my niece and her husband."

A moment of silence, and then, "Of course, of course. It's just that we had no idea who—"

"I understand, Edith. But as a general rule, civility costs you nothing."

"Yes. Thanks for the reminder, sir. I will personally insure that all their needs are met."

"That's good to hear. I will be there tomorrow afternoon to check on the situation myself. I look forward to meeting you in person. Now, could you please put my niece back on the phone."

"Uh, yes, yes...of course. Here she is."

I heard the phone changing hands and mumbled apologies from dear Edith.

Cassie said, "What did you say to her?"

"I merely explained the situation to her in a manner that she could understand. I don't think you'll have any further problems."

She laughed, "You did that mental Jiu Jitsu thing on

her, didn't you?"

"Who could say. So, listen, call Michael's publicist and tell him to get the media onsite as quickly as possible."

"Seriously? I thought we wanted to keep them out of it."

I said, "I changed my mind. The hospital needs to see a show of force before I get there tomorrow."

"So, you're really coming?"

"Yes, I am. But not unless I get going."

"Okay. I love you, Uncle."

"Love you more, little girl."

I had just disconnected the call when Aaron walked in.

"What's up?" he asked.

"Change of plans."

He rolled his eyes.

"What a shock."

CHAPTER 33

6:30 p.m.

The pain had been unspeakable. The humiliation even worse. Charles wasn't bleeding, and he didn't think there were any broken bones, but the things Oksana had done to him in her efforts to determine his truthfulness had left him trembling, whimpering and basically willing to sell out his own mother if the pain would just stop. He was not a brave man. And he was largely okay with that. In his world, bravery was highly overrated.

"How you doing, Charlie-boy?" Oksana asked, her voice tinged with concern.

He stared up at her from where she had strapped him into the cushioned comfort of one of the Learjet's Corinthian leather seats.

"I've been better," he wheezed.

Kneeling down so her face was even with his, she said, "I'm sorry I had to do that to you—really, I am. You see, I kind of like you, Charlie. I can't explain it, but I do."

"If that's true, then I'd hate to see how you treat people you dislike."

"Yes, it's not pretty."

"I can't imagine that it would be." He stared through the window. "Where are we, anyway?"

"Vacaville, California."

"Vacaville? Why? And do you think you can untie me

now?"

She immediately began freeing him from his bonds.

"Vacaville doesn't have a tower. Therefore, we can land and take off without having to deal with official logs and stuff like that. We'll be hanging out here until around ten p.m."

Charles sat up, massaging his wrists.

"Why so long?"

Oksana stood, reached for a bottle of water and handed it to him.

"Because where we're going *does* have a tower, but it closes at eleven."

"Why is that significant?"

"After the tower closes, we can land and not have to deal with anything official."

After taking a long drink of water, he said, "Are you satisfied now that I'm telling you the truth?"

"I am. And, as I said, I didn't enjoy doing that to you. Sometimes I do, but that wasn't one of those times."

"How is that even possible, you know, to enjoy someone else's pain?"

She sat down in the seat across the aisle.

"I can't really explain it. I suppose it has something to do with being an expert in interrogation—a practitioner of a very rare craft."

"So, you're a practitioner of pain?"

"Very poetic, Charlie-boy. But, yeah, I guess I am. But it's not pain for pain's sake. I mean I'm not a sadist."

"Could've fooled me."

"The big difference is that sadists enjoy hurting people, while I enjoy the results the pain produces."

"Well, no offense, but having been on the receiving end of the hurt, I can't honestly say that I see all that much difference."

She regarded him silently for a few seconds.

"I don't expect you to understand—for *anyone* to

understand, for that matter."

He started to stand up, but stopped and asked, "Is it okay if I stand? I really need to use the restroom."

"Of course. We're in this together now, Charlie-boy. Partners. You have nothing to fear from me. I'm on your side."

He stood slowly, stiffly and stepped tentatively into the aisle where he paused, staring at her in confusion.

"I've never been afraid of a woman before. But I'm sure as hell afraid of you."

She stood suddenly, pulled him to her and kissed him full on the mouth.

Stepping back, she said breathlessly, "I've been wanting to do that ever since I first met you."

"I'm so confused right now, Lib...Oksana. I'm not a sophisticated guy. I'm a smart guy, but not sophisticated. I don't understand you. I don't understand the whole pleasure and pain combo thing. And I feel like you're just trying to manipulate me, maybe like I'm some form of diversion for you, or something."

She kissed him again, this time pressing her body into his.

"What's wrong with a little diversion, Charlie boy? I'm sure you could use it, and I know for damn sure that I could. What say we have a little fun before we take off?"

His eyes widened in bewilderment.

"Wait, are you suggesting that we, what...have sex? Here? On the plane?"

"Why not?"

"But, you just tortured the hell out of me. And now I'm supposed to be attracted to you sexually?"

She grinned.

"Supposed nothing. You already are. You think a girl can't tell when a guy is attracted to her? I may be young, Charlie boy, but I know what's up."

Much to his chagrin and utter shame, he found that

everything she said was true. And he hated himself for it.

"I really have to pee," he said and walked quickly toward the restroom in the rear of the plane.

As she watched him go, Oksana smiled. It was the smile of a master manipulator. She now had Charles Sutton right where she needed him to be in order to carry out the rest of her plans.

Pleasure and pain. Keep them off balance. It was a mantra that had been drilled into her for years by her father—a father who, early on, had recognized his daughter's beauty, natural intelligence and near total lack of conscience, qualities that made her perfectly suited for the role he had predetermined she would serve in the organization. How she hated him. For he was the one who had practiced what he preached on her, arguing that it was all part of her training.

She would kill him one day.

Soon.

CHAPTER 34

After working out the details with Muriel by phone, we had driven south to Carlsbad, arriving at Michael's home around 8:00 p.m. Once there, we all sat down and briefly discussed the gravity of the situation we were facing on both fronts: Tommy's case and Michael's illness. I say briefly, because we didn't really have any time to lose. First of all, the only flight I could get for Muriel left at 10:30 p.m. and arrived in Jacksonville about 8:30 a.m. It was a brutal way to spend the night, but Muriel was more than willing to do whatever was necessary to help her best friend. And since it was now moving on toward 8:20, she needed to be on her way if she was going to make that flight.

Which brought up the other issue. If, in fact, Oksana planned to land at Palomar Airport after 11:00 p.m., there was no way I could take Muriel to the San Diego Airport—a forty-minute drive each way without traffic—and be back in time to greet our Russian assassin. The only logical thing to do was to have Bridgett, Vanessa and Eddie drive Muriel. Logical. Simple. A perfect division of duties to accomplish a common goal.

If that were all true, then why did it bother me so much?

Of course, everyone had an opinion, which, at present was being voiced simultaneously and enthusiastically.

I hollered, "Hold it! Everybody just stop and let me figure this out."

Vanessa asked, "What is the problem? I mean it's a trip to the airport and back. It's not like Eddie and I are children. Plus, Bridgett *is* an FBI agent."

"Yes," Bridgett agreed. "I am."

"I know. It's not that."

"Then what? You worried about my lingering impairment? Because if you are, I can still shoot the eyes out of a hawk at two-hundred feet."

Around a sigh, I replied, "It's not about you, Bridgett. Something's just off."

Aaron said, "Look, we got two pressing needs: get Muriel to the airport—and she needs to leave..." he checked his watch, "...like right now—and be ready for Oksana to arrive. You can't do it all, bro. Let them go and let's get on with it."

Eddie's phone buzzed. When she looked at the caller ID, her eyes lit up.

"It's Pete."

Pete, as in Pete Tolles. Our former enemy now turned family friend, sometime associate in our adventures and newly acquired suitor to Eddie.

An idea suddenly presented itself.

I said, "Let me answer it."

I took the phone from her.

"Pete, it's Jake."

Pete's slow, southern drawl oozed through her phone's earpiece like sweet molasses.

"Mr. Moriarity sir. I sure didn't expect to hear your voice. Is everything okay with Miss Eddie?"

"Yes. Listen, where are you?"

"Why, I'm just down the street and was hoping to take Miss Eddie out for some coffee, that is if she's available."

I laughed.

"Oh, she's available. So, listen, I need a huge favor."

"You only have to ask, you know that."

"I need to get Muriel to the San Diego airport right now, and we've got some heavy stuff going down on a case we're working. Bottom line, I can't do it and for reasons I can't explain, I don't feel good about Bridgett being the only line of defense for Muriel and the girls. I can't explain it, but I just don't like it."

He said, "Well, hell's bells, Mr. Moriarity. I'd be plum tickled to do that for you. Where are you right now?"

"We're at Michael and Cassie's."

"Okay. I'm five minutes away." He whooped like a cowboy who had just roped a calf. "Man, oh man. And here I thought this was just gonna be a little 'ol date with my girl."

"Thank-you for this, Pete. I owe you one."

"You don't owe me anything, Mr. Moriarity. You gave me my life back. That right there is payment enough for the *rest* of my life. And I mean that, sir."

"Well, thank-you anyway. See you in a few minutes."

I terminated the call and handed Eddie's phone back to her.

"What's happening?" Bridgett asked.

"Pete is five minutes away. He's going to come by and drive you guys to the airport."

Bridgett was nodding her head slowly.

"Okay. I feel much better about that, because, to tell you the truth, in spite of what I said a few minutes ago, I wasn't feeling great about this either. Not because of any sense of danger, but just because I still don't know my way around San Diego all that well and I just don't like driving at night."

Eddie concurred, "Me either."

Muriel said, "Then, I guess I better get my stuff and say a proper goodbye to my man."

Aaron grinned.

"Now, sugar, you know we don't have time for no proper goodbye."

Muriel wrapped her arms around him and purred, "It wouldn't take all that long, baby."

Vanessa shouted, "Hey! You know we all can hear you

two, right?"

Aaron laughed.

"We just messin' with y'all."

The doorbell rang.

Eddie jumped up and ran to answer it, returning with a grinning Pete Tolles in tow. Pete is nearly as large as Aaron, with a pleasant, country-boy face that, when coupled with his shaved head, completely disguises the fearsome, tactical operator inside.

"Evenin' gents, ladies," he said in greeting. "I'd love to stay and chit-chat, but we gotta get down the road pronto if Miss Muriel is gonna make that flight."

I introduced Tommy.

"Pete, this is Tommy Marshall. He's—"

"Mr. Perry's bass player. Yes, sir. I saw you at Cassie and Michael's wedding. I am an admirer of your work. I used to play myself back in the day."

Tommy grinned widely.

"Is that a fact? Well, when the dust settles, we should get together and talk shop."

"I'd be honored, sir."

Hugs and kisses were exchanged all around and as they were walking out the door, Pete turned back.

"Mr. Moriarity, sir, is there something happening that I should be aware of? You know, like any danger to look out for?"

I said, "We're dealing with the Russian mafia, Pete. And the answer to your question is, maybe. I just don't know. Bridgett can fill you in on the way."

"Okay. What else do you need me to do after I get back with the girls? Because I am more than willing to lend a hand."

I thought about that for a minute, and in the process realized that I had completely forgotten to account for Tommy's safety while Aaron and I went after Oksana. My original idea had been to have Bridgett and Muriel watch out for him. And given their physical prowess and expert-level marksmanship that would have been enough. But now...

I turned to Tommy.

"Tommy, I need you to go with Pete and the girls."

"Why's that, Jake?" he replied, confusion wrinkling his brow.

"I can't take the risk of leaving you here alone while Aaron and I go after Oksana. Pete and Bridgett will be formidable guardians."

He nodded his head slowly.

"Okay. I mean I don't understand any of this, but, okay."

"And Pete, Bridgett, do you think you could stay here with Tommy and the girls until we wrap this up?"

Bridgett nodded as Pete said, "It would be my pleasure, Mr. Moriarity, sir."

"You know you don't have to keep calling me Mr. Moriarity, right?"

"Yes sir. But my momma told me to always treat people we respect with honor. And I respect you, Mr. Moriarity, yes I surely do."

"Okay. Then we'll see you guys when we see you. And we'll keep you up to speed on whatever is transpiring on our end."

"Sounds good to me. Adios," he said, drawing out the 'a.'

Once they were gone, Aaron asked, "How are we gonna play this?"

It was a great question.

And, true to form, I had absolutely no idea.

"Well, I thought we'd go on over to the airport and wait for Oksana's plane to land."

"Yeah? Then what?"

"I don't know."

"So, business as usual?"

"Pretty much."

CHAPTER 35

I've never been any good at just sitting around waiting for something to happen. I'm not saying that it's a good thing. It's just the way it is. I suppose my philosophy could be described like this: suppose you're trapped in a cage with a sleeping lion. Eventually he's going to wake up and do what lions do, which is to devour any prey within reach. So, since the end result is going to be the same, why not prod the lion, wake him up and get it the hell over with.

As it turned out, unbeknownst to me, I had already prodded the "lion", and he was not happy.

My phone rang.

It was Pete.

"What's going on, Pete?"

"Well, sir, we've got ourselves a tail."

I put him on speaker so Aaron could listen in.

"Interesting. How long has it been there?"

"Oh, ever since we left Michael's place."

"And I assume you're packing?" Aaron asked.

"Oh, yes sir. Me and Bridgett. Muriel has her weapon as well. She planned to leave it with Vanessa and Eddie after they dropped her at the airport."

Vanessa had been going to the range with Muriel for the past couple of months as part of Muriel's rehabilitation, and had developed a basic proficiency level. But, she had never been involved in anything close to a live fire situation.

I said, "Can you see how many bad guys are in the car?"

"Two guys in the front, for sure. There may be another guy in the back, but I can't be sure. It's a black, Cadillac Escalade. One of those stretch versions."

"Where are you right now?"

"Just passing La Jolla Village drive."

"You're making good time."

"Yes sir. It sorta helps when you've got some Russian mafia chasing you. At least, I assume that's who they are."

Aaron said, "So, you're about twenty minutes from the airport. Doesn't seem to me that they would try anything while you're on the freeway. How's traffic?"

"Well, sir, it's pretty heavy but moving right along."

I thought through a few scenarios and suggested, "I'm pretty sure it's Tommy they're after. So, why don't you just keep to the plan, only instead of dropping Muriel off, valet the car and go inside with her, make sure she makes it to security. They'll be less likely to try anything at the airport, and especially if you stay in a group."

"Good to hear you say that, because it's exactly what I was thinkin'. I'll let you know if the boys behind us get squirrely."

"Thanks, Pete."

After terminating the call, Aaron asked, "If they've got a tail on Tommy, seems likely that they'll have a few more boys lurking around here somewhere."

He was right about that.

"Then, we need something to smoke them out and neutralize the threat."

"Got any ideas?"

I checked my watch.

"It's a little after nine, and we need to be on our way to Palomar by no later than ten p.m. So, we don't have much time." I thought for a few more seconds. "Michael spent a bundle on his security system, so, short of disabling everything there's no way for anyone to get inside. Besides which, they don't know where we are."

"But they must have followed us from Dana Point. How else would they have been able to set up a tail?"

"What I meant was, with the guard shack out front—and having to stop and explain why they should be given permission to enter the complex—there is no way they'd know which house we're in. The tail on Pete's car had to come about purely by them seeing Tommy in the vehicle."

Aaron asked, "Do you think the guys they left behind could be on foot?"

Good question.

"Seems likely. I mean think about it. Unless they dispatched additional foot soldiers, it'd be hard for multiple vehicles to set up surveillance without attracting unwanted attention."

"Sounds like we need to go fishin', bruh."

"Indeed. Since I told Oksana who I am, it's highly probable that she has already alerted her father. If so, he would've sent people who will know me by sight. Less likely is the possibility that they know you."

"So, you want me to go have a look-see?"

"I want both of us to go, but I think you should go first and let me come along behind you from another direction."

"Okay," he said. "How we gonna do that?"

"If, in fact, they left a couple of guys behind on foot, they won't be hard to spot. If you want to know the truth, they'll probably stick out like sore thumbs."

"What the hell does that even mean?"

"What?"

"Sticking out like a sore thumb. Apart from the obvious pain involved with having a sore thumb, there's nothing particularly noteworthy about the condition."

I said, "While I don't consider myself an expert on the phrase's etymology, it occurs to me that sustaining an injury to one's thumb—or any digit for that matter—would prompt one to attempt to protect the injured digit. In order to do that, doesn't it seem that the tendency would be to, I don't know, hold it in an unnatural position?"

He nodded his head slowly.

"I think you might be on to something. I remember hurting my left thumb once, and I had to put on this big ol' bandage. Sucker felt like I had a tennis ball stuck on the end of it."

"I know what you mean," I replied. "I remember when I broke my right index finger once, it felt like a target. I kept banging it on stuff. Hurt like hell."

He stared at me.

I stared back.

He finally said, "Well, all right, then. Glad we got that settled. Let's go get some bad guys."

I said, "Hang on. I want to tell Zack what's happening."

I called him.

He answered immediately.

"Jake. What's up?"

"Well, long story, but I had to send Muriel back to Jacksonville to be with Cassie."

"She okay?"

"Cassie is, but Michael's in ER due to some complications from his injury."

"Oh, no. Is he going to be all right?"

"We don't know. Anyway, I had Pete Tolles and Bridgett drive Muriel to the airport. Vanessa, Eddie and Tommy are with them. But, as soon as they left Michael's, they picked up a tail."

"Interesting. So, if someone is tailing them, someone else must have been left behind to keep an eye on the house."

"Exactly."

"Do you want me to send some guys over there?"

"Yeah, I do. We're going to go flush them out, but I don't have time to sit around and babysit them once we take them into custody."

"Not if you're going to get out to the airport and be in place when the Learjet lands. I'll send a couple of guys from the San Diego office right away. Shouldn't take them more than thirty minutes. Think you can manage until then?"

I checked my watch.

"It'll be tight, but we'll be okay."

"All right, Jake. I'm on it."

After hanging up, I said, "Okay. *Now* let's go get the bad guys."

CHAPTER 36

Charles was sitting in his seat, his mind reeling from what had happened to him over the course of the past two hours. A trained assassin working for the Russian mafia had tortured him mercilessly, but then that same woman had kissed him passionately—suggestively, even—stopping just short of promising a more intimate encounter to come. He was ashamed to admit that in her expert hands, he had been as helpless as a spring lamb being led to slaughter.

Charles watched Oksana as she stood in the aisle fiddling with her phone, feeling a sense of disappointment that the moment had passed and would, most likely, never come around again. For in order for that to happen, he would have to live. And he suspected that given who he was dealing with, the likelihood of surviving more than a day or two was slim at best.

"What?" she inquired under the intensity of his gaze.

"Oh, nothing. I was just thinking how beautiful you are."

Sitting on the armrest, she leaned over, ruffled his hair and kissed him, cupping his face in her hands.

"What a sweet thing to say, Charlie-boy. Thank-you. Seriously. Thank-you. As you can imagine, in my line of work, I don't very often have the opportunity to feel pretty, or sexy. Mainly I feel, well, evil."

"But, what if you're not evil? I mean not really. What if you just have a job to do and you happen to be good at your job?"

She sat back and regarded him levelly.

"I *am* good at my job. Maybe the best ever." She stood and shook her hair out, pulling it back into a ponytail. "But the other thing—the thing about being evil—I don't know. It's never really bothered me. Until now."

"What's different?" he inquired.

"You mean, besides you?"

"Me?" he exclaimed incredulously. "What could I possibly have to do with anything?"

She finished arranging her hair and sat down across the aisle from him.

"That's a good question. When I met you yesterday morning, you were just another mark, you know, another assignment to complete by any means necessary."

He sat up, leaning back against the bulkhead so he could face her.

"What changed?"

Her expression hardened for a second, and then relaxed.

"Well, first of all, I don't want you thinking that I'm okay with this...this thing that I feel happening to me. I like me. I like what I do. And I don't walk around feeling guilty about it. But then you come along with your innocent little middle-aged face and your crappy little middle-aged body and your stupid little vulnerable eyes and, well, shit Charlie! You've messed me up."

He grinned shyly.

"I'm uh...sorry?"

"Yes, you are. You are one sorry mess. But I like you. God help me, but I do."

His grin vanished.

"So, does this mean that you aren't going to kill me when all of this is over?"

Her gaze hardened once again.

"Best not to ask me about that, Charlie-boy. Just let

things be. Either I will, or I won't, and there's really nothing you can do about it either way. Just enjoy the moment, because that's all any of us really have."

"I actually know what you mean, because as soon as the stuff with—well, your bosses I guess—started happening, I kind of figured that my life was what I'd made of it; choices and consequences thereof, you know? And whatever was going to happen was completely out of my control. The only thing I was really worried about was Helen. I got her into this without her consent. And it's just killing me that she paid for my stupidity with her life."

"Well," Oksana said, "it hasn't killed you yet."

He nodded and turned to glance out the window.

"Where are we?"

"About thirty minutes out from San Diego."

"And what's going to happen once we get there?"

"Well, that depends."

"On what?" he prompted.

"On whether Jake Moriarity has figured out what I plan to do."

"And what if he has?"

"Then I have to kill him before we can move on."

"Just like that?"

She turned to stare out the window, pondering Charles' question.

"If he is as formidable as his reputation suggests, then no, it won't be," she snapped her fingers, "...just like that. It will require a considerable amount of effort."

Charles was quiet for a few seconds, and then said, "What if I helped you?"

Around a laugh, Oksana replied, "And how would you do that, Charlie?"

"By letting him believe that he is rescuing me from you."

She stared at him for a long time without speaking, trying to work the suggestion out in her mind.

"You know...that just might be worth some serious consideration. And you'd do that for me? Not knowing whether I'm going to let you live or die?"

Charles took a deep breath and said, "Yes, I would. Because there's enough money in those offshore accounts that we could go somewhere and start completely new lives. No one would ever find us. And somehow, I think that idea appeals to you."

In fact, it did. But she wasn't sure it was time to let Charles in on that little secret just yet.

"I'm going to think about it, Charlie-boy and by the time we land, you'll have your answer."

And why had he said that? Why was he willing to so glibly hand over the money—money that Helen had died protecting—to a woman who had just caused him more pain than he had believed possible? It was because even with all of that, he felt more alive in her presence than any time in his life.

And he would do anything to make the feeling last.

Even if it meant selling out Helen *and* her sacrifice.

CHAPTER 37

As it turned out, they weren't hard to spot—the bad guys. It's not like Michael and Cassie live in the slums. I'm pretty sure the average home in their development goes for somewhere north of five million dollars. And Michael's was probably closer to eight. Put a couple of hard looking guys with shaved heads and copious tats into that environment and the sore thumb analogy becomes self-explanatory.

Aaron had walked out ahead of me as planned and immediately spotted the two sitting and, of course, smoking on a low wall that ringed the outer parking area. All Russian bad guys smoke. At least the ones I've encountered. So, he walked toward them and asked if he could help them find someone. At first, they pretended not to hear him, so he came closer and repeated the question.

That's when the fun started.

They were fairly large men, say six-one or six-two and well over two hundred pounds. And, as is true of many men of that size, they apparently believed that since they were large, burly men—and that it was two to one—that they could intimidate Aaron and get him to go away. But to win the fight game, you have to have more going for you than size and strength. I came around the corner of the development just in time to see one guy take a swing at Aaron. He broke that guy's arm and put the other one on the ground clutching his throat and gurgling as if he were drawing his last breath. All of which took less than thirty seconds.

Not bad for a piano player.

I approached and said, "You're slowing down in your old age."

"Wha'chu mean, slowing down?"

"Hell, Aaron, time was when it would have taken you no more than twenty seconds to deal with something like this. I timed you. Thirty seconds on the dot. Slowing down, bro."

"I suppose you could've done better?"

"I didn't say that. Unlike you, I never claimed speed."

The guy with the broken arm was speaking Russian; the substance of which I assumed was directed toward our persons in an unflattering and deprecating manner.

Aaron sighed and yanked the guy to his feet by his bad arm, saying, "I know enough Russian to know that what you said is very unkind, son. So, you best be keeping your mouth shut unless I, or my friend here—who is actually way meaner than me—asks you to speak. Are we clear on that?"

His face frozen in a grimace, the man nodded.

His partner had recovered enough to have rolled over onto his right side but still struggled to breathe.

"Damn, Aaron. What'd you hit him with, an elbow?"

"Two fingers, bruh. That's all that was required. But then, bein' a piano player, I have very strong fingers."

I squatted down beside the man on the ground and felt for a pulse. It was rapid, but steady and strong. Aaron had hit him directly below his Adam's apple, which caused the larynx to convulse and constrict the airway. It would relax eventually, but he'd be out of commission until it did.

I asked the man standing if he spoke English. He stared balefully at me and puckered up his lips to spit. But, before he could complete the action, Aaron had twisted the broken arm, which, in turn, caused him to think better of his decision.

"That right there is education at work, my man," Aaron said. "You can't win this. You're done, so just relax."

Just as I was asking the man if there were any more of his colleagues around, a black SUV with Federal license plates pulled into the parking lot and came to a stop right beside us.

Three agents exited, led by my old friend, Special Agent Gerald Redfern with whom I had worked many cases.

I said, "Don't they ever give you a day off, Gerry?"

"They do," he replied while shaking my hand. "But when Zack told me what was going on, I couldn't just sit at home and let you and Aaron have all the fun."

"How you doin', bro?" Aaron said in greeting.

Redfern glanced down at the fallen vory.

"A damn sight better than that guy. Did you have to lump him up?"

"Nah, man. Just a little love tap to the throat."

Redfern issued instructions to his guys to get the Russians secured and then pulled us a few feet away so we could talk privately.

"Zack filled me in a bit on what's happening, but I'd like to hear it from you."

So, I walked him through what I knew of the story thus far.

"Aaron's bass player, Tommy Marshall, lost his wife two days ago as a result of complications from a massive stroke—which, by the way, we believe was induced by operatives from the Russian mafia. The reason we believe this, is because she had reconnected with a high school sweetheart named Charles Sutton; not his real name, but it's what he was going by, so we'll just stick to that. Charles has been working as a venture capital adviser for a firm in Orange County. About a year ago he was given a client who turned out to be the grandson of one of the Russian mob's top stateside bosses.

"Of course, Charles didn't know this at the time and began making investments on his client's behalf—investments that started paying generous returns. After a few successes, the guy requests to make a substantial investment off the books. Charles agrees only to learn that all of the money he had been making for the guy was going to support the mob's human trafficking enterprises in Southern California."

"Damn. So, what did he do?"

"He took the money; invested it; made a substantial profit and promptly stashed it away in several offshore accounts."

"Wait," Redfern said. "Are you saying that he stole the Russian mob's money?"

"That's exactly what I'm saying. At some point he got Tommy's wife, Helen, involved by having her open a safe-deposit box at a bank in Lake Forest where they put the USB drives with all the offshore account information."

"And the Russians found out about Helen?" he asked.

"Apparently, because she's dead."

"Did they get the information from her before she died?"

Aaron said, "Based on some other stuff that happened in the aftermath of her death, we don't believe they did."

"For instance?" Redfern prompted.

"For instance," I replied, "they sent a couple of goons to Tommy's place in Dana Point with instructions to find the location of the box and the key that opens it. Zack has those guys in custody now. Also, Charles Sutton—who, by the way, is in WitSec as a result of testifying against the Russians—has disappeared."

"Okay, hang on. Your guy's in WitSec? Have the Federal Marshalls been notified that he's missing?"

"Oh, they know he's missing. Seems he dismantled his phone leaving them with no way to track him."

He ran his fingers through his hair.

"Well, they can't be too pleased with that. So, any idea where he is, or is he still in the wind?"

"We believe he is being held by a female Russian assassin named, Oksana Orlov who is, as we speak, headed for Palomar Airport."

"Oksana Orlov?" he repeated. "Vasily Orlov's daughter?"

I said, "That name mean something to you?"

"Oh, just chatter you hear now and then. From what I've heard, she's one of their top assassins, if not *the* top."

"Also," Aaron interjected, "there are trafficked women involved—some already in the LA area and another load coming in via a big-rig sometime soon."

Redfern scrunched up his eyes and replied, "Exactly what I would have expected. Okay, so we need to intercept Oksana when she lands; release Charles from her custody; find the women currently being trafficked and stop that big-rig from dropping off its load. Oh, and get the USB drives from that safe-deposit box. Does that about cover it?"

"Almost."

"Almost? You mean there's more?" he asked incredulously.

"Well, I don't want to get into all the details right now, but Cassie and Michael are in Jacksonville, Florida. Michael is in ER due to serious complications from the accident. Cassie is falling apart, so I have Muriel on her way to lend some emotional support. I can't really walk away from this right now, so I had Pete Tolles and Agent Polk take Muriel to the airport. Vanessa, Eddie and Tommy Marshall are with them. The problem is that they picked up a tail as soon as they left Michael's place—unquestionably the Russians. I would appreciate some help keeping them safe."

"Absolutely. And I'm so sorry to hear about Michael. I'm very fond of that guy." He paused for a moment and then continued, "Here's what I want to do: tell Pete to stay put at the airport until my guys arrive to give him an escort back to Carlsbad and stay with them until we know they're safe. I'll also have an intercept team meet us at Palomar to assist with taking Oksana and Charles into custody. I assume Zack has everything else covered?"

"He's working on it. We're going to the bank in Lake Forest tomorrow morning to deal with the safe-deposit box, but as far as the trafficking issues go, we have zero information. One of the guys Zack took into custody up in Dana Point is willing to cooperate if we can rescue his girlfriend from the mob. I promised him that I would do that. So, I'm sure he will be able to provide us with everything we need to know in order to release the girls currently in slavery and stop the arrival of the new shipment."

Redfern blew out a long breath and ran his hand through his hair again.

"That's a lot to do. Let me make a couple of calls and get some things rolling."

As he walked away Aaron said, "I don't know how you keepin' it together, bro. It must be killin' you to stay here when things are going all to hell back there with Cassie and Michael."

"You have no idea. But, what else can I do?"

My phone buzzed.

It was Gabi.

"Hey beautiful."

"Hey yourself. What are you doing?"

I laughed.

"Oh, just stopping the Russian mob from engaging in wanton human trafficking and securing the release of a guy in WitSec who is in their custody."

"So, nothing important?" she teased.

"No, nothing like that. How about you?"

Around a yawn she said, "I just finished up some work and was actually thinking about going to bed."

I suddenly realized that I hadn't updated her on Cassie and Michael.

"Hey, listen...Michael is in ER."

"What?"

"It's a long story, but he's in rough shape; Cassie is falling apart; Muriel is on her way back there and will arrive around eight-thirty tomorrow morning." I paused and then added, "I'm dying because I can't just drop everything and go."

"Oh, Jake, I'm so sorry."

"But, my sense is that we will wrap this thing up before morning and I can hopefully be on the first flight out."

She was quiet for a few seconds before asking, "Would you like some company?"

"You mean, like, go back there with me?"

"Yes."

"That would be amazing. Can you pull that off with your work schedule?"

She said, "I have a substantial amount of PTO accrued. I'll just let them know that I am going to be using some of it."

"You think they'll be okay with that?"

After a laugh, she replied, "After what I pulled off for them last night, they have no choice."

Things were suddenly looking much brighter.

"Okay, I'll take your word for it. How about you get some flights organized and call me back with the details. And, thank you for this, Gabi."

"I get to go to Florida with the man I love and, hopefully, serve a young couple in distress whom I also love. No thanks are necessary. It is my great pleasure."

"Well, I get it, but thanks anyway."

She gasped and said, "This means that I get to see you tomorrow. I'm not sure I will be able to sleep at all tonight."

"Well, try, because I have plans for you that require a significant level of energy."

"You, sir, are possessed of an immodest imagination."

"I was talking about touring St. Augustine. What did you think I meant?"

"Okay, mister. I'll remember you said that."

"Goodnight, Gabi. I love you today."

"Love you every day, Mr. Moriarity."

I disconnected the call and checked my watch.
10:30 p.m.
So much needed to happen.
So little time.

CHAPTER 38

Aaron and I were following Gerald Redfern down Palomar Airport Road and heading for the airport.

It was just a few minutes before 11:00 p.m., but I figured Oksana would wait until at least midnight before attempting to land. Why? I couldn't begin to tell you except that it's what I would do were I in her position. As for how we were going to take her into custody, when, and if, she did as I expected...well, that was going to have to be a game-time decision based on the level of resistance she provided. And if you want to know the truth, it didn't really matter all that much unless she had a full tactical crew onboard. Even then, the element of surprise would weigh heavily in our favor.

Aaron, who had been researching flights as we drove, said, "Gabi was right, getting both of you into Jacksonville at the same time is going to be next to impossible."

"Yeah, I kind of figured. I appreciate you jumping in for Gabi and taking care of this. That thing at work didn't leave her with much choice than to hand it off."

"No worries at all. From Vegas, there are no non-stops. So, I think about the best we can do for her is a Delta flight that leaves at six a.m. and gets in mid-afternoon."

"Damn. Anything later in the morning?"

"About the only other thing I'm seeing is a seven-ten a.m. that gets in about five o'clock."

"Do the seven-ten. It's not much, but it sounds better

than six."

"Okay." He was silent for a few minutes as he confirmed the flight. "Done. Now, as far as you're concerned, it's gonna be hard because you don't know when we gonna be done with this mess."

"Just find the best options after noon tomorrow."

"I'm looking at…well, there's a two-oh-five p.m. that'll get you into Jacksonville around eleven."

"That will be tight. What else?"

"About the only other options all have you arriving Tuesday morning."

"Shit."

"Right?"

I didn't really want to wait until Tuesday morning. I mean late Monday night was bad enough.

"Book that two-oh-five. I'll just have to get this wrapped up by then."

"Well," he said, "one thing in your favor is that with your FBI credentials you can zip through security."

"There is that."

I called Gabi and had Aaron give her our itineraries and then asked her to get in touch with Cassie to let her know what was happening. We talked for a few minutes trying to come up with a plan to deal with the logistics of the trip and decided that she would take care of securing lodging and a rental car. By the time we had said our goodbyes, Aaron and I had arrived at Palomar Airport and found it all but deserted.

As we climbed out of the Range Rover, we saw Gerald Redfern walking quickly in our direction.

"What's up, Gerry?" I asked.

"The two bad guys we picked up at Michael's?"

"Yeah?"

"They're both in the hospital and the one guy whose throat Aaron attempted to crush is in the ICU."

We both stared at him.

"What?" he said defensively while throwing his arms

out the side. "All I did was give the dude a little love tap."

Redfern grinned.

"If that was a love tap, then please, don't show me any love."

"Duly noted."

"Also, I just got off the phone with Zack, and your boy, Iosif, has given up the location where most, if not all, of the trafficked girls are being kept. Get this, it's in Pacific Palisades."

"So much for subtlety," I replied. "How about the big rig?"

"He didn't have any specifics on the exact truck, but he did tell us where it would most likely offload the girls."

"And?" I prompted.

"Somewhere around the docks in San Pedro."

"Makes sense," Aaron declared. "Nobody down there pays much attention to anything other than their own damn business."

I said, "I assume that Zack is going to manage all that drama?"

"He is."

"Then I need him to watch out for Nastasiya and make sure she's safe."

"Is that Iosif's girlfriend that you mentioned?" Redfern asked.

"Yes. I made him a promise."

"No problem, Jake. Nastasiya will be taken care of."

I checked my watch.

11:15 p.m.

In the distance, I could just make out the sound of a jet descending toward the landing strip.

CHAPTER 39

Oksana stared through the window in the Learjet's bulkhead and spoke into the intercom, "See anything that looks unusual?"

The pilot answered, "Tower is dark. Tarmac empty. One or two cars visible in parking lot. Light traffic on the street."

"Good. You may proceed with the landing."

Charles said, "What if Jake Moriarity is down there waiting for us?"

Oksana replied, "I *know* he's waiting."

"And you're going to land anyway?"

"Sure."

Charles stared uncomprehendingly at her.

"You seem pretty cool."

"I am."

"May I ask why?"

"Oh, let's just say that I have a little surprise planned for him."

Charles asked, "And what if he's not alone? I hear he works with the FBI."

She waved her hand dismissively.

"Alone, FBI, it doesn't matter."

"I hope you know what you're talking about."

She reached over and mussed his hair.

"Don't worry, Charlie-boy, it's all going to be fine."

With a laugh, he asked, "How do you do it"

"Do what?"

"How do you project as much confidence as you do? On my best day I was never as sure as you."

She seemed to think it over for a few seconds.

"Well, I guess after you've done the things I've done —and have been successful doing it—you get to know who you are and what you're capable of." After a wink and a smile, she added, "You also learn to stack the deck whenever possible."

"What does that mean?"

"It means that I never play fair, Charlie-boy. I always play to win."

"Kind of like you did with me?"

"Yeah, kind of like what I did with you. Although with you—and please don't be offended by this—I didn't really have to work that hard."

"What, because you recognized that I was a lonely, confused middle-aged man you could have your way with?"

"Well, that, plus all of the research I had available to me. It's not like you are unknown to the Russians, you know. Why do you think that stupid kid contacted you anyway? I mean do you really think you were chosen at random? Far from it. They vetted you for months before he first reached out to you."

"Apparently you don't think very highly of Alexei."

She spat in the aisle.

"I despise the little prick."

"Why?"

Her brow furrowed over, eyes suddenly grown as cold as a Dakota winter.

"He thought that because his grandfather was one of the big bosses he could have anything he wanted."

Charles said, "And, let me guess. He wanted you?"

"Yes."

"And I'm also guessing he wasn't exactly successful in acquiring what he wanted?"

"No...no, he wasn't. But his wounds healed eventually."

"Wounds? Eventually? What did you do to him?"

"I cut him, what do you think?"

Charles raised his eyebrows in understanding.

"You *cut* him?"

"Yes. Down there. It was not pretty."

"But, didn't you get in trouble with grandpa? With your father?"

She spat into the aisle, saying, "My father is a pig. I care nothing for what he thinks. And as for the grandfather, I own him. I made sure of that when I first started working."

"You mean—"

"That I slept with him on numerous occasions? Yes. Whenever he wanted, actually."

Charles blew out a long breath.

"That seems a high price to pay."

"Not if it gets you what you want."

"And what did you want?"

She said, "I wanted immunity from things like cutting his grandson."

"No offense, Lib...Oksana, but sex is sex—family is family."

She shook her head.

"You don't understand. The old man is obsessed with me and would do anything to have me. Besides, I do his dirty work. I know things no one else knows about him, my father and the entire Russian mob. If anyone ever tried to take out any form of retaliation or revenge for me nearly gelding his little pussy of a grandson, I would take them down. After I cut them too, of course."

Charles sat in silence as the plane made its final approach. Craning his neck in an attempt to see more clearly, he noticed three identical sets of headlights moving quickly in single file down the southern side of the landing strip. Then, with a slight bump they were down and racing down the runway as if they had no intention of stopping. He suddenly realized what was happening. The three sets of head-lights belonged to three SUVs that were paralleling their progress down the runway as if they intended to rendezvous with them at the extreme western end. Through the SUVs windows he could make out at least four people in each. That meant that Oksana had arranged for a small army to es-cort them away from the airport.

He felt the powerful engines kick into reverse thrust and it felt as if the pilot was virtually standing on the brakes. Whatever the case, the plane finally began slowing allowing the SUVs to catch up to them. When they came to a complete stop, one SUV pulled up directly in back, while the other two flanked them.

Oksana turned to him with a big smile.

"Okay, Charlie-boy. It's show time!"

CHAPTER 40

We watched as the Learjet touched down. But instead of slowing, it seemed to maintain its speed.

"What the hell?" Redfern muttered.

Aaron grabbed my arm and pointed. Three black SUVs had just come squealing around a corner and were paralleling the Learjet's progress on the opposite side of the runway from us.

"Well, shit," I exclaimed. "That can't be good."

Redfern started hollering into his radio for local law enforcement to send reinforcements.

Aaron said, "I don't suppose you've got anything more substantial in the car than my three-fifty-seven do you?"

I shook my head.

"All I have is my Sig. But at least I've got a few boxes of ammo in the back."

"Not gonna do us much good if those boys open up with the kind of firepower I suspect they're packing."

Redfern said, "I should've seen this coming."

"What do you want to do?"

"CHP and San Diego Sherriff's department are all coming to help, but I'm not sure they'll get here in time to do us any good."

Aaron gestured at the SUVs, "Probably a minimum of three guys in each."

"And every one of them with long guns," I added. "Not sure how much of a deterrent we can provide with pistols."

Redfern's radio crackled to life with a metallic voice saying, "Our chopper can't be there for at least thirty minutes and the Sherriff's chopper is deployed chasing a stolen vehicle. Please advise."

Redfern replied, "Then have CHP and the Sherriff's department start blocking freeway onramps and surface streets in a one-mile perimeter from Palomar. We'll attempt to contain the—"

He stopped speaking because I grabbed his arm and pointed to a helicopter inbound from the west toward where the Learjet was surrounded by the three SUVs about a half-mile from our position.

"That's brilliant tactical thinking right there," Redfern said grudgingly. "Risky as hell, but brilliant. They know there's not a damn thing we can do to stop them."

In the glow of headlights and landing lights we could see a man and a woman running from the jet toward the chopper surrounded by five or six heavily armed men. Once the man and woman were onboard, the helicopter lifted off and went dark, disappearing into the night sky while their escort hustled back into the SUVs and took off overland. The Learjet made a quick about face and then took off the opposite direction from which it had landed.

I shook my head in frustration at how badly we had been outfoxed.

"Where can they go from that western end of the runway?"

"Well," Redfern replied, "there's some self-storage buildings at the end there, but where they're headed looks like they plan to go off-road and use the golf course access roads."

"Is there a main road they can access?"

He was looking at a map on his phone.

"The only main road is College Boulevard, but my guess is that they plan to head into this industrial area," he tapped the screen, "right here. Once they get in there, the options for concealment, transferring of vehicles, et cetera are substantial."

I thought it over for a few seconds, feeling more and more like a tactical rookie.

"Look, I don't care all that much about the foot soldiers. I want Oksana. I suggest we attempt to track that chopper and let those guys go."

Redfern nodded his head in agreement.

"I'm with you, Jake. Let me see what I can get going."

As he walked away, Aaron said, "Bro, we got played like a honky-tonk piano."

"Yes. We did. And I find that I'm not overly fond of the feeling."

"Where could they land that chopper? I mean they got to come down at some point."

"True, but given its range and ground speed—and the fact that we have absolutely no identifying information—they could literally go anywhere and simply blend into the crowd, so to speak."

Redfern returned, running his hand through his hair, his face registering frustration.

"My guys are telling me that with all the air traffic in the area, we're back to the needle in a haystack scenario. In short, there's no way either the chopper or Learjet can be tracked."

"And Oksana knew that would be the case when she put this little drama together," I replied. "Okay. Then we need to focus on the most logical end destination."

Aaron asked, "What's she really after? The stuff in the safe-deposit box, right?"

"Right. So, I suppose we don't have to go to her. She'll eventually come to us."

Redfern said, "Agreed. But in the meantime, she has shown herself to be a fairly brilliant tactician, so we really need to be thinking creatively about this."

I have established, through trial and error, that there

are two unarguable rules when dealing with situations such as this: the first is to never underestimate an opponent. The second is like unto the first: never overestimate yourself.

Thus far I had violated each liberally.

I said, "She's already got Charles—or whatever the hell his name is—in her custody. If I were her, I would at least try to take Tommy, if for no other reason than to have added leverage when it came down to negotiations."

"Well," Redfern replied, "there's little chance of that happening."

"How can you be so sure?" Aaron asked.

"Pete and Agent Polk are with him, plus I've got two of my guys escorting them back to Carlsbad."

"Two guys?" Aaron responded with incredulity. "Two guys after the small army we just encountered? Where do you think those guys are going next? Out for coffee?"

"Shit," Redfern exclaimed and started hollering into his radio.

"It just keeps getting better and better," I said.

"We'll get on top of this, bro."

My cell buzzed.

It was Cassie.

"Hey, little girl."

"Uncle," came her wailed response. "Michael just went into cardiac arrest."

CHAPTER 41

The ground felt as if it had suddenly tilted and I was struggling to maintain my balance.

I said, "When did this happen?"

"About ten minutes ago."

"So, they're working on him?"

"Yes," she sobbed. "There's at least eight or nine people crowded around his bed. They've already shocked him twice and now it looks like they're going to inject something with a big needle."

I grabbed Aaron and pulled him away from the small group of FBI agents huddled around Gerald Redfern.

I told him, "Michael is in cardiac arrest."

"Oh, my sweet, Lord Jesus," he breathed somberly.

"That's almost certainly epinephrine they're injecting. Anything happening?" I asked Cassie.

"Well," she said, her voice trembling with emotion. "It looks like there's a heart rhythm. Hang on..."

I could hear a deep, male voice speaking indistinctly in the background and Cassie's mumbled replies.

After thirty seconds or so, she came back on the line.

"Okay. They've got him stabilized."

"Good to hear, Cass. Did the doctor give you any indication as to why this happened?"

"He said that it was directly related to the issues Michael is experiencing."

I could hear the exhaustion and hopelessness in her voice.

I checked my watch.

11:45 p.m.

I said, "Muriel is on her way; Gabi will be there by mid-afternoon tomorrow and I'll be there by tomorrow evening. Help is on the way, Cass. Just hang on a little longer."

She sobbed, "I'm not a weak person."

"I know you aren't."

"But this..."

At no time in my long career had I ever hated my job. Until now.

"I'm so sorry that I can't be there for you, sweetheart."

"You didn't see this coming. *I* didn't see this coming. It just is, and there's nothing we can do about it except ride it out and hope for a good outcome." She paused to blow her nose and then continued, "I'm going to be fine. I'm just, you know, beyond exhausted."

"Well, try to get some sleep. And when you wake up, Muriel will be there."

"Yeah," she replied around another sob. "That will be really good."

The silence stretched between us. Only, it wasn't tense or awkward. Communication was happening, only it was on a soul level.

"Listen," she said. "Don't beat yourself up over this, okay?"

I blew out a long sigh.

"You realize that you're talking to a lifetime self-flagellator, right?"

"Yes, I do. So, stop it and finish your work so you can come and hug me."

Someone, without my knowledge, had suddenly crammed a wad of cotton the size of a melon down into my throat.

"I will definitely be doing that when I see you. Bye, little girl. I love you."

"Love you more."

She terminated the call, and I stood there with one hand covering my face and the phone still pressed against my ear.

"You okay, bro?" Aaron asked softly.

I couldn't speak. If you want to know the truth, I didn't *want* to speak for fear of breaking down into uncontrollable sobs. So, I just nodded my head unconvincingly.

Aaron stepped around in front of me and wrapped me up in a bear hug. I don't mind telling you that I wept. Right out there on the tarmac in front of five, very manly FBI agents.

Redfern approached cautiously and asked, "Is it Michael? He okay?"

I stepped back from Aaron and patted his shoulder appreciatively.

"He just went into cardiac arrest and it took them a while to revive him."

Redfern was quiet for a few seconds before saying, "Look, Jake, if you need to go, we can handle this."

"There is nothing I would like more than to do just that, Gerry. But the way the schedules are set up, I can't get a flight until two o'clock tomorrow afternoon. So, I'm sort of stuck here until then. Might as well try to be useful."

He hesitated slightly and then asked, "What if there was a way to get you there before that? Would you take it?"

Now that was a great question. Would I?

"Well..."

"Dude," Aaron said. "Why would you even hesitate? If we can get stuff settled with Oksana tonight, there's no reason you shouldn't be out of here just as soon as Gerry can arrange it."

It was the being "out of here" that bothered me. And why did it bother me? Is it because I am, by nature, a control freak and have a nearly obsessive need to be up to my elbows in everything that happens? Or was it something deeper? Like, if I were to leave and things were wrapped up successfully without me, would that reflect negatively on my worthiness; my effectivity—the extent to which I am even needed?

I said, "I don't want you to think that I am unappreciative of the offer, Gerry. It's just that I kind of have a thing about finishing what I start."

"Understood," he replied. "But what if we get this finished by, say, mid-morning? Would you allow me to arrange transport for you?"

"Of course. But that's a tall order, my friend."

He slapped me on the back.

"How about if we just move forward and do what we can do. If it turns out that fortune smiles on our efforts and we get things done in a timely manner, then we put you on a Bureau jet and get you reunited with your family. If not, then you've still got your original plan."

"Okay. That'll work. Now, while we've been talking I think I figured out what Oksana is going to do next."

Aaron said, "Pray tell."

"She has Charles. And I'm betting that willingly, or unwillingly, Charles has told her everything about the safe-deposit box and the location of the key."

"Then, why does she need Tommy?"

"She doesn't."

Redfern said, "But, she has someone tailing him."

"Think about it. Through Charles, she knows about the Bible and, therefore, the location of the key. The tail is not meant to do Tommy harm or even an attempt to snatch him."

"It's to keep an eye on him cuz she's gonna break into his condo," Aaron replied.

"That's exactly right. My sense is that the chopper will drop her off somewhere around Dana Point where she will meet up with her team. From there, they'll go to Tommy's— probably pick the lock—and secure the key."

"But," Redfern said. "The key's not there. You have it."

"That, I do. But they don't know that, so they will still make the attempt."

Aaron asked, "But, even if they had the key, how could they use it to access the safe-deposit box? I mean don't you need ID in order to do that?"

"If you went in during business hours," I replied. "But that's not what Oksana has planned." I thought for a few seconds and then continued, "My guess is that her operatives already have the manager from *Tenshi Community Bank* in their custody."

"That makes total sense," Redfern agreed. "That way, they can go in under cover of darkness and not trigger any alarms. They probably plan to kill the poor bastard when they're through with him, though."

"Just as she will kill Charles when he has served his purpose."

Iosif's phone buzzed with an incoming text.

It was from Oksana.

I said, "It's a text from Oksana."

"What's it say?" Aaron asked.

"'*I don't have much time. She'll kill me if she finds me using her phone.*' That has to be from Charles."

I texted back, '*Charles, this is Jake Moriarity. What's going on.*'

Redfern said, "You think this is legit?"

"I intend to find out."

Charles answered, '*I have been kidnapped and tortured and Oksana plans to kill me. Helen told me that if things started going sideways to reach out to you.*'

"Ask him where he is," Redfern suggested.

I wrote, '*Tell us where you are so we can come and get you.*'

"That chopper has only been airborne for ten or fifteen minutes, so unless they set down somewhere, he's still onboard."

His return text said, '*I don't have any idea, but I know she's headed for Helen's condo in Dana Point. She's coming back!*'

We all stared at the screen as if willing another text to appear.

"So, was that legit?" Redfern inquired.

"Not a chance."

CHAPTER 42

Oksana took her phone from Charles' trembling hands.

"Do you think he bought it?" Charles asked.

Oksana shrugged.

"No way to know for sure, but we'll find out soon enough."

"I'm not sure how me telling him about your plans is going to be helpful."

"Oh, Charlie-boy," she said with a laugh, "he already knows my plans."

"How can you be so sure?"

"Rumor has it that he is almost psychic when it comes to figuring things out. He knows we're going after the key. And, he probably knows about the bank manager, although that would require him knowing about the bank. And the only way he'd know about the bank is if Helen's husband had figured it out, or—"

Charles interrupted, "If they have the key."

"And how would they even know where to look for the key? And even if they had the key, how would they know what bank the safe-deposit box is in?"

"I don't know. I know for sure that Tommy didn't know about the key *or* the bank and in our communications with each other, Helen and I were ridiculously cryptic."

"How cryptic?"

"Well," he said, "we never directly mentioned anything about the safe-deposit box, the bank or where she had hidden the key."

"Then how did you communicate?"

"We used a Bible verse."

Oksana raised her eyebrows.

"Really? Which one?"

"It was Revelation twenty, verse one."

"You're going to have to clue me in, Charlie-boy. I'm not exactly up on my biblical knowledge."

"It says, 'And I saw an angel come down from heaven, having the key of the bottomless pit and a great chain in his hand.'"

"Okay," she said, drawing out the word. "That's pretty damn clever. But don't forget, we're dealing with Jake Moriarity here. My guess is that he's cracked that code and is already one or two steps ahead of us."

"There's no way," Charles argued.

"Don't kid yourself. Like I said, Moriarity is legendarily intuitive."

"I get that, but even if they found our communications, how could anyone pick up that the key is hidden in her family Bible at that verse in Revelation, and that angel is referencing Tenshi Community Bank?"

"Moriarity works with the FBI, which means that they would have torn Helen's phone apart and retrieved all of her emails and texts."

"But, how could anyone read that verse and—"

"Look, we can debate the point—which I have no interest in doing—or we can just move on under the assumption that he knows what we plan to do and adjust accordingly."

Charles said, "Like me calling and reinforcing that I am your captive?"

"It's a start. If he believes that you need rescuing, he'll never see you coming."

Charles was suddenly sober. Sober and terrified.

"I don't know if I can kill someone."

"But, that's the beauty of it, Charlie-boy," Oksana said, running her fingers through his hair. "All you have to provide is distraction. I'll take care of the rest."

He stared at her.

"You think you can pull this off even with the FBI there?"

She winked at him with an evil grin, "How about you just let me worry about that."

"But you said you'd never faced anyone like Jake Moriarity before."

"True, but he's just a man. And in case you hadn't noticed, I know how to handle men."

He blushed and turned away.

"Yeah, you do."

She started barking orders to the pilot who responded by banking the helicopter sharply to the left, which made Charles' stomach threaten to empty itself of everything he had consumed in the past twelve hours. When they finally leveled out he could make out the lights from a densely populated area on the right juxtaposed with dense darkness on the left.

"Where are we?" he asked.

"Just passing over San Clemente. We'll be landing in ten minutes."

"What happens then?"

She mussed his hair again and replied, "Then, it's showtime, Charlie-boy."

No matter how hard he tried, he couldn't shake the sense that his life was drawing to a close, and that Oksana was going to end it. He had tried to fool himself into thinking that he had somehow ingratiated himself to her and that even if her original plan had been to kill him, that she liked him well enough now to have changed her mind.

But it was no use.

He was, as they say, a dead man walking—or in this case, flying. The pretty girl who had picked him up at the coffee shop was a heartless killing machine completely devoid of any conscience whatsoever. Kind of like that woman cyborg in one of the Terminator movies. When the time came, she would terminate him as easily as he would squash a hapless bug that happened to randomly wander across his path.

He had always been smart—smarter than everyone else, actually. It's what made him so good at his job. He could think critically and incisively, delving into even the most complex situations and finding advantages that no one else could see.

And what about this situation? Why hadn't he employed his secret weapon—his intellect? Simple. In the short time he had known Oksana, he had fallen totally and completely in love with her. Oh, it wasn't a deep, heart-level love like he had possessed for Helen. This was visceral; primal; more along the lines of obsession than anything else. Maybe that was it. He was obsessed with her. And why, because of one bit of kindness following on the heels of cruel and horrendous torture?

"Oksana?"

"Yeah, Charlie?"

He stared at her, his mouth working to form an appropriate follow-up.

"Never mind," he finally said.

She reached over and cupped his face in her hands—hands that were surprisingly soft for an assassin.

"Look, I know you're worried about what is going to become of you."

"Wouldn't you be if you were in my position?"

"Probably, but I have good news."

"You do?"

She grinned and kissed him. It was long. Passionate. It literally took his breath away.

Pulling back, she said, "I've decided that I like you too much to kill you."

Whether she meant it or not, there was nothing he could do either way to change the final outcome. He was a pawn, and she was the chess master.

And he was okay with that.

CHAPTER 43

And how do you know it wasn't legit?" Aaron said, as I returned Iosif's phone to my pocket.

"Think about it: we're supposed to believe that Charles somehow got Oksana's phone away from her, sent and received multiple lines of text without her knowledge while seated right next to her inside a helicopter? Please!"

"Then why the charade?" Redfern asked. "It doesn't make any sense."

"You're wrong, Gerry. It makes perfect sense."

"You're going to have to explain that one to me."

I said, "This was Oksana telling me that *she* knows that *I* know about her plans."

Aaron replied, "But, if the girl's that confident, why would she even bother with that?"

"Because she wants to make sure I know that she's better than me. And the best way to do that is for her to say, 'Okay, Moriarity, here's exactly where I'm going and what I'm going to do. But even with that knowledge, you can't stop me.' Which tells me that somehow, the deck is stacked."

"Stacked, how?"

I thought about the question for a few seconds before answering, "I'm not completely certain, but I think it has something to do with Charles. Maybe...maybe she's completely turned him and he's now working with her."

Redfern said, "The text mentioned that she had tortured him and threatened to kill him. If he is working with her it's out of abject terror, not willingness."

"I'm not so sure, Gerry."

"So, are you suggesting some kind of twist on the Stockholm Syndrome?"

I said, "Capture-bonding is an established fact. No one can explain it, but case study files are filled with examples where people who have been taken hostage and, quite often, tortured horribly develop emotional bonds with the very ones doing the torturing."

"If you ask me," Aaron offered, "this is starting to sound like the plot of a really bad movie."

"But what if it's true?" I asked. "What if Charles is, in fact, exhibiting textbook symptoms of capture-bonding?"

"Patty Hearst," Redfern remarked without explanation.

Aaron screwed up his face.

"What?"

"Patty Hearst. She was the nineteen-year-old heiress to the William Randolph Hearst fortune. In the mid-seventies an extreme left-wing revolutionary organization, calling itself the Symbionese Liberation Army, kidnapped her from her Berkley apartment, beat her into unconsciousness, sexually assaulted her, brainwashed and threatened to kill her."

I said, "If I remember correctly, she ended up joining them, right?"

"Correct. Two months after the abduction, an audio-tape was released with her announcing that she had, in fact, joined the SLA. She even participated in a bank robbery."

"How you know so much about this?" Aaron asked.

Redfern grinned, "My dad was a reporter for the San Francisco Chronicle and was actually assigned to the case. According to him, his work on the Patty Hearst SLA story established his career, so, as you can imagine, he talked a lot about it when I was a kid. As a result, I grew up with an innate fascination for what had happened. Then, when I got to Quantico I read everything I could find. It was really interesting having heard my father speak from the perspective of a reporter to then read the actual case files."

"I bet," I said. "So, you agree that capture-bonding could be occurring in this instance here?"

"Oh, absolutely," he replied.

I said, "So, let me think out loud for a few minutes: I'm guessing that Oksana isn't exactly hideous. So, for the sake of discussion, let's say that she's beautiful—consummately lethal and cruel, but beautiful. Charles is a lonely, isolated middle-aged guy whose partner, and former high school sweetheart, has just died. Oksana targets him; plays on his grief; his loneliness; somehow wins his confidence and convinces him, either through coercion or manipulation—maybe both—to go to LA and retrieve the safe-deposit box key." A thought suddenly occurred to me, so I ran with it. "I believe she did, in fact, torture him and has kept him on a short leash by threats of death, but—and this is pure speculation—I also believe she is working the pleasure-pain axis."

"Now this is something I know about," Aaron remarked. "Sylvie, my ex-wife, went to a Tony Robbins seminar once and heard him talk about the pleasure-pain axis; you know, the need people have to avoid pain and the desire to gain pleasure. That was some weird shit right there, bro."

"It's not far-fetched at all," I replied. "I've never heard Robbins, but in my somewhat limited experience, I understand the principle. Specifically, as it regards Oksana and Charles, I believe she is causing terrible pain, but then turning around and giving him a level of pleasure that, perhaps, he's never known before."

Redfern said, "That would be phenomenally addictive. And it would also keep him constantly off-balance."

"Exactly," Aaron said in agreement. "And if the boy's emotionally unstable anyway..."

He let the sentence trail.

"So, what are we concluding from this little Dr. Phil session?" Redfern asked.

"It's like I said," I replied. "The deck is stacked, and Charles is her ace in the hole. She's expecting us to move forward on the basis of believing that Charles needs rescuing."

"Which," Redfern added, "will leave us blinded to her actual intentions."

"Using Charles as, what, a Trojan horse?" Aaron asked.

"That's exactly what Oksana is counting on."

"But, we not gonna do that, are we?" Aaron said with a smile.

"No, we're not."

My phone rang.

It was Zack.

"Zack, what's up?"

He chuckled lightly before replying, "Well, I got to thinking about the situation and how we had made plans to go to Lake Forest tomorrow morning and deal with the safe-deposit box."

I put him on speaker and the three of us crowded around.

"Zack, you've got me, Aaron and Gerald Redfern here."

"Great. This is something you all need to hear. Anyway, I started wondering, why wait until tomorrow to go to the bank? I mean it's late, but why not just arrange to pick up the manager—a very nice and very accommodating man named Thomas Enoki, by the way—and just get it over with tonight?"

"Do you have him?" Redfern asked.

Zack laughed again.

"That's just the thing. We do have him, but we had to fight off four vory to get him."

"I knew it," I said. "I knew Oksana was going to try to get him before us."

"Well, you were right. As it turns out, Mr. Enoki is only too happy to be in our custody."

Redfern replied, "I just bet he is."

I said, "We believe Oksana is headed for Dana Point and Tommy's condo."

"Because she thinks the key is there?" Zack asked.

"Yes. We think her plan was to get the key, kidnap Mr. Enoki and hit the bank sometime tonight."

"So, we need to stakeout Tommy's condo and wait for her."

"That's probably not going to work, because I'm pretty sure she has people there already," I replied.

"Damn! I'm starting to get the feeling that we've been outsmarted and outplayed on every level of this thing."

"Sadly, she's been out in front of us the whole way, which, in and of itself is not uncommon in well-planned and executed things of this nature. It's just that she's still managing to pull stuff off even after I figured out what she was going to do and when she was going to do it."

Redfern said, "She's either damn smart, or damn lucky."

"Probably a bit of both," Aaron replied.

Zack was silent for a few seconds before saying, "Okay, how about this: we take out her people in Dana Point, intercept her communications so she believes that everything is a go, and then when she shows up, we snatch her."

Even though he couldn't see me, I shook my head.

"That's not going to work."

"Why not?"

"Because she's not going to Dana Point."

"She's not?" Zack replied nearly in unison with Redfern and Aaron.

"No. She's coming to Carlsbad. She's coming after me."

CHAPTER 44

K eeping Zack on the line, I pulled Iosif's phone from my pocket, located the list of recent calls and stabbed a finger at Oksana's number. It rang a few times before she answered.

"Mr. Moriarity, I presume?"

"Yes, it is. Listen, I thought I'd go ahead and save both of us some time, energy and frustration."

"And how do you propose to do that?" she asked in a bored tone of voice.

I couldn't hear any noise in the background, so I assumed the chopper was on the ground.

"I've got something you want. You have something I want. I propose a trade."

She laughed, "You have nothing I want."

"I have the key."

A cold silence hung between us as she processed this information.

"That isn't possible," she finally replied.

"Isn't it?"

The silence returned and seemed to stretch on for minutes, even though I know it was merely seconds.

"Okay," she said, "let's say you're telling the truth."

"Oh, I am."

"But how can I possibly know that?"

I pulled the key from my pocket, snapped a pic and sent it as a text attachment. I heard her phone buzz on the other end of the line and then some muted conversation with a male who I assumed to be Charles Sutton.

"Okay. You've got the key. Congratulations. But I still have Charles and if you ever want to see him alive again, you will do what I say."

I laughed.

"You seem to be forgetting that Charles Sutton means nothing to me. In fact, he means nothing to anyone here with me. In short, you have no leverage."

"Really? What if I kill him slowly and painfully? Won't that weigh on your conscience?"

I sighed and pretended boredom.

"I assume you've done your homework on me, Oksana. And if you have, you will almost certainly have found that I can be one heartless son of a bitch when the situation calls for it. And this situation is definitely calling for it. Because of that prick, one of my best friends is dead. He means less than nothing to me. So, do what you have to do."

"Hang on," she said quickly and then handed the phone to someone.

A voice said, "Mr. Moriarity? It's Charles Sutton."

"And why should I believe that this is really you?"

He quoted the Scripture verse from Revelation to me and asked if that was sufficient documentation.

"I suppose," I said in reply. "All right, what do you want?"

"I just want out of here and away from this woman."

"Well, Mr. Sutton, if it coincides with our plans, I will see what I can do to accommodate your release. If not—"

"You don't understand. She's going to kill me."

"And what makes you think she won't just kill you anyway when you have served your purpose. By the way, since I have the key, you're not much good to her anymore, are you?"

I heard the phone being snatched away.

Then, "Listen, Moriarity, I'm not playing games here."

"Oh, please. This whole thing is a game to you, isn't

it?"

I heard someone cry out in the background.

"Does that sound like I'm playing?"

I heard Charles sobbing, saying something about how she had cut him.

"Well, I'm not playing either. In fact, I'm hanging up. Goodbye."

"What?" she said, alarm coloring her voice. "You can't just hang up."

"Really? Watch me. Goodbye, Oksana. It's been nice—"

"You're signing his death warrant! I'm warning you."

"Kill him; let him live; it doesn't matter to me. Goodbye."

I hit the red "end" button on Iosif's phone.

Zack said, "I can't believe you just did that."

"Yeah," I replied. "I can't either."

Aaron shook his head, saying, "I've seen you do some crazy-ass stuff, bro, but that was a bit extreme even for you."

Redfern asked, "What were you going for?"

"I'm betting that she will take the bait and call me back. If not, I just killed Charles Sutton."

CHAPTER 45

Oksana stared incredulously at her phone.

"He hung up on me. He actually hung up on me."

Charles was clutching a handkerchief to his hand, attempting to staunch the flow of blood from a cut Oksana had scored across the top of his knuckles.

"Was this really necessary?" he asked, his voice trembling.

Leaning toward him, her eyes filled with anger, she replied curtly, "Yes," and then relaxed, reaching out and stroking his hair. "But, the only reason I did it was to convince Moriarity that I was serious. It's not so bad. If I would've really wanted to hurt you, Charlie-boy, I think you know that I could have."

He nodded silently.

"So, what now?"

The helicopter had let them off in the parking lot of a grocery store in Oceanside that had obviously been closed for quite some time. The entire maneuver had required no more than sixty seconds, with the chopper coming in fast, setting down just long enough for them to exit toward a waiting SUV and then lifting off once again into a night sky blessedly cloaked by a marine layer.

Oksana pondered Charles' question for a few seconds and then asked, "What happens once they get that safe-deposit box opened? Are the USB drives just tossed in there, or are they in their own cases? What?"

"No. They are all inside a small, fireproof and tamper proof case. It has a digital code that only Helen and I knew."

"So, they couldn't, like, smash it open or something like that?"

"Well, I mean, sure, if they had the right tools. But not without damaging the drives."

Her original plan—which was to go to Dana Point, break in to Tommy's condo and get the key—had been unfortunately scrapped due to Moriarity and the FBI's meddling. How they had gotten to Thomas Enoki, the bank manager before her men was a mystery. Then again, so was Jake Moriarity being in possession of the key.

"So," she mused, "even though the FBI has Mr. Enoki and Moriarity has the key, there's nothing they can do with the USB drives because they can't access them, right?"

"That's right."

She smiled and kissed him on the lips.

"You're in luck, then, Charlie-boy. I still need you for a while, so you can relax."

He nodded and dabbed at his bleeding hand.

Oksana said, "Do they know about the case inside of the safe-deposit box?"

"No. No one knew about it. Not even the banker. Just me and Helen."

Moriarity. How she loathed the man, and she had never even met him. Oh, she'd heard the rumors about him, but passed most off as typical, over-stated hyperbole—the stuff of myths and legends told and believed by those more gullible than she. But now? She wasn't so sure. He had surprised her, and she wasn't easy to surprise. What this adventure needed was something to knock him off his stride; get him stutter-stepping and attempting to regain balance. As for what that would look like, she wasn't quite sure.

But an idea was forming.

"How's the hand?" she asked with genuine concern.

"It's okay. Not as deep as I had thought and the bleeding is slowing."

"That's good, Charlie-boy."

The SUV was driving south toward Carlsbad on Interstate 5. The intel provided by her father's assistants said that Moriarity had family there and that he was actually house sitting for his niece and her new husband. The plan was simple: arrive on scene and create as much chaos as possible in the shortest amount of time possible. That way, while he was dealing with the chaos, she and Charles could be working on finishing what they started.

But, what form would the chaos take?

While she couldn't be absolutely certain, she had a feeling that only one of them would walk away from the encounter.

And it wasn't going to be him.

CHAPTER 46

I felt Iosif's phone vibrating in my pocket. I pulled it out and hit the speaker.

"Yes?"

"Mr. Moriarity," Oksana began, "it seems that you and I have gotten off on the wrong foot, as they say. I would like to...oh, how should I put it...start over."

I glanced at Redfern and Aaron, who, true to form, rolled his eyes dramatically.

"Okay, I'll bite. What did you have in mind?"

"I propose a face-to-face meeting. Just you and me. No Charles. No FBI. Just us two."

Redfern was nodding vigorously for me to accept her proposal.

"That's a definite possibility. But, I'm curious as to why you would want to put yourself in danger?"

She chuckled.

"Are you so sure it would be me who is in danger?"

I liked the sound of her voice. I liked it a lot. It was rich, refined, colored by dark undertones that brought to mind sweet chocolate and sultry, summer nights.

"Well, with all due respect, Oksana, I am unaccustomed to feeling fear in any form. And if you have done your homework on me, you will know that my sense of well-being is not at all hyped, nor is it unfounded."

"Are we having a—how do you Americans say it—a pissing contest, Mr. Moriarity?"

"No. Not on my end, at least. I am simply stating fact."

She said, "Well, here's a fact for you, Mr. Moriarity: I have personally killed over fifty enemies of our organization in just six, short years."

"And how many of those were given a fair chance to fight back? None, right? Because, isn't that how assassins like you work? You target unsuspecting people and kill them before they know what hit them? If you were going for impressive, I'm afraid you failed miserably."

She suddenly shouted, "Every one of my kills have been done up close, and personal. I do not believe in sneaking up on people."

"Nor, I am suspecting, do you believe in taking on your victims as opponents on a level playing field. My impressions of you thus far, Oksana, is that you mainly excel at stacking the deck."

She was silent for a few moments before replying, "Stacking the deck is for amateurs."

"Really? Can I quote you on that?"

"Quote me? I—"

"Isn't this exactly what you are trying to do right now? To stack the deck in your favor?" Before she could answer, I pressed on, "Even as we speak, your natural and deeply held insecurity has caused you to take drastic measures to do just that. Come on. Admit it."

"I will admit no such thing," she countered, although I knew it was exactly what she was attempting.

"Oh, please. You are terrified to go up against me on your own; because in your heart you know you would fail. Isn't that it?"

She screamed, "I. Am. Not. Afraid of anyone."

"It sounds as if you are becoming unhinged, Oksana. I thought we were just having a pleasant conversation. What's wrong? You afraid I'm going to best you?"

She screamed.

It was a long, drawn out shriek of frustration.

"I am going to kill you, Moriarity, and I will enjoy

every single second of the experience. And before I kill you, I will kill your—"

"Family? Damn. You know, I've never heard that one before. I'll give you this, you are nothing if not original."

I heard someone scream in the background. No doubt Charles again.

"Did you hear that, you piece of shit?"

"I heard a man scream—and I am guessing that, as per usual, it was an unarmed man. Probably Charles. But, then, we've already had this conversation about him."

"Apparently you don't take me seriously, Moriarity."

"Oh, I take you seriously," I said. "You are a manipulative, insecure, fearful bully who experiences pleasure in hurting men. What's the matter, Oksana? Did daddy mess with you?"

She screamed. I heard what sounded like a heavy object colliding with a human skull; Charles cried out and then the phone went silent.

"Damn," Aaron said. "You got to her. You definitely got to her, bro."

Gerald was laughing.

"Jake, my man, I've heard some master manipulators in my time, but nothing close to that. You have her completely tied up in knots."

I stood there, nodding my head in agreement, but secretly lamenting the horror I had most likely visited on Charles Sutton.

"Yeah, I know. But I'm worried about Charles."

"Charles?" Aaron said. "The boy brought all this on himself. Whatever he gets falls under the category of unintended consequences."

"I know you're right, but still..."

Redfern asked, "So, what's the next move?"

I glanced at my watch.

1:25 a.m.

"I don't know about you boys, but my next move is to

grab some sleep somewhere and by any means necessary. Because, I have a feeling that this is far from over."

"I couldn't agree more," Redfern answered. "Why don't you and Aaron go back to Carlsbad? In the meantime, based on what Iosif told us, we'll concentrate on closing down the human trafficking organization and intercepting that inbound semi-truck and trailer with the new recruits."

I learned early on that rest is a weapon. I hadn't had any; therefore, if I was going to be even close to being equal with Oksana, I had to get some sleep.

"Okay, Gerry. Let us know if anything starts popping."

"You got it, Jake."

And so, we left for Michael's condo.

I wish that we could've known then what we know now. We would have done things much differently.

CHAPTER 47

Charles was slumped over in the SUV, his head bouncing painfully against the side window.

"Charlie-boy, are you okay?" Oksana asked with seeming genuine concern. "Listen, I know I shouldn't have done that, but, see, I have this temper and sometimes it gets the best of me. Say something, Charlie."

Charles reached up and felt the knot forming behind his left ear. If she had merely punched him, he would've been okay. But she had hit him with the butt end of an overly large knife, sending him immediately into unconsciousness.

"I, uh...I'm really nauseous."

"You probably have a concussion," she said. "It's common in head injuries. The nausea will pass in a bit."

Charles stared at her as if attempting to make up his mind regarding Oksana.

"How do you do that?"

"Do what?" she replied.

"Just knock someone into unconsciousness, cut their hand open—torture them—and then turn around the next minute and express concern for their well-being?"

"Call it a gift. I don't know. It's just the way I am."

And was she concerned for him? This was an uncommon and uncomfortable situation for her. Charles Sutton was an assignment, someone from whom information needed to be extracted and then terminated in the same heartless manner that had marked her career and elevated her above other operatives. But it had gotten messy and there was no one to blame but herself.

Moriarity had mentioned daddy issues. If he only knew. But, no one could ever know. Maybe that was a contributing factor in these feelings about Charles that had wedged the doorway of her emotions open and now demanded attention.

"How old are you, Charles?"

"Fifty-three," he groaned.

A year younger than her father.

She thought about what she had done to Charles—what she continued to do to him—and suddenly felt like a sick and twisted monster for whom there were no boundaries when it came to getting what she wanted.

"I really do regret hitting you," she said in a rare show of emotion.

He inclined his throbbing head slightly in her direction and immediately regretted the movement.

"Then, do me a favor and don't do it again."

She nodded.

"Fair enough." She took a breath; started to express the thought that had been forming in her mind; dismissed it; and then decided to say it anyway. "Those USB drives represent a lot of money, don't they?"

"Uh, yeah. About twenty-seven million dollars."

She nodded slowly and then said, "Remember the conversation we had on the plane about going somewhere and starting a new life?"

"Yeah, I do. And then you sliced my hand open and tried to bash in my skull. I'm not sure I'd survive a week with you let alone a life."

She softened her tone.

"But, you've also seen the other side of me; the loving, pleasurable side."

"Yes, I have."

"That's not normal. No one *ever* gets to see that

Oksana. No one. But for some reason, you are drawing that person out of me. And I've been thinking: why should I continue to put my life on the line for people who don't really care if I live or die, only that I complete my assignment."

Charles squeezed his eyes shut against the onslaught of pain.

"So, what do you have in mind?"

"What you suggested."

"Which is?" he prompted.

"That we get those USB drives and go somewhere so far away that no one will ever find us. Maybe Argentina, or somewhere like that. Or find an island where we could just live in comfort; eat, drink, and just be happy."

He stared at her for a long time without speaking before saying, "You are the most confusing woman I have ever met. I can't tell right now if you're just playing me in order to get something, or if you, in fact, are experiencing some sort of come to Jesus moment and genuinely desire to change your life."

"I'm not sure if this is a come to Jesus moment, but I definitely am considering a change."

"Why? Like you said, you are at the top of the food chain in your profession; your conscience obviously doesn't suffer from the horrible things you do; you are well-paid—"

"And completely expendable as soon as they have gotten their use out of me."

"Funny you should say that," he mused, "because that's exactly the way I feel with you."

As the SUV slowed to take the Tamarack Avenue exit off of Interstate 5, Oksana contemplated the truth of his statement.

"Well," she said, "it definitely started out like that, Charlie-boy. But it's different now. I mean I could finish what I started—"

"Which includes killing me?"

"Yes," she replied simply.

"But?"

"But, I fear that what little soul I have left would be forever lost in the process."

With a supreme effort, he shoved himself into an upright position in the seat.

"Are you saying you're falling in love with me?"

"No, not love. It's just that I really like you, Charlie-boy. I can't explain it, but I do."

He nodded, causing his head to throb so violently that the nausea he had somehow managed to hold in check threatened to erupt. Several deep breaths later, it had subsided and he thought about the surreal nature of what he was currently experiencing.

Shifting his eyes without moving his head, he regarded Oksana who sat staring straight ahead through the front windshield, her eyes seemingly focused on something far away. What a strange woman. Strange, lovely and absolutely lethal. Why should he trust anything she had said?

Because he wanted to, and that was the damnable hell of the matter.

He wanted to trust her and be with her with nearly the same intensity as he craved his next breath.

But at the same time, a little voice in his head repeated a phrase over and over again like something stuck on a digital loop: *You're going to die...and she's going to kill you. You're going to die...and she's going to kill you. You're going to die...and she's going to kill you.*

He wanted the voice to shut up, but there was no stopping it. Just like there was no way to stop the events he had set in motion from playing out to whatever conclusion awaited him.

He was so screwed.

CHAPTER 48

Aaron and I arrived back at Michael and Cassie's place to find Pete, Bridgett and their charges safely inside and four of Gerald Redfern's finest agents posted outside. I explained to them that their presence was no longer necessary, but they insisted on staying, citing Redfern's orders to ignore everything I said. It was probably for the best, because I really did need some sleep. Hell, we *all* needed some sleep.

Pete told me that Muriel had gotten onto her flight without incident and that as soon as the FBI agents had shown up, the car that had been tailing them disappeared.

Vanessa and Eddie were already asleep in one bedroom and after a brief discussion we decided that Tommy would sleep in the third bedroom, and that Pete and Aaron would sleep in the den, a scene that—given the fact that they were attempting to fit on furniture not designed to accommodate NFL linebacker-sized men—would have been deemed comical under other, less life-threatening circumstances.

Bridgett had agreed to take the first watch.

I walked into the master bedroom; checked my phone for messages; found none; fell onto the bed and was asleep within thirty seconds.

It lasted all of forty-five minutes before I was jarred awake by my phone's insistent ringing.

I picked it up, stared at the number, didn't recognize it and was just about to turn it off before realizing that under the circumstances, that was probably an irresponsible thing to do.

I answered.

"Jake Moriarity."

"Mr. Moriarity, this is the security company for Cassandra Harvey's condo. We are calling to report that the alarm has been triggered and we suspect a break-in in progress."

I was suddenly on high alert. This was a very reputable company and Michael had spent a lot of money on the condo's security system. False alarms were few and far between. If they said there was a break-in, then there was a break-in.

It had to be Oksana.

I said, "Do you have any of your people on the scene yet?"

There was a slight hesitation before he replied, "Yes, we do, only I can't raise them at the moment. Must be some sort of equipment failure, or something."

"There is no equipment failure. Do you know who I am?"

"Uh, yes sir, I do."

"Then you know I work with the FBI. This is almost without question something related to a case we are on. Please don't send anyone else to check on your man. Call the Carlsbad PD and inform them of the situation and make sure they know that I am on my way."

"Roger that, sir," the man said and then hung up.

Since I was still fully clothed, I paused only long enough for a quick restroom break before charging into the other room.

Bridgett was immediately on high alert.

"What's happening, boss?"

"I'm not completely sure, but the security company for Muriel's condo just called. There is a break-in in progress."

"And you're thinking that it's Oksana's doing?"

"No other explanation will fit."

Aaron and Pete had come around and were already up and prepping for whatever came next.

Aaron said, "What's the plan?"

"The security company can't raise their man by phone or radio, so we need to get down there and check things out."

"Want me to stay here and hold down the fort?" Pete said.

"That would be a tremendous help, Pete. Aaron, grab our go-bags and meet me in the garage. Bridgett and I will explain what's happening to the agents outside."

The "go-bags" were duffels kept in a constant state of readiness containing weapons, ammunition, passports and ten thousand dollars cash. While it was doubtful that we'd need passports or money, it was a dead certainty that we'd need the weapons and ammo.

Pete said, "You think there's any chance that woman will make a run on us here?"

"It doesn't make any sense for her to do that," Bridgett replied.

I said, "But then, she is entirely unorthodox in her methods, so to answer your question, yeah, be ready for anything."

"Yes sir, Mr. Moriarity. I'll keep things nice and tidy here. Don't you worry none about Tommy or your girls."

Aaron threw the bags in the back seat of the Range Rover while Bridgett and I told the FBI agents what was going on.

By the time we were driving toward Muriel's condo, it was almost 3:15 a.m.

"How you feelin' about all this?" Aaron asked.

I shook my head slowly, trying to come up with a suitable answer.

"Honestly? I feel like I'm sleepwalking. The thing with Cassie and Michael has me so stressed that I'm missing

TEARS IN A BOTTLE

things I normally would be on top of."

"You doin' just fine, bro. We'll get through this and everything will be all right."

"I wish I shared your confidence, Aaron. But, I don't. I feel a sense of dread that I can't really explain. It's like… like something's coming—something horrible—and even if I throw everything I have at it, there's nothing I can do to make it stop."

Bridgett said, "Do you think that has to do with this case, or something to do with your niece and her husband?"

"I don't know, Bridgett. I really don't know."

Aaron reached over and squeezed my arm, saying, "Look, all we can do is what we can do, Jake. Sounds overly simplistic, but it's the truth. All we've got is the next breath, the next step; don't know anything beyond that. Right now, we got to deal with this thing at Muriel's place. After that, who knows? I guess my point is, beating yourself up for things that are out of your control just doesn't make any sense to me. Be a better use of your time and energy to just stay in the moment until the moment changes."

I glanced sideways at my friend.

"You're getting philosophical in your old age."

He grinned widely.

"I got game, bro."

CHAPTER 49

When we pulled in to the parking lot of the condominium complex, two cruisers from the Carlsbad Police Department were parked by the car from the security company.

I said, "All right, let's go do this."

The three of us got out and walked toward where the two officers were standing and the security guard sitting in his car holding gauze to his bleeding head.

"Are you Mr. Moriarity?" one of the young officers inquired.

"That's me," I replied while shaking his hand.

"Officer Lopez. Sir, we haven't entered the condo, but we have confirmed that there has definitely been a break-in. I understand that you are with the FBI, but protocol dictates that we clear the unit before allowing anyone else inside."

"I understand, officer, but this is not just a burglary. It is related to a case the FBI has been working since yesterday that involves the Russian mob and human trafficking. This, therefore, falls under our jurisdiction."

The two officers glanced at each other without speaking.

I continued, "I would be happy to get Special Agent in charge, Gerald Redfern, on the phone if you would like someone to explain the situation further."

The first officer said, "That won't be necessary sir. We'd be happy to be your backup."

"You're good men. Give us a minute to get strapped

up."

The young man from the security company asked what he could do to help, so I told him that if he felt up to it, he could set up a surveillance of the condominium complex's parking area and alert us if any suspicious vehicles or personnel arrived on the scene. It wasn't really necessary, but it made him feel like he was being useful.

I pulled Bridgett aside and said, "Listen, I know you're not a hundred percent, and if comes down to a physical confrontation, you're going to be at an extreme disadvantage given your limitations."

She said, "I can hold my own."

"I know you can, Bridgett. But I cannot in good conscience ask you to go into a situation like this."

She smiled slyly.

"Actually, boss, as the only Special Agent on site—and given that this is an official FBI operation—I am required to not only go with you, but to lead."

I wrinkled my brow.

"Is that true?"

"I don't know, but it was worth a shot."

That made me smile.

"Okay. You can come." I turned and hollered at officer Lopez, "Hey, you guys have an extra vest that Agent Polk can use?"

"Yeah, I do," he replied and started digging around inside of the trunk. After a few seconds, he found what he was looking for and trotted over to our position. "It might be a bit big on—"

He had started to say that it might be a bit big on her, but when he noticed that she had at least two inches in height on him, just handed it over with an embarrassed smile.

Aaron and I strapped on our own body armor and checked our Sig's. Aaron also brought along a Standard DP-12 tactical 12-gauge shotgun and a Heckler and Koch

416 for me. All in all, a quite lethal arsenal.

Bridgett looked at her service pistol and said, "I think I have weapon envy."

So, I handed the H&K over to her.

"There. Feel better?"

"Thanks, boss."

"You don't have to call me boss."

"Okay, boss."

As we walked back toward the two police officers, Lopez whistled.

"That's some damn fine hardware there, gentlemen."

I said, "Yes, it is. A friend of ours in France introduced these firearms to us a while back and we've been using them ever since. Okay, you boys ready?"

They both nodded and we moved down the side of Muriel's condo toward the entrance in a tight, tactical formation. I was in the front with Aaron right behind me, the two Carlsbad officers behind him and Bridgett bringing up the rear. As we approached the door, I suddenly stopped.

"There's nothing here," I said, turning to face the others.

Aaron shook his head.

"What do you mean?"

"This was a feint. They are going after Tommy. Officer Lopez, can you and your partner clear the residence? We've got to go."

"Roger that, sir. We'll take care of everything."

As the three of us took off running toward the parking lot Aaron asked, "How do you know they're going after Tommy?"

"It's the only thing that makes any sense. This was just a diversion to get me out of the way."

"But they've got four FBI agents, plus Pete to go through in order to get to him," Bridgett said.

"Aaron, call Pete," I said as we jumped into the Range Rover.

Aaron had his phone out and was dialing Pete's number even before he had the door shut.

"I'm not getting any answer."

"Okay, that's not good. Try Vanessa's phone."

As I raced out of the parking lot and onto the street, he scrolled through his list of favorites and punched her number.

He put the phone on speaker and held it closer so I could her.

It rang once. Twice. Three times and then Vanessa's sleepy voice answered, "Hello?"

"Vanessa," I hollered. "Are you okay?"

Suddenly on high alert, she answered, "Jake? What's happening?"

"Listen, I need you to grab Eddie and whatever firearm is within reach and get into a closet, a bathroom, under a bed—anywhere safe."

"Okay, but can't you tell me what's going on?" she asked, her voice trembling with tension.

"Nothing good. Too complicated to explain. Just do what I said and we'll be there in a minute."

"But, isn't Pete here? And those FBI guys? Shouldn't we be safe?"

"Just get Eddie and do what I said."

"You're really scaring me, Jake."

"Sorry, Vanessa, can't be helped. See you soon."

Aaron terminated the call as I drove like a maniac down the coastal road toward Michael's home.

He said, "You need to tell me how in the hell Oksana could fight her way through four tactically trained FBI agents *and* Pete Tolles, the toughest son of a bitch I know outside of you and me."

"She didn't fight."

"Wha'chu sayin'?"

It normally takes ten minutes to drive from Michael's to Muriel's.

I made it in five.

We came squealing into the lot, causing the FBI agents a moment's panic before they realized who we were.

The lead agent asked, "What's going on, Jake?"

"I'm not sure. Just follow me."

We all took off at a run toward the house, taking cover positions as we approached.

Signaling for silence, I checked the front door.

It was locked, so I inserted the key as quietly as possible and turned the doorknob slowly. Opening the door a crack I listened for anything out of the ordinary. The lights that were on when we left were still on and I could hear the sounds of a television playing from the den.

I pushed the door open all the way and walked in with Aaron and the FBI agents close behind.

We nearly gave Pete a heart attack.

"Whoa, buddy," he yelled while diving for cover behind the sofa. He then poked his head over the top. "Mr. Moriarity? What the hell's goin' on?"

"I don't know, Pete. Aaron, go check on Tommy. I'm pretty sure he's not there, but go check on him."

Aaron and one of the agents moved swiftly down the hall as I went toward Vanessa's bedroom.

I knocked, and then opened the door.

"Vanessa, honey? It's Jake. You can come out."

She came running from the bathroom and threw her arms around me with Eddie close behind.

"Jake, what's happening? We've been so scared," she said, her voice trembling.

"I'm not sure, sweetheart, but we'll figure it out."

Aaron and the FBI agent came down the hall shaking their heads.

"He's gone," Aaron said dejectedly.

"That's what I thought. I remembered that before we left for Muriel's condo, we didn't see him. With all the commotion, he should have come out to investigate. It was so obvious, but I was so focused on what we were doing, I didn't bother to check on him."

The lead agent said, "Given the circumstances, I think it's best if we return to our posts. Let us know if we're needed in here."

"Will do. And thanks for your help."

As they left, Bridgett asked, "So, you're saying that while all of us were here, that someone came in and took Tommy right out from under our noses?"

"That's exactly what I'm saying," I replied.

"But, how is that even possible?"

I asked Vanessa if she had heard anything.

"Nothing. Eddie and me were sound asleep just like the rest of you. I didn't even know you and Aaron had left. That's why I was so startled when you called."

"This is really bad," Aaron said, falling heavily into a large chair.

It was, but not as bad as what I had just remembered.

"It's a little worse than bad." Everyone stared at me waiting for an explanation. "Earlier I was thinking about things that could possibly go sideways during the night, so, before I went to bed, I gave the safe-deposit key to Tommy."

CHAPTER 50

Y ou did what?" Aaron said unbelievingly.

"I gave the key to Tommy."

Pete exclaimed, "Well, that right there's enough to make a preacher cuss."

Vanessa screwed up her face.

"What?

He laughed and said, "Sorry. That's an old southern expression that means it's messed up."

"By the way," I said, "Aaron tried to call you from Muriel's condo, but you didn't answer. Is your phone working?"

Pete threw his hands up and exclaimed, "I wouldn't know. I've looked all over hell 'n half 'a Georgia and I can't find it."

Eddie reached into her pocket and came out with a cell phone.

With an embarrassed smile she said, "I, uh, took it earlier so I could, you know, take a selfie for you to have."

"Well, now, that's right sweet of you, darlin'," Pete replied while giving her a hug that looked as if it would crush her small frame.

"That explains why he didn't answer the phone," Aaron offered.

Bridgett said, "I'm still stuck on how Oksana was able to get in and take Tommy without us hearing her."

"Yeah," I agreed. "And why didn't she try to inflict casualties in the process?"

Pete added, "And how did the girl even know what

room he was in?"

Vanessa said, "Maybe she used a drone—you know, flew it around outside until she saw him in that bedroom."

I smiled.

"You know, Vanessa, I'm willing to bet money that that's exactly what she did."

"But, wouldn't those FBI boys have noticed something like that?" Pete asked.

"Not necessarily. Rumors have swirled for years now about the government developing micro air vehicles—also known as MAVs—for surveillance use, some as small as mosquitos."

"Is that for real?" Vanessa inquired skeptically.

"I don't know about the mosquito thing, but I know for sure that some models exist as small as fifteen centimeters."

"That there'd be about the size of a bird," Pete suggested.

I affirmed, "About that."

Aaron said, "That still doesn't address Bridgett's question of how she got in and out without us hearing her."

"No, it doesn't. But, if she's half as good as I think she is, then she can move like a ghost whenever the situation requires it."

"Guys?" Eddie said. "I just looked in Tommy's room. You should come and see this."

We all trooped down the hall and into the generously sized bedroom. There was a small balcony that provided a view of the coastline looking south. The French doors that provided access to that balcony were both open.

"Well," I said, "that explains that."

"Do you think that woman jimmied those doors, or that Tommy left them open on purpose so he could hear the waves?" Pete asked.

"Tommy left them open," Aaron answered. "I'm pretty sure of it, because he loves the sound of the ocean."

Iosif's phone started vibrating in my pocket.

"Speaking of the devil," I said as I pulled it out and put it on speaker.

Oksana laughed lightly.

"I see you found out that your friend is missing."

Turning toward the open doors, I strained to spot the drone.

"Funny, I never would've pegged you as a voyeur, Oksana."

"Oh, once you start getting into it, it's really quite addicting."

I turned and shooed everyone out of the room except Aaron.

"So, you have Tommy and I'm sure that by now you've figured out that he has the key."

She laughed again.

"You're making this too easy for me, Moriarity. I thought you'd provide more of a challenge."

She was right. I had been so distracted by Michael's medical emergency that I really *had* made her job easy.

"I admit it. You caught me on an off day. So, now what?"

"Well, I've been thinking about that quite a lot."

"And?" I prompted.

"And I have a proposal."

"Okay, let's hear it."

She spent the next five minutes telling me about her role in the Russian mob; the odd affinity she had developed for Charles Sutton; and her desire to walk away from her past and start over somewhere. She also said she'd be willing to divulge all the specifics of the entire trafficking structure in the LA basin.

"Okay," I said. "That's all very interesting. But what do you want in return?"

"If I promise to take Mr. Marshall back to his condo in Dana Point unscathed, will you agree to let me walk away without trying to pursue me?"

"And how do you plan to do that? Seems to me that at this point, *I* will be the least of your worries."

"Yes, my father typically takes a dim view of people he once thought loyal turning on him and betraying his confidence."

"Right. So, what are you going to do about that?"

"That's where you leaving me alone comes in."

I asked, "And how's that?"

"In order to pull this off, I need resources. Charles has enough money hidden offshore to do just that. Money that he basically stole from the Russian mob. We just need to get it and do whatever is necessary to disappear, which means that if I'm simultaneously trying to fight you off, it's going to prove very challenging."

I said, "So, let me see if I'm understanding you correctly: you are asking me and the FBI to just look the other way while you steal twenty-seven million from the Russian mob?"

"That's exactly what I'm asking. After all, why should you care? With all the information I'm willing to provide, plus the loss of those resources, their trafficking operations will be virtually crippled. You can't lose with the deal I'm offering."

She was right. I didn't care about the money. And as long as it was kept away from the Russians, why should it matter to me how that was accomplished?

"Look, Oksana, even if I sign off on everything you've proposed, what makes you think you can stay alive? Last time I checked, the people you work with are among the most ruthless on earth when it comes to exacting revenge."

"That is true, but the reason it's true is because of people like me. And I am at the top of that particular food chain, so to speak. There is no one better than me, so anyone they send after me will be tremendously disadvantaged. Besides, I have insurance."

"I just bet you do. Okay. Let me think about this for a bit." Something suddenly occurred to me. "You already have the USB drives, don't you?"

She was silent for a few seconds.

"Maybe you really are as good as they say you are."

"So, I take that as a 'yes?'"

"Yes. Once I had the key it was just a simple matter of breaking into the bank and disabling the alarm system. I could have done it in my sleep."

"I'll call you in a little while."

"Don't take too long, Moriarity. This offer has is time sensitive."

And with that she hung up.

Aaron said, "Girl's got some cojones."

"That she does," I agreed. "But, she also has a very agile, inventive mind and considerable skills to go along with all that bravado."

"So, what are we gonna do?"

I shook my head and laughed without humor.

"I think I'm going to let her do it."

"Just walk away?"

"Yep."

"Just like that?"

"Why not?"

Aaron sighed and threw his arms out to the side.

"Just seems wrong, somehow. I mean the girl's a stone-cold killer. Doesn't seem right to let her walk away without paying for her crimes."

"She commit any of those crimes against you?"

"Uhh…none that I am aware of."

I grinned.

"Then, what's the problem? Like she said, in a very direct way this will cripple the Russian mob's operation in the LA basin, while at the same time bringing justice against the ones who killed Helen."

"Well, there is that."

"So, we good?"
"Ah, hell, Jake. Okay."
I hit redial and called her back.

CHAPTER 51

Oksana's phone rang, sounding incredibly loud in the confines of the small diner.

"That didn't take long," she said to Charles.

She and Charles Sutton occupied a booth in the rear of an all-night fifties-style diner while her five bodyguards had positioned themselves at various points with Tommy Marshall under the care of the two in the next booth. All had ordered breakfast and were waiting for their food to arrive.

"Mr. Moriarity?" she said lightly. "Do we have a deal?" She listened intently for a few moments, nodding her head slowly as if in agreement. "I suppose, if that's the only way to get this done."

After a few more seconds of listening she said goodbye and terminated the call.

Charles asked, "Well, what did he say?"

"He agrees to the plan. But, he wants us to hand Mr. Marshall here over in person."

"And you agreed to that?" he exclaimed.

"Yes, I did."

"But, why?"

"Because he agreed that he wouldn't try to stop us from taking the USB drives and leaving. In exchange, I will give him information on how to finish dismantling my father's human trafficking operation in LA."

Charles couldn't believe what he was hearing.

"And, you trust him to keep his word?"

She laughed and said, "Probably about as much as he trusts me to keep mine."

"So, what are we supposed to do?"

She answered, "He wants us to meet him at Crystal Cove State Park in Newport Beach at six a.m."

Charles glanced at his watch.

"It's almost five right now. Can we do that?"

"No problem," she said confidently. "We have a chopper, remember?"

"Oh, yeah."

Turning sideways in her seat, she talked across the next booth.

"Good news, Mr. Marshall. It looks like you're going to survive after all. We're going to be taking you to meet up with Moriarity."

He nodded his head slowly and then asked, "I need to ask you something and obviously you don't have to answer, but I would appreciate it."

"Okay. Ask."

"Did either one of you have anything to do with Helen's death?"

Charles choked back a sob and said, "Tommy, I...I loved Helen in my own way. I guess I've loved her since high school. Never stopped, actually. So, I give you my word that I had nothing to do with it."

Oksana waved the guards away and moved into the booth next to Tommy, laying her hand on his arm.

"It wasn't me, Mr. Marshall," she whispered. "But I know who did it and, better yet, I know who ordered it done."

"Then, do you think you could tell Jake who that is?"

"It would be my pleasure." She paused, thinking something over and then said, "It was my father, Vasily Orlov. And I hope Moriarity kills him."

Tommy stared long and hard at the woman sitting next to him, finding himself unable to reconcile her beauty and obvious refinements with what he knew of her profession.

Finally, he said, "You must hate the man something fierce."

Her eyes hardened as she replied, "You have no idea! I would like to kill him myself—and take my time doing it—but I'm just enough of a Catholic to fear that I'd burn in hell for it."

As much as Tommy wanted to hate her for everything she represented, he found an inexplicable compassion arising from his core.

"I'm genuinely sorry for whatever happened to cause that depth of emotion."

She stood and beckoned him to join her in the booth with Charles.

"I'm not. It made me the woman I am today: cold, cruel and heartless—all essential qualities if one is to be the most successful assassin of her generation. And I am."

The server brought their food and Charles asked if they had time to eat.

"Of course we do, Charlie. We'll enjoy our meal, and then we'll go finish what we started."

Charles fingered the USB drives through the material covering his pants pocket. Could it really be happening? Would they actually be able to walk away from life as they both knew it, twenty-seven million dollars richer and start all over again?

He stared at Oksana's lovely face and thought to himself once again, *I'm going to die...and she's going to kill me.*

CHAPTER 52

We left the four FBI agents in place to watch over Vanessa and Eddie, while Aaron, Pete, Bridgett and I drove toward Newport Beach and Crystal Cove State Park. I had chosen the site for the express purpose of staging the meeting away from populated areas because I had a feeling that while Oksana was willing to cooperate, her father might not be so charitable.

Aaron said, "So, you thinkin' we gonna have some company besides Oksana?"

"It is a near dead certainty."

"If you don't mind me askin', Mr. Moriarity sir, how can you be so sure?" Pete inquired.

"Let me ask you a question," I said in response. "If someone had twenty-seven million dollars of your money, and you sent a trusted operative to retrieve the money and eliminate the individual keeping it from you, only to find out that your operative is now working in concert with the person she was supposed to terminate while at the same time planning to keep the money—and especially if the operative was your daughter—would you just let it go?"

"Hell no! I'd track those suckers to the ends of the earth." He nodded silently for a moment and then added, "I see what you mean."

"Let's say the Russian bad guys do actually show up," Bridgett mused. "How can you be sure that Oksana isn't behind it and that they're there to help her, not take her down?"

"The simple answer is that I *don't* know." I thought for a few seconds. "The way Oksana reacted when I mentioned daddy issues makes me wonder how deep those issues run."

"In what sense?"

"What if her childhood was similar to Vanessa's? Only complicating the issue is the fact that her father is now also her boss?"

Pete blew out a long whistle from the back.

"I'll tell you what, old son, that would make for a very complicated working relationship."

"It would, indeed. What has just occurred to me is that making off with that money is only a part of this. I'm thinking that her reason for agreeing to meet face-to-face is that she knows daddy is tracking her and will show up at the meet."

"And if, in the process, we wind up killing him off, all the better?" Aaron asked.

"Let's just say it wouldn't surprise me."

Pete said, "Now, I've never tangled with the Rooskies before, but I'm just gonna take a wild guess that these guys aren't amateurs."

"No, they're not. They will come prepared to do battle. And, by the way, that's not an offensive term to them."

"What, Rooskie?"

"The Russian word they use for themselves sounds like rooskie. It's spelled r-o-o-s-s-k-i-y."

Aaron was staring at me from the passenger seat.

"What?"

"You did it again."

"Did what?"

"Just pulled an unbelievably random fact out of your butt."

"I knew you'd be disappointed in me if I didn't."

As we shared a good laugh, I began planning some strategy to deal with what I feared we'd be facing when we arrived at the state park. Given the firearms we had brought along with us, I didn't fear being outgunned, just out manned.

I was also concerned for Aaron's safety.

I was *always* concerned for his safety.

Even though he had training as a combat Marine, the fact still remained that he was arguably the premier jazz pianist of his generation and it just wouldn't do to have him shot while helping me with a case. We'd had the conversation many times before regarding the level of danger he risked every time accompanied me. He knew the risk and accepted that I would never willingly put him in harm's way.

And it usually wasn't a problem.

But this was an exceptional situation.

I exited off I-5 Northbound at Dana Point so we could come up Pacific Coast Highway and enter the park from the south.

"You think we can count on any help from Oksana?" Bridgett asked.

"I've been thinking about that."

"And?" she pressed.

"Possibly. I'm sure she has at least a couple of guys with her, but when the shooting starts, there's no way of knowing where their loyalties lie."

Pete leaned forward.

"Speaking from my own experience as a gunslinger for hire, I can tell you for damn sure that my loyalties have always been with whoever was paying me."

"Which is exactly my point," I replied. "So, I suppose we have to assume there will be no help forthcoming from anyone else and prepare to do this with just the four of us."

"You got a plan for that, boss," Bridgett said, "or are we just going to wing it?"

Aaron chuckled.

"My boy Jake here is a legend when it comes to winging it. Truth is, he's turned it into an art form."

"You messing with the new girl, or are you serious?"

"Totally serious," Aaron replied.

I said, "I'm afraid it's true, Bridgett. The problem with having an elaborate plan is that having expended the effort to make it, your tendency moving forward is to carry it out."

"So, you're saying that's a bad thing?" Bridgett inquired.

"Only in the sense that when your focus is on the plan, then by definition it would conversely have to be *off* whatever is happening peripherally. Understand?"

She seemed to ponder my question and then nodded her head slowly as she answered, "Yeah, I do. It's like putting something into your phone's map program and then keeping your eyes on the program instead of where you're going."

"Basically, yeah. I like to deal more in the realm of purpose."

Aaron said, "And what, pray tell, is the difference between a plan and a purpose?"

"For example, the purpose, or objective, in this case is to get Tommy back from Oksana. There could be twenty-five plans on how that could be accomplished, but still only one purpose."

"Kinda like Bridgett's map example," Pete suggested. "The destination is the purpose, but there may be four or five ways to get there. And if you get goin' the wrong way somehow, the little lady in my phone will tell me she's redirecting my route. That what you're talking about?"

"Exactly."

"Well, like my little 'ol Pentecostal grandmomma would say, 'That'll preach, son.'"

Aaron made a humming sound deep in his throat.

"You know something? We do that all the time in jazz. We start with a twelve or sixteen bar chord progression that has an established melody. The *purpose* of the quintet is to all arrive at the end at the same time having played our butts off in the process. The *plan* on how to get there after the initial sixteen, however, is almost never the same. It's called improvisation. We travel by many routes, but the purpose is always the same. If our focus stayed on just what was written down musically for those sixteen bars, we'd never arrive at a satisfactory outcome for us *or* our fans."

Pete asked, "All that being said, Mr. Moriarity—our purpose being clear and all—you got any sense at least on how we're gonna start?"

"Yes. When we get to the park, we'll wait to see what happens and then respond appropriately."

Aaron turned halfway around in his seat and said, "It's like they taught us in the Marines, Pete: improvise, adapt, overcome. Get used to it, guys. This is just the way Jake rolls."

Pete settled back in his seat.

"I got no problem with that whatsoever. No sir. Fact is, the more I think about it, sounds like we're gettin' ready to have ourselves some fun."

That isn't exactly what I had been thinking, but I was relieved to hear Pete speaking positively.

"How far we got?" Aaron asked.

We had just passed through north Laguna Beach.

"Three or four miles, so figure ten minutes or so."

"Might be a good idea to arrive ready to boogey. Can you hand me my bag, Pete?"

Pete handed it through the opening between the front seats and he and Aaron began hurriedly checking and re-checking weapons, magazines, weapon lights, laser sights, in-ear radio comms as well as extra ammunition, then handing it off to Bridgett who did the same.

In short, we were prepared for war.

CHAPTER 53

The park entrance was just ahead on the left, and as I slowed to make the turn, I found that I was a mess of conflicting emotions. On the one hand, I was praying that we wouldn't be required to engage in a firefight. But on the other hand, I found myself hoping we would.

Why?

Good question.

Mainly, I think it was because I carry a personal vendetta against human trafficking in any form and have dedicated my life to doing whatever I can, *whenever* I can, to see it eradicated from the face of the earth. Besides, how often does the opportunity come along to take down a genuine, honest to goodness Russian Mafioso kingpin like Vasily Orlov, especially when the man had promised to end my life? And as an added bonus, he was not only a sex trafficker, but had also committed sexual abuse against his own daughter.

Having agreed with Oksana that we would meet by the restrooms at the extreme southern end of the parking lot, we moved slowly past the empty guardhouse in the fog-shrouded half-light of the early morning. All of us were on high alert as I drove slowly around the circuitous drive and then headed back in a southerly direction. The restroom structure wouldn't be much, but between that and my car, we would have at least some level of cover in case the shooting started.

Indistinct, nearly spectral shapes swam in and out of focus in the mostly empty parking lot. A dumpster; a landscape barricade; a stand of low, windmill palms; a few cautionary A-frame signs.

But no cars.

"How we gonna do this?" Pete asked.

The thick, coastal fog was both a blessing and a curse: it would make it harder for them to see us, but the converse would also be true. I surveyed the area, looking for defensible positions that would also offer good sightlines.

"Are you seeing any obvious firing positions?"

I had Pete bring his MSSR. That stands for Marine Scout Sniper Rifle. He was one of the best snipers the Corps ever had, and his skills have only improved over time.

Pete quickly surveyed the area and said, "Only viable position is the roof of the restrooms. Probably positioned over the entrance yonder."

I followed his gaze.

"I don't like it. You'd be too exposed. How about prone and firing under those partitions in front of the entrance? Looks like about a twelve-inch gap at the bottom. Because of the elevation, you could maintain good sightlines and be almost invisible in this fog."

Aaron scoffed, "Only problem is, that partition wouldn't stop a BB Gun and you got nowhere to hide if things get dicey."

"Then I guess I'd better make sure I can duck inside that bathroom if necessary," Pete replied with a grin.

"You tellin' me you got a lock pick set with you?" Aaron said.

"Now, son, I am a professional and a professional is always prepared."

I checked the time.

5:50 a.m.

I pulled the Range Rover to a stop in proximity to the restrooms and said, "Better get in place, Pete. They'll be here any minute."

"Roger that."

As Pete exited the car and hustled into position I gestured toward the right front of the SUV.

"Aaron, I want you behind that fender so you've got the engine block and wheels between you an any incoming fire."

"Got no problem with that."

"Bridgett, stay with me until Oksana shows up."

"Roger that, boss."

I started to tell her once again that she didn't have to call me boss, but stopped because an SUV was emerging out of the mist, looking like a large, black beast lumbering toward us.

"Okay," I said. "Here we go."

As Aaron got out and crouched down behind the wheel well, I glanced toward the restrooms. Even knowing that Pete was there on the ground, I still couldn't see him.

The SUV stopped about twenty feet away parallel to our position. I could just make out two men in the driver's and front passenger's seats. However, the rear windows were so dark I couldn't make any assessment regarding the other passengers or even if there *were* additional passengers.

Over our comm, I said, "Pete, you copy?"

"Yes sir, I'm ready to rumble."

"Okay. Let's just play this cool and see where it leads."

The right rear passenger window came down slowly to reveal three people in the back seat, one of whom was Tommy Marshall.

"So far so good."

I saw Oksana. She saw me. Our eyes met and she raised her brows inquisitively, so I nodded and we both exited our respective vehicles walking slowly toward each other.

She was striking. 5'7" or 5'8"; her platinum, blonde hair hanging loosely to her shoulders set off a face that, by anyone's estimation, would have been deemed beautiful.

She moved with a dancer's grace and yet I could tell that underneath there was a tightly coiled power that could be unleashed swiftly and lethally.

In short, she was formidable.

Something familiar about her. Something...I had seen that face before.

"Did you come alone?" she inquired in a low voice completely devoid of accent.

"Whether I did or didn't is no concern of yours. Just release Tommy and we'll be on our way."

"Ahh, so you aren't alone."

"I may or may not have a couple of friends who have your guys in their sights as we speak," I replied with a smile.

After staring at me for several uncomfortable seconds, she smiled and said, "You are much bigger than I imagined. And you have the eyes of a killer."

Now, *that* was a first.

I had been holding the HK loosely, but my grip suddenly tightened as I saw movement out of the corner of my eye. Two SUVs had just pulled off the road and were making their way slowly past the guardhouse and around the driveway.

"Did you bring anyone else with you, Oksana?"

Her eyes widened slightly, but she didn't waver.

"I knew he would come."

"Your father?"

"Yes. The pig."

This last statement was spat as if removing something poisonous from her mouth.

"If it comes down to a firefight, will your guys fight for you or him?"

She glanced quickly over her shoulder.

"They will fight for me."

"Are you sure of that?" I asked skeptically.

"There is no question. They hate him as much as I do."

I said, "You guys picking this up?"

They all responded that they were.

"Okay, here's what I want to do. Oksana, if you can have your driver pull around until your car is right next to mine facing the opposite direction, it will give us double cover."

She started barking orders and the SUV immediately moved around and into position.

"Aaron, Bridgett, keep an eye on that trail behind us. It's possible they could have people coming up from the beach."

"Roger that," they both replied.

"Oksana, get Tommy and Charles out of your vehicle and have my associate, Pete let them in to the restrooms over there. It'll be better cover behind those block walls than anything we've got out here."

She nodded and pulled the two men from the SUV.

As soon as I saw Charles, I knew.

Portland.

On the street outside of the coffee shop.

The couple I had observed in fierce debate.

Charles saw me and rocked back a step.

"You," he breathed. "I saw—"

"Yeah. I know. Portland. We can reminisce later. For now, take off."

Oksana ran them over to the restrooms where Pete already had the door open behind him. Once they were safely inside, she rejoined us behind the vehicles.

We watched as the two SUVs approached at a snail's pace, stopping about fifty feet away where they sat idling.

"Pete, you got a shot if they exit?"

"Yeah, I do. Just give me the word and I'll light 'em up like Christmas."

I asked Oksana if either one of her guys had sniper training. She said that they didn't, but she did. So I handed her my HK and pulled the DP twelve-gauge from the back of my car. When it came right down to it, given the proximity of PCH and the houses lining the hills above us, I didn't really want there to be any shooting, primarily because I wanted to keep local law enforcement out of it as long as possible. Ultimately, with my FBI cred's and Zack Hastings backing me up, I could pull rank, but it would be a needless complication. Then again, none of that was within my control.

All I could do was respond to whatever action Vasily Orlov chose to initiate. I had gone into this thinking that we had a better than even shot at walking away unscathed. But if you want to know the truth, I liked our chances less by the second.

And if I were forced to put a number on it, I gave us no more than a three in five chance.

CHAPTER 54

T he SUVs suddenly moved forward about twenty feet and parked nose to nose. Four heavily armed men emerged from the front seats and took up tactical positions behind the vehicles. The rear doors opened and four more men got out escorting Vasily Orlov, a short, balding, corpulent man in his fifties.

I said, "Do you know about Portland?"

Oksana smiled evilly and replied, "If you are referring to the way you humiliated my father, then, yes. It was exquisite."

"Do you also know that I saw you and Charles in the Starbucks in the Pearl District?"

A quick glance my way, then, "No. But how?"

"I will tell you afterwards."

Vasily stood in the middle of his four escorts as if waiting for us to make a move.

"Oksana," I said, "I need to go talk to him. Do you want to come with me?"

She hesitated and then shook her head no.

"Okay. Pete, when I give the signal, I want you, Oksana and her two guys to put laser sights on Mr. Orlov. Just let him know that if anything goes sideways, he dies first."

"Roger that," Pete answered as Oksana and her men nodded their affirmation.

"Aaron, Bridgett, don't take your eyes off that beach path."

I moved out from behind the SUVs, the shotgun held

loosely in my hands, and walked slowly toward where Vasily and his men were standing.

When I got to within ten feet, one of the men in front held up his hand indicating that I should stop.

"Okay, now."

Suddenly, four dots appeared on Vasily's chest. He didn't even blink.

I'll say this for the man, he was not easily intimidated.

"Moriarity," he said in a low, sonorous voice that brought to mind some of the great Shakespearean actors I had heard over the course of my life. Men with voices so richly modulated that it made you want to just sit and listen to what they had to say for the sheer pleasure of hearing them speak. He sounded nothing like he had in our previous encounter. I wrote it off to laryngitis or some other respiratory malady.

I replied, "I'm still standing, Orlov. You can't beat me. You have tried and failed. Most men with any intelligence at all simply give up at this point."

"Are you saying that my presence here indicates a lack of intelligence?" he asked, indignation coloring his face.

"Now that I think about it...yes. That's exactly what I'm saying. Walk away now, or we will kill all of your men. I don't like *your* chances of survival either."

I jacked a shell into the shotgun and aimed it directly at his head, as soon as I did so the dots of the laser sights moved to the foreheads of the four men surrounding him.

"At this distance, and with the loads I'm shooting, there is no way I can miss. You'd be dead before you hit the ground, as would your men. The men behind you might be able to take me out before my people also take them down, but they would still be without an employer. This is a zero-sum game for you, Vasily."

He sighed, signaled for his men to stand down and walked slowly toward me stopping when he came within two or three feet of my position.

"As much as I wish for you to be dead, it is not necessary for this situation to escalate into violence. You have something I want. If you give it to me, I will withdraw and we never have to see each other again."

"And what do you want?"

His eyes shifted toward Oksana.

"I want my daughter and the man that she is helping to steal vast sums of money from me."

"I see. And what are you offering in return?"

"It is as I said. You give me what I want and we," he paused to indicate his men, "will go away without an altercation."

"And If I refuse?"

His brow wrinkled.

"Why would you refuse? You have nothing to gain by continuing to shield her. You get what you want—which is Mr. Marshall's safe return."

I suddenly shoved the shotgun up under his chin, which prompted the men behind him to shoulder their weapons.

"No, what I want, you sick son of a bitch, is for you and all the other scum like you to pay for the horror you inflict on young, helpless girls." I paused and then added, "And especially for what you did to your own daughter."

His eyes widened. He tried valiantly to maintain his exterior calm, but I had been doing this long enough to know when someone is falling apart internally.

"The girl," he said slowly and articulately, "Oksana, has always had an overactive imagination. Always a problem child—making up fantastic stories of things that never happened. Perhaps this is what you are referring to?"

I leaned in until I was literally hovering over him.

"You know exactly what I am referring to, you piece of shit. And *that* is why I'm going to blow your worthless head off."

His right eye jerked spasmodically, but other than

TEARS IN A BOTTLE

that, he managed to remain calm.

"You wouldn't shoot me, Moriarity."

"And why is that?"

"Because you would also die."

I grinned.

"And this would happen because your men would shoot me?"

"What do you think?"

I said, "Pete, do you think you can level the playing field a little?"

I heard the MSSR spit in rapid fire and saw three of the four men standing behind Vasily drop to the ground clutching various wounded appendages, their weapons skittering across the asphalt. Then, the fourth man, who had acted as the squad leader, crumpled to the ground from a shot placed right between his eyes. My guess was that the shot had come from Oksana and that she'd had good reason to take out that particular man.

"Four down, four to go," I announced calmly, seeing Vasily's eyes widen. "Now, we are evenly matched, and I have you standing in between me and your men. Do you still want to discuss how advantageous it is for me to walk away?"

"Perhaps I underestimated your resourcefulness."

"A common and often fatal mistake made by those who oppose me."

Shrugging, he suggested, "I am not without resources. It is possible we could come to some sort of financial arrangement?"

I jabbed him with the barrel of the shotgun.

"Not a chance."

"Come now, Moriarity. Everyone has their price. What is yours?"

I shouldn't have done it, but the man disgusted me and I don't do well when people disgust me.

Keeping the shotgun firmly against his chin, I grabbed

him behind the head, forcing his throat down onto the point of the gun.

As he started choking I said, "My price is that you give Tommy Marshall back his wife."

He sputtered, "I don't know—"

"To you, she was nothing—just another expendable life. To him...she was everything."

As I released the pressure, he nodded slowly and said, "So, I suppose you now expect me to just walk away empty handed?"

"Whoever said anything about you walking away?" As his eyes widened, I continued, "I said I was going to blow your head off and you had been instructing me on why that was a bad idea. If you want to know the truth, for someone who is about to die, you don't present a very compelling argument."

A pronounced tremor had started in his cheeks and his voice was hoarse when he spoke.

"You cannot just kill me in cold blood, Moriarity. You are with the FBI. It's illegal for a member of American law enforcement to indiscriminately kill an unarmed man."

"Oh, this is good. I have a Russian Mafia kingpin lecturing me on the illegality of the indiscriminate taking of life. Maybe I should be taking notes."

"I could give the order for my men to kill you," he muttered lamely.

"You and I both know that isn't going to happen. First of all, they'd have to be damn good shots to shoot around you and hit me. Second of all, in order to come anywhere near having a shot like that, they'd have to expose themselves to the people behind me equipped with automatic weapons, each with a laser sight. And, thirdly...in case you haven't figured this out by now, my ace in the hole is a Marine Scout Sniper who was the best of his generation. Pete, can you demonstrate your skills to Mr. Orlov?"

I heard a spit, and simultaneously a tuft of fabric blew

off the shoulder of Orlov's three-thousand-dollar suit without harming him.

I said, "And lastly, this firearm has had its trigger pull altered so that it is now what they call in the trade, a hair-trigger. The slightest twitch of my finger will discharge it into your head. Face it, Vasily, you're finished." I pressed harder with the shotgun. "The only thing left for you to do is to try and convince me to turn you over to the FBI instead of killing you where you stand."

He shouted something in Russian and then all hell broke loose.

CHAPTER 55

We were suddenly plummeting down a rabbit hole where time seemed to speed up and slow down simultaneously.

Vasily leaned backwards to pull away from the pressure of my shotgun under his chin while at the same time gunfire erupted behind me. He tripped and fell hard onto his hands and knees, crying out in pain.

Seeing that I was now a wide-open target, his men rose from behind their respective SUVs intent on perforating my body with a wide variety of quite powerful ammunition. And since I had no desire to be selectively slaughtered, I hit the ground behind Vasily, throwing an arm across his back and pulling him in front of me.

I heard gunfire coming from the access trail that ran behind the restrooms and down to the main beach. As I had suspected, he had sneaked his operatives up the trail, hoping to catch us in the crossfire. No matter. I was confident that between Aaron and Oksana's guys, the threat would be neutralized.

The man to my far left suddenly disappeared, felled by a round that took him just under his chin. That left two bad guys behind the SUVs and whoever was lighting things up behind the restrooms. Even though all the weapons were suppressed, there is no way to completely dampen the sound of a high-caliber rifle on full automatic. This had to end quickly or we'd be overrun with local law enforcement within minutes.

From my position on the ground, I could easily see under the SUVs and what I saw made me very happy. Almost directly in front of me was a man's leg from mid-shin down to his feet. Using Vasily's body as a prop, I fired the shotgun and was rewarded by a loud scream followed by the man falling to the ground clutching his leg that had nearly been cut in two by the blast.

One guy left.

He took the easy way out by jumping into one of the SUVs and tearing off with tires squealing, leaving behind a trail of smoke and a screaming colleague whose injured leg he had driven over.

The live fire behind me had ceased, so I stood and pulled Vasily to his feet and said, "Now it's just you and me, Vasily."

I had just started to walk him toward my Range Rover when Oksana came out of nowhere and hit him full stride with some sort of flying kick to his face.

What happened next wasn't pretty.

I'll spare you the details, but in the end, Vasily Orlov died.

Horribly.

I'm not sure what Oksana did or how she did it, but once he was down she pounced on him like a predator on its prey and began to administer a series of sequential cuts any one of which would have been sufficient to cause exsanguination. But the most chilling part of it all was that she did it in a cold and remorseless silence, her face completely devoid of emotion.

The entire attack had taken less than ten seconds. Even if I had wanted to stop her—which I didn't—it happened so quickly that there was virtually nothing I could have done.

When she was through, she stood slowly to her feet, stepped back to stand by my side and then spat on her father's dead body.

Trembling with emotion, she looked up into my eyes.

"It is done," she said simply, quietly.

And then she wept.

She was such a pathetic figure standing there, that I didn't know what to do. So, I put my free arm around her and pulled her close just letting her cry.

I heard someone calling her name and turned to see Charles running toward us. She turned and opened her arms pulling him into an embrace. He wasn't much to look at; probably the same age as her late father; a bit shorter than her with a very slender build. But I sensed tenderness in the man that I'm sure Oksana found very compelling given the circumstances of her upbringing.

"Jake," Aaron shouted. "Come have a look."

I jogged toward where he and Bridgett stood with Pete and Tommy behind the restrooms.

"What do you have?" I asked.

Aaron pointed toward the footpath leading to the beach.

"You were right to have me and Bridgett keep surveillance on that bad boy. Those three jokers came up after your boy over there shouted."

Pete said, "I figured y'all guys had the situation out front well in hand, so I decided to give Aaron here a hand."

One of the three was quite dead; another seemed to be nursing a shoulder wound, while the third appeared to have a dislocated elbow.

I looked questioningly at Aaron who simply shrugged and said, "Didn't really want to shoot anyone, so Pete shot the rifle out of his hand and I gave the boy a lesson in basic human anatomy."

Bridgett said, "Boss, you just *have* to let me train with Aaron. That nerve and joint stuff he does is the coolest thing ever."

While Oksana's men were collecting weapons from Vasily's fallen soldiers, she and Charles walked around the

Range Rover and joined us.

She stared up at me.

"Thank-you for not interfering."

"You're welcome. But the truth of the matter is that you acted so quickly, I couldn't have stopped you even if I wanted to. Which, for the record, I did not."

She smiled mirthlessly.

"Well, they are dead now."

"They?"

"My father and his pig of a lieutenant."

"That the guy you shot in the forehead?"

She nodded, explaining, "He would also, uh, have his way with me when I was a little girl. My father would watch and...he..."

"You don't have to say anymore, Oksana," Charles said. "I think we get the picture." He turned to me and asked, "So, about Portland?"

I shrugged and replied, "Not much to tell. I was there on a case and was just walking to dinner when I randomly saw you two through the window of Starbucks. You seemed to be in a fairly intense conversation. At the time, I didn't think a thing about it, except that there was quite a bit of difference in your ages and figured that you probably weren't a couple. But, I almost never forget a face, so when I saw both of you again, I remembered the moment."

"I remember it as well," Charles said. "Do you remember making eye contact with me?"

"Yes, I do."

"Well, when it happened, I nearly fell off my stool! There was something that passed between us; almost a transference, or something."

"Huh," I said. "And, here we are. Speaking of which, we need to wrap this up."

Oksana asked, "So, what happens next?"

"Well, in a perfect world, you and Charles would just leave before I call the FBI to come and clean up this mess."

"But, this is not a perfect world?"

I paused for a few seconds to consider her question, and then answered, "Today it is."

Tommy gestured toward the bodies of Vasily Orlov and his lieutenant and said, "Are those the people responsible for Helen's death?"

Oksana nodded.

"It was Grigori, his lieutenant—the one I shot in the head. But my father ordered it. It wasn't necessary, Tommy. My father...he just enjoyed killing and ordering people to be killed. It made him feel powerful."

Turning to Charles, Tommy said in a voice trembling with emotion, "Everything in me wants to blame you for this."

Charles covered his face with both hands and shook his head slowly, remorsefully, his shoulders shaking with sobs. After a few seconds he pulled his hands away and stared at Tommy through red-rimmed eyes.

"I can't think of anything to say that would even come close to being appropriate right now, Tommy." He paused and then continued, "But I just need you to understand that none of this was supposed to happen. I was trying to do a good thing, you know," His voice broke. "Doing well by Helen and her investments. Then when I learned what was really happening with the Russians, my focus turned toward trying to deprive a group of monsters of the funding they needed to continue their monstrous acts. And Helen, being Helen, wanted to help. I don't know why she tried to keep you out of it—probably just trying to protect you. She loved you with everything she had, you know."

Tommy stood with eyes closed, his lips trembling involuntarily and nodding slowly as if trying to work through what Charles had just said.

Finally, he replied, "I know that's right—about Helen. It's just who she was. She hated injustice. My nickname for her throughout our marriage was..." his voice broke, "Crusader Helen, because of all the causes she took up."

And then, without another word, Tommy stuck out his hand. Charles hesitated slightly, but then clasped Tommy's hand. They shook once, sincerely, nodded at each other and, just like that, the tension was broken.

I said, "I hate to spoil this moment, but I need to call in the FBI before the locals show up."

I walked a few feet away and called Zack Hastings.

After three rings his sleepy voice answered, "Do you ever sleep?"

"Apparently not. Listen, I'm in Newport Beach at the Crystal Cove State Park. We had an altercation with Vasily Orlov and his boys."

"And?" he prompted.

"And, Oksana killed Orlov along with his main lieutenant. The other soldiers he brought along are suffering from various forms of gunshot wounds and general physical trauma."

"Hold it! Oksana killed—"

"It's a long story."

"I bet. So, how many guys are we talking?"

"Two fatals and nine wounded."

"What?" he exclaimed. "How did you pull that off?"

"I had a little help."

"A little help? Sounds like you had an army of your own."

"No, just me, Bridgett, Aaron and Pete Tolles. Oh, and Oksana helped."

Zack said, "You know, this is way too much information for me to process before coffee. You need to tell me what went down in detail. Oh, and by the way, we got a report that someone broke into *Tenshi Community Bank* last night, but only one safe-deposit box was found open and empty in the vault. Nothing else was missing. I don't suppose you know anything about that, do you?"

"Now, how would I know anything about that? I have

been busy fighting Russian bad guys most of the night."

"Uh-huh," he intoned skeptically. "Okay, I'll have some people on the scene shortly. But I'm going expect a full report from you, Moriarity."

"It'll have to wait until I get back."

He was silent for a few seconds before replying, "Going back to be with Cassie?"

"Yeah."

"Listen, Gerald Redfern alerted me last night to what's going on and he's got a Bureau jet that was already headed to the east coast standing by to take you along if you want to go."

I checked my watch.

6:25 a.m.

"I definitely do. I should be wrapped up here and back in San Diego by eight. Can they wait until then?"

"Absolutely. All right, Jake. We'll talk soon."

He terminated the call and I started doing some quick calculations. Muriel would be landing in Jacksonville in a couple of hours; Gabi's plane should have left at six would arrive mid-afternoon. I knew from previous experience that it's close to a five-hour flight to get to Florida on a Learjet. If we were airborne by 9:00 a.m., that'd put me in Jacksonville by five or so, which was better by far than my scheduled late-night arrival by commercial airliner.

I suddenly didn't want to go. If you want to know the truth, I was terrified to go. Something was off. A sense of...I don't know what it was, but I sensed disaster looming. And based on my experience, that was never good.

CHAPTER 56

As I walked back to rejoin the group Bridgett asked, "What about that truck full of girls that's supposed to be coming in, boss?" Oksana cleared her throat.

"It could be that someone anonymously alerted the California Highway Patrol that a big-rig was driving erratically and posing a danger to other drivers and that the truck was pulled over just west of El Centro."

I said, "And, could it be that human cargo was discovered onboard?"

"Umm, who could say?" She smiled, waited a few beats and then added, "Thank-you, Jake. This was...unexpected. I had thought we would be enemies, but now..."

"Not enemies. Definitely not enemies. You guys should go."

"I owe you one," she said.

"Oh, you owe me more than one, but who's counting?"

Oksana and Charles glanced at each other, nodded and walked to their SUV where her associates were waiting.

As they drove off Tommy asked, "What's going to happen to them, Jake?"

I watched the SUV take off like the devil himself was after it.

"They are going to go someplace far away, assume new identities and attempt to avoid being discovered by the Russians."

"Is that even possible?"

"Under normal circumstances, I'd say no, but with the resources they are going to have at their disposal they definitely have a chance."

My phone vibrated signaling an incoming text.

It was from Oksana. I read it out loud.

Tell Tommy to check Helen's bank account tomorrow. Charles is transferring all of Helen's assets that were a part of the investments he made on her behalf, plus a substantial amount he wants him to have. It won't, of course, bring Helen back or justify what happened, but it's what he wants to do. Farewell.

"What am I supposed to do with that?" Tommy asked when I'd finished reading.

Aaron rolled his eyes.

"Take it. Man wants to give you what's yours, that's all."

"Aaron's right, Tommy," I said in agreement.

"But, that's Russian mob money. It's dirty."

"I understand how you could feel that way," I replied. "But when Helen originally invested her portfolio with Charles, it was because she wanted to help provide for your family's financial future. Well, she did that and then some. Money is neither clean nor dirty, Tommy. It's just, money. What you do with it makes it one way or the other."

I could tell he was still wrestling through the ethics, but he nodded in agreement and then shook my hand.

"I can't thank you enough for this, Jake. I don't know what I would have done without you."

"Well, it was my—our—pleasure to help out, Tommy. Like Aaron is fond of saying, you're family. And we take care of our family."

Pete affirmed, "That right there is God's honest truth, Mr. Marshall."

"Not to be insensitive, but I have a plane to catch in San Diego," I said.

Aaron asked, "What's going on? I thought your flight wasn't until this afternoon."

"Redfern has a Bureau jet that was scheduled for an east coast run anyway, and he's going to let me tag along. Hopefully we can be on our way by nine o'clock or so."

"Then we better get on down the road," Pete replied.

Just then, four Bureau vehicles came roaring into the lot and the place was suddenly overrun with FBI agents. Gerald Redfern was in the lead car.

He walked slowly toward me surveying the carnage.

"Well, it would appear that you've been busy. What happened?"

I briefly related the details of the incident, after which he asked me what had happened to Charles and Oksana.

I said, "Somewhere in all the chaos I guess they decided they'd had enough and disappeared."

He glanced sideways at me.

"Disappeared, huh? You have anything to say about this, Agent Polk?"

Bridgett looked around dramatically.

"They must have. I mean I don't see them anywhere, do you, sir?"

He was nodding slowly as a small smile made its way onto his face.

"And I suppose I'm just supposed to tell the US Marshall's Service that they've got one of their WitSec charges is still in the wind? And report to Zack Hastings that Oksana Orlov—a person of interest in several dozen Russian mob hits—has vanished without a trace?"

I shrugged.

"Well, Zack sort of already knows."

"Sort of?"

I shrugged again.

"Yeah."

He glanced around at the dead and wounded, shaking his head in consternation.

"I suppose I should just be happy that we saved a truck-load of young girls from the horrors of sexual slavery and took down one of the most important Russian mob figures in the contiguous United States. Right?"

"Sounds good to me," I replied encouragingly.

He pulled up his sleeve to check his watch.

"If we're going to get you on that jet, we need to go. You okay with Aaron taking Pete and Tommy back to Carlsbad?"

"Of course."

"Aaron," Redfern hollered, "I need you to drive Pete and Tommy back to Carlsbad in Jake's car. Agent Polk and I are going to take him directly to the airport."

"Got no problem with that."

"Okay. You ready to go?" Gerald asked.

Good question.

"Yeah, I guess I am."

"You need to stop by home to get anything?"

"No. I always keep a couple of changes of clothes along with toiletries in the go-bag."

"All right. I'm ready when you are."

I approached Aaron and gave him a bear hug.

"I love you, brother."

"And I love you. I'll be praying for Michael."

I simply nodded, walked away and got into Redfern's car, secretly hoping in my heart that Aaron had some pull with the Almighty.

It was 7:15 a.m.

As Gerald Redfern merged with the early Monday morning freeway traffic, I texted Gabi, Cassie and then Muriel to let them know what was happening and then rode the rest of the way in silence.

For one of the first times in my life, I had nothing to say.

CHAPTER 57

I was having a dream—a very realistic dream. And in my very realistic dream I was falling. Actually, it was worse than that. I was plummeting! Dropping like a stone.

Caught in a nosedive.

"Sorry about that," came the captain's voice over the cabin intercom. "We hit some not-so-friendly-skies and dropped about five hundred feet. The air should be calm the rest of our flight."

I shook my head, rubbed my eyes and checked my watch. I had been asleep for close to four hours. Probably would *still* be asleep had it not been for the damn air pocket. Glancing around the cabin, I noticed that my three fellow passengers, all FBI agents based on the east coast, were alert and drinking coffee.

That suddenly sounded like the best idea ever.

So, I unbuckled my seat restraint and headed for the galley situated in the rear of the plane. As I poured a steaming cup of java, I reflected on the events of the past two days, marveling that I had managed—for one of the only times in memory—to escape the confrontations unscathed. Which was a good thing because, if you want to know the truth, I'm just plain over getting shot, punched, stabbed and treated in a generally deleterious manner.

As I was on my way back to my seat, the captain's voice announced that we had picked up a significant tailwind along the way and would be landing about fifteen minutes ahead of schedule. We had taken off from San Diego around 8:45 a.m. PDT and, thanks to the tailwind, were now scheduled to land in Jacksonville around 4:15 p.m.

Being on an FBI Learjet meant that I had access to cell service, so I sat down and sent a group text to my girls to let them know of my early arrival. Then I drank some coffee and waited for a response.

Nothing.

Not even from Gabi.

I checked the text to make sure that it went through. It had.

"Huh," I said out loud. "That's weird."

The reason it was weird is because Cassie, Muriel *and* Gabi were prolific texters. To the extent that you can typically expect a reply in mere seconds after you hit send. But it had been nearly five minutes. Something was wrong—terribly wrong. Of course, I expected the worst.

I don't know about you, but I hate not knowing what's going on. Especially in situations such as this thing with Michael, where someone you love is facing life-threatening circumstances.

Silence is *not* golden.

It's distressing.

I texted Aaron and asked if he had heard anything from Muriel. He answered back right away to say that it had been a while, like maybe an hour. I inquired as to whether everything had been okay the last he'd heard. He said that it had and wondered why I was asking.

I called him.

"You're spooking me, bro. What's going on?" he asked.

"I texted all three girls and haven't heard anything back."

"Well, they could be involved in something that is requiring their attention, or they're not paying attention to their phones—"

"Not paying attention to their phones? You *do* realize

who we're talking about here, right?"

"Okay, okay," he granted. "I admit that it's a bit out of the ordinary."

"A bit?"

"You're right. It's weird. Want me to try?"

I said, "I think you should."

"All right, hang on."

I heard him put his phone on speaker and then the sound of his fingers tapping on the screen.

"There. I sent it. And now we wait."

"Thanks, Aaron. You doing okay after our all-night adventure?"

"A little tired, but I'm all right. Tommy is a wreck. He's a sensitive guy anyway, but Helen's death accompanied by all this drama just about put him over the edge. Gerald dropped Bridgett back by here after taking you to the airport and told her to help out wherever she could."

He chuckled and I said, "What's funny?"

"It's just that, she took Tommy on like a professional caregiver, or something. Just being there for him, you know? Sitting with him; fetching him stuff; just a presence. A very caring presence. She's really something."

"So I'm beginning to believe."

He paused and then said, "I got nothing from that text. Now *I'm* worried."

The captain's voice announced that we were beginning our initial descent into the Jacksonville area and to make sure we were strapped in.

"I gotta go, Aaron. I'll let you know if I hear anything before I get to the hospital and you do the same."

"Roger that. And Jake?"

"Yeah?"

"I got a terrible feelin' about this. If it turns out I'm right, Cassie is going to need you like never before."

I was about to say that he didn't need to tell me that, but I just went with, "Thanks, my friend. I'll talk to you soon."

It was a bumpy ride into Jacksonville Executive thanks to a weather system that had decided to mosey through the area, and by the time we were finally on the ground I had all but determined that air travel just wasn't for me. We taxied for a bit, finally coming to a waiting ground crew and three Bureau SUVs on the tarmac.

After exchanging farewells with the other agents and thanking the pilot for waiting for me, I exited the Learjet and was surprised to learn that one of the SUVs was designated for my use.

"That's not necessary," I explained to the junior agent who had driven it to the airport. "I have a rental reserved."

"Assistant Director Zack Hastings called me personally and arranged to make this available to you, sir. And he's accustomed to having his orders followed."

"Then, I'll take it."

He handed me the keys and walked away as I climbed inside and took a minute to familiarize myself with the layout of the dashboard. It was while I was thus occupied that my phone rang.

It was Gabi.

"Gabi, did you get my text."

She sobbed and then said, "Jake...we're losing him. Get here as soon as possible. It's bad. Very bad."

My heart nearly stopped. I wanted to ask for details, but that wasn't the time.

"I'm in my car and on my way. Even with the best traffic conditions, though, it's going to take me thirty to forty minutes to get there."

"Just hurry, please. Cassie needs you."

"I'll do my best. I love you."

"I love you too."

She disconnected the call and I sat staring, trying to calm my breathing before I left. It was no good. The dread, the premonitions of doom I had been fighting for two days suddenly descended like a noxious cloud intent on choking the life out of any remaining hope.

From the recesses of my subconscious mind came a taunting notion that perhaps a bit of prayer would be in order—a notion that I summarily dismissed as being entirely irrelevant given my history with the Almighty. Prayer hadn't worked when I had needed it the most. I had cried out to God until my throat was bloody on behalf of my precious Abby.

And then, she died.

If He hadn't responded to my pleas then, why should it be any different now?

As I keyed the hospital's coordinates into my phone's maps program, my ears heard my voice saying, "Listen... God, I know you and me have issues, but my issues are not Michael's. I know he believes in you. The question is, do you believe in *him*? Are you in a saving mood today? Or, will you let Michael die just like you let Abby die? For Cassie's sake, I sure hope you intervene."

It wasn't exactly a prayer, but it was the best I could summon.

I put the car in gear and glanced at the vehicle's emergency lights wondering if the gravity of the situation was sufficient to employ their usage. I thought not and pulled away from the airport, my FBI credentials at the ready should any overly eager local law enforcement personnel deem it necessary to pull me over.

"Hang on, Michael," I breathed. "Hang on, brother."

CHAPTER 58

Even though I didn't use the lights and siren en route, when I got to the hospital I turned them on as I drove around to the emergency entrance and pulled into a parking slot marked, "Police Only." After texting Gabi that I had arrived and asking her to come and meet me in the waiting room, I got out of the SUV and walked toward the entrance doors, my body feeling progressively heavier with every step. A security guard glanced at my car and then raised his eyebrows questioningly, but I flashed my FBI credentials and he waved me through.

I had just walked into the waiting room when I saw Gabi emerging through a set of double doors off to my left.

If a picture is worth a thousand words, then the expression on her face made words unnecessary. Her earlier warning had *not* been an exaggeration.

It was bad.

Really, really bad.

She approached me quickly and threw her arms around my waist, sobbing quietly into my chest.

Finally, she was able to manage, "They're doing everything they can to save him, Jake. But they've already revived him three times. I don't know if they can do it again."

It took me a moment before I was able to speak.

"How's Cassie?"

Stepping back, Gabi wiped her eyes with a well-used wad of tissue.

"She's trying to be strong, but I think she's reached the

end of her strength. I'm afraid of what's going to happen if he, you know..."

I nodded and asked, "Have you heard any status reports directly from the medical staff?"

"Just that they're employing every technique known to medical science to save him. His publicist is here, by the way. Arrived about an hour ago, which I hear is about three hours after the media."

I said, "And have the media been intrusive?"

"Surprisingly, no. It's almost as if everyone is genuinely concerned for Michael's life and are keeping a respectful distance."

"*That's* a switch. How about Michael's parents, are they here?"

"Not yet. I guess they had trouble booking a flight. Even the charters were difficult, but Bernie worked his magic and finally managed to snag one. The last I heard, they won't be getting in until late this evening."

"Probably around the time I was originally scheduled to arrive."

I paused, willing myself to move forward.

"Okay. Let's go see my girl."

We got to the security station outside of the ER and my mind was suddenly taken back to another ER two thousand miles away and the night of the accident that turned Michael Harvey from a 6'7" towering giant into a wheelchair-bound paraplegic. Now, as then, the guard issued me a nametag, noted my FBI status and entered my name into his logbook before waving us through.

The doors opened into a world of chaos. Medical staff moving at full speed in every direction in a frantic effort to save just one more life; trauma patients crying out in pain; a mother and father weeping over the loss of a young child; a young man being rushed past us on a gurney suffering from a gunshot wound in his upper torso; a middle-aged man doubled over in pain from some abdominal distress.

It was simply overwhelming.

We moved carefully down the hallway, seemingly taking forever to arrive at the area where Michael was being treated. Even as we were approaching I could tell that things weren't going well. When you've had as much experience as I've had around trauma units, you develop an ability to read micro expressions and body language in the emergency personnel. What I was seeing in that medical staff was exhaustion and frustration—the look of people who had done everything they knew to do and had, thus far, failed to make even the slightest improvement in the condition of their patient.

And then I saw Cassie.

The one I loved above every other human on earth.

My heart nearly burst inside of my chest.

She sat bravely erect with Muriel's arm around her shoulders, staring straight ahead, her eyes seeing nothing. Her face was a complex mask of sheer exhaustion and worry coupled with unmitigated despair.

I gave Gabi's hand a squeeze and walked toward Cassie.

Muriel saw me first and sprang up to hug me tightly. Cassie turned her eyes on me slowly, as if every movement were causing her excruciating pain.

And then, she fell apart. Not all at once, but sequentially. Her tragic, beautiful face seemed to collapse in on itself as she raised her arms to me, just like she had done when, as a little girl, she had suffered great hurt and needed a father's comfort.

"Uncle," she sobbed and tried to stand.

She only made it halfway before I scooped her up in my arms and clung to her shaking body, willing my strength into her. We stood like that for a solid minute, not speaking. Just holding on to each other.

Finally, I backed up a little, brushed a few stray strands of blonde hair away from her eyes and said, "So, where do we stand?"

Composing herself, she blew out a long breath before answering, "Well, that depends on who you ask. The charge nurse suggested that we notify family members that they should arrive as soon as possible, while the cardiologist said he believes Michael is stable and if he can keep him that way for another few hours his chances of survival are good."

We sat down with Gabi and Muriel scooting their chairs around until we were in a loose circle.

"When did the cardiologist say that?" I asked.

Cassie looked to Muriel who replied, "I think it was about thirty minutes ago, but as you can see, the situation in there looks anything *but* stable."

At that moment every member of the ER staff was staring at a bank of monitors, one of which displayed a very erratic heart rhythm. I really hoped Cassie wasn't seeing what I was seeing.

Cassie's head fell against my shoulder.

"I don't understand any of this, you know? After everything he's been through, why does he now have to endure all of this pain and suffering?"

I stroked her hair and said, "I wish I had answers for you, little girl. I also wish Aaron was here. He's much better than me at putting things like this into perspective."

She sat up slowly, rubbing the heels of her hands into red-rimmed eyes.

"I wish he was here too, Uncle."

"He wanted to be. We just couldn't work it out."

Cassie nodded slowly.

"I know. By the way, is Tommy okay?"

"It's a long story, but, yeah, he's going to be fine."

"Cassie," Gabi said gently, "why don't you tell Jake what happened when you were standing by Michael's bed?"

Cassie smiled sadly.

"Yeah, I should. Well...I was standing there holding his hand and talking to him. He was totally out of it, of course, but the doc said I should talk to him every chance I could. So, I was telling him how much I loved him and that I couldn't wait to take him home so we could get on with our lives. And he…" She stopped to allow a wave of emotion to pass. "He opened his eyes and stared at me. They were clear, and I knew that he was actually seeing me. And then he whispered something I couldn't quite make out, so I leaned in closer and asked him to repeat it. He, uh…he said, *'Let me go, Cass. It's okay. In this life…I was loved by you. I'm good.'*" She sobbed for a few seconds before finishing, "And then, he was back to wherever he had been before speaking to me, you know, unresponsive. The whole thing was so surreal that I actually questioned whether or not it had happened."

"And now?" I queried, while brushing a stray tear from my sun-roughened cheek.

She nodded slowly and then said, "I know it happened and I know he knew what he was saying."

Suddenly pandemonium erupted in the treatment room as multiple monitors began beeping and medical staff scrambled to bring order. Above Michael's bed the heart monitor displayed a flat line.

CHAPTER 59

Cassie gripped my hand, squeezing hard, her breathing having turned ragged and sporadic.

I saw a doctor place paddles on Michael's chest and then yell, "Clear." Michael's body jerked, but the flat line remained unbroken and nurses began tag-teaming chest compression.

A couple of minutes later the doc tried it again with the same results.

Cassie said in a voice tight with emotion, "This is what we've been going through for the past two days. Counting those two, I think the number of times they have used the defibrillator is now up to somewhere around twenty. Right before you got here, the cardiologist came out and had a very frank and honest talk with me. He said that with continued defib you run the risk of turning Michael into a 'cardiac cripple' in his terminology."

I said, "I read once that every defibrillation has the same effect on the body as running a mile."

"Well, if that's true, then Michael is almost a marathoner."

After two further unsuccessful attempts at resuscitation, the doctor ordered the chest compression to continue and then walked toward us.

Coming through the swinging doors of the cardiac intensive care unit he pulled the surgical mask away from his mouth and stopped in front of Cassie.

"This is the conversation I told you was coming," he

said.

Cassie sniffed, "I figured as much."

"So, listen, we can put him on life support and keep him clinically alive for, well, let's just say that we can do that for a long time. But, it's not life, Mrs. Harvey. And my medical opinion is that, well…that Michael's great heart is done."

Cassie nodded slowly, wiping tears away from her face with the back of her sleeve.

"Can I go in and see him before you do whatever you have to do to make it official?"

"Of course."

She stood slowly and walked with the doctor, weariness and grief wrapped around her like a sodden winter coat. I wanted to rush to her side, but something told me that this was a private moment.

Once inside the Cardiac Intensive Care Unit, the doctor shooed away the nurses who stepped back a respectful distance to allow Cassie unfettered access to Michael's prone and pathetic form. At first, she just stood and stared at the bank of monitors as if willing a sinus rhythm to disrupt the stark reality of the flat line. Then she looked at his face, with the hideous intubation apparatus taped to his mouth.

Gesturing at the device, I saw her mouthing something to the doctor who turned and gestured for the nurses to remove it. It took a few minutes for them to get the thing completely removed and then wipe his mouth clear of residue. Cassie seemed to thank them and then moved a step closer, her hand hovering over Michael's face. She then stroked his brow; his hair; traced the outline of his mouth. I could see her saying something to him as a couple of the nurses wiped tears from their eyes.

Laying her hand lightly against his cheek, she leaned close and kissed his poor, dead lips, lingering slightly. Then, she rose up, brushed his cheek one last time and turned toward me, her eyes pleading. I rushed through the doors to her side and caught her just before she fell.

There was no dignity in that moment. Just raw, terrible emotion.

She didn't cry.

She shrieked. It was the sound of a soul in utter anguish. I had never in my life witnessed grief of that intensity. It was a palpable force in the room felt by the entire medical staff.

I finally was able to get my arms under Cassie and picked her up, cradling her as a parent would cradle a small child. With my lips pressed against her hair, I stared down at the dead body of my dear friend, feeling so lost and helpless in the face of such a terrible tragedy. In my heart I told him that I would see him on down the road, but wondered immediately if there was any reason to hold out for that mystical hope.

I walked out of the CICU with Cassie sobbing quietly in my arms and saw Bernard Rothstein, Michael's publicist standing behind Muriel and Gabi—each of them dealing with grief in their own way. Bernie was on his phone, no doubt alerting media outlets of the passing of one of America's greatest novelists. Once I cleared the doors, I just stood in place, holding Cassie tightly, never wanting to let her go, almost daring something—anything—to even try coming against her.

Gabi and Muriel ran to my side, kissing Cassie; telling her how sorry they were for the loss she had just experienced; saying other things that never quite translated to my ears. Mainly because internally, I was railing at the heavens.

Actually, that description is prodigiously inaccurate. I was cursing. Yes, cursing.

I cursed fate, and the late Paul Morgan for creating the freak accident that had turned Michael into a paraplegic.

I cursed the dead driver of the vehicle that had hit him.

I cursed the limitations of medical science that left

the doctors unable to save his life.

And, last but definitely not least, I cursed the non-interventionist God I had once served and in whom I had invested so much faith and hope early in my life.

I decided then and there that it is far better to never have believed in God at all, than to have believed and been abandoned.

But, most of all, I cursed myself. Because every single one of the sad and sorry events that had conspired to bring about this present, heartbreaking reality could be traced directly back to me and were, in fact, ultimately my fault.

I stood, frozen in place, holding Cassie in my arms and feeling the physical manifestations of her terrible grief while battling an internal blitzkrieg of emotion. My legs suddenly felt shaky, so I sat and attempted to slide Cassie into the chair next to me, but she wouldn't let go, clinging to my neck as if her very life depended on that contact. Muriel and Gabi moved in, attempting to console her.

As for me, I had been rendered speechless. It was all too much. Just too damn much! I couldn't summon a single thing to say that would make even the slightest difference in the way my Cassie was feeling.

Gabi stood and came around behind me, leaning into my ear and whispering, "It's okay to not say anything, Jake. What she really needs right now is what you are already providing—an anchor in this raging storm."

I glanced at her and nodded my head in understanding.

At some point, although I can't tell you how long it took, my arms began to cramp and I knew I needed to transfer Cassie into her own seat.

I said, "Cass, I'm going to put you down next to me, okay?"

That only made her cry harder.

"Honey, I *have* to set you down. My arms are cramping."

So, I leaned over and placed her in the seat without

breaking contact. She seemed okay with that.

Muriel asked if there was anything she should be doing and I told her that since Michael's parents would have their phones available on the charter—and they would no doubt be desperate for any information—to go ahead and make the call so they didn't inadvertently walk in and find their only son dead without having been warned ahead of time. I told her she also should call Aaron so he could pass along the news to everyone else. Muriel agreed and walked away to place the call.

Gabi sat down beside me and grabbed my right hand, squeezing tightly and laying her head on my shoulder.

It was a pitiful sight: Cassie with her head on my left shoulder, completely undone by grief; Gabi with her head on my right shoulder, weeping softly; and me, fighting to hold it together so I could be strong for my girls, because that's what I do, right?

No time to fall apart.

No time to feel, just act.

Feelings would come later, if they came at all.

I felt my chest heave with an unbidden sob, and the tears came in a torrent.

Manly?

Who the hell cares!

My friend was dead. My niece was devastated. Life as we had all known it was suddenly and irrevocably altered.

Cassie lifted her head and stared at the tears coursing down my cheeks. And then my beautiful, brave girl cupped my face in her hands, stared into my misty eyes and kissed me on the forehead.

"I, uh, I can't fix this, Cass," I stammered.

She pulled back and with one hand still cupping my cheek, said, "I don't need you to fix this. It's enough that you are willing to weep with me."

I laughed ironically.

"Well, mission accomplished. I haven't cried like this

since...you know."

Putting her arms around me, she whispered, "We'll get through this, Uncle. You and me. We always do."

Suddenly, it was Cassie giving *me* strength.

Can you fathom it?

I had no words, just feelings. Love? Well, yes, but so much more than that. It was also ineradicable respect. For in that moment, something changed; a switch was flipped; the fixer became the one in need of fixing. I suppose it happens eventually in all parent/child relationships, where the nurturer and protector find themselves in need of just that. Cassie was not only telling me that she was going to be okay, but that if I was *not* okay she'd be there to help me along.

It was impressive.

It was impressive as hell.

Gabi said, "And you've got me, Jacob Moriarity."

I leaned my head into hers.

"Yes, yes I do."

Cassie glanced through the windows into the CICU, and shook her head sadly.

"I think I always knew this was going to happen. He just—you know, after the wreck—he just wasn't ever right. And it wasn't just the physical challenges." She tapped her head. "But in here." Then her chest. "And in here. It was like he had lost the fire—the drive, passion, I don't know—to live. Especially after he finished that damn novel! Even before the onset of autonomic dysreflexia, I could feel him slowly giving up. And then there was what he told me yesterday, you know, about letting him go. I think in his mind he had become this hideous burden to me and that..." she paused, sobbing, "and that I would be better off if I didn't have him to worry about."

"Well," I said, drying my eyes, "whether any or all of that is true, we will never know. But what we *do* know, little girl, is that he loved you with everything he had. And even if he did make a conscious decision to let go—to leave—even that was driven by love."

She nodded her head, still sobbing.

Gabi suddenly whispered softly, "Can't forget, won't regret what I did for love."

"Excuse me?"

"It's an old, sad song from a Broadway musical—*Chorus Line*, I believe."

Cassie sobbed, "Michael loved that song. In fact, he'd quote it to me." She laughed through her tears momentarily. "He tried to sing it once and I requested he just stick with quoting it."

"Yeah," I replied. "The boy was a genius writer, but possibly the worst singer I've ever heard."

Turning pensive, she continued, "I wonder if he was trying to prepare me for this? Because I would see that one line, 'What I did for love...' scribbled across the top of his notes; sometimes on a piece of paper discarded in the trash; just in odd places, you know?"

"It sounds like it was definitely on his mind."

I stopped speaking due to a meandering memory strolling through my consciousness that had temporarily robbed me of my ability to speak.

After a few seconds I managed, "When you two were classmates in high school, I remember Michael stopping by the house one day after school with a very important question. He said, 'Mr. Moriarity, how do you know when you're in love?' Even though I knew the source of the question, I played along and explained it the best I knew how. As I was talking, I could see his smile getting wider and wider. Finally, he nodded, thanked me, and walked out of the house like he was walking on air. He loved you then, Cass, and he kept loving you right through the very end."

She nodded through her tears.

"I know that, and I know that him choosing to stop fighting was, in the end, an act of love. But...knowing doesn't lessen the pain."

What was there about our family that seemed to invite tragedy? Losing my mom while still in high school; Cassie losing her mom and dad at the age of seven, and me losing my only sibling at the same time; losing my wife, Abby to cancer; and now losing Michael. Was there some cosmic edict in place designed to periodically and sequentially drop horror, pain and calamity onto our lives just to keep us in our place? I mean, what the hell?

It was a question for which I intended to seek answers as soon as all of the ancillary details had sorted themselves out and Cassie was stronger.

CHAPTER 60

Bernard Rothstein finished his call and came over to offer condolences and ask if there was anything he could do to help.

I had Gabi slide over and take my place next to Cassie and then took Bernard by the elbow, steering him toward a far corner.

When we were alone, I said, "Bernie, I need you to promise me that you will keep people away from Cassie."

With his lower lip trembling, he nodded.

"Yeah, I can do that, Jake. And I have his power of attorney, so I can deal with the requisite hospital forms and anything else that needs to be signed. I'll deal with transport to the mortuary and funeral arrangements as well, if you'd like."

"That'd be very helpful. It goes without saying that the funeral will be in San Diego."

"Of course." He paused, staring through the windows into the CICU. "I just, you know, can't believe he's actually gone. He just always seemed…bigger than life."

"He was one of a kind, that's for sure."

"I was a nobody when he first hired me. I had no credentials. No form of success to point to. Just a lot of confidence and bravado. But Michael saw something in me and," he paused to choke back a sob, "I just remembered what he said to me when we signed our first contract."

I laid a hand softly on his shoulder.

"What was that, Bernie?"

Blinking away the tears he said, "He told me that I was going to be the greatest publicist that had ever worked in publishing. That I was going to do things I never dreamed I could do."

"Well, you are, and you did."

It was as if he had been holding back the emotion and something suddenly gave way. Covering his face with both hands, he bent slightly forward and sobbed.

I put my arm around his shoulders and gave him a quick hug.

"Michael loved you, Bernie. He used to tell me that he wouldn't have ever become Charleston Hawthorne if it hadn't been for you."

He straightened up, wiped his eyes and took a deep breath.

"Okay. I'm okay. I just had to get that over with. Thanks for being here, Jake. And I want you to know that I will be there for Cassie—whatever she needs, she can count on me. Please tell her not to worry about any of the business stuff. I will take care of all of it: the probate, the will... everything." He hesitated as if something had just occurred to him, and then added, "Maybe you should think about taking her somewhere, you know? Just the two of you. A long trip somewhere."

It was an idea that had merit.

"I'll give it some serious consideration." I shook his hand. "Thanks for everything, Bernie. I'd better get back to Cassie."

"Sure thing, Jake. I'll be in touch."

And with that, he was off, his phone in its usual place glued to his ear and talking a mile a minute.

Inside the CICU, I could see the attending physician filling out the pronouncement of death form while the staff prepped Michael's body for organ harvesting. It was something about which he had cared deeply, and in spite of a furious argument with Cassie over the subject, he had insisted that, upon the occasion of his death, any organs that could be used be donated.

Time to get Cassie out of there.

I walked over to where Cassie sat with Muriel on one side and Gabi on the other and said, "So, I just talked to Bernie. He has Michael's power of attorney, so he's going to take care of all the official stuff."

"Can we go, then?" Cassie asked. "I think I'd like to go."

A quick glance into the CICU and I replied, "I think it's time. Muriel, did you get in touch with everyone?"

"I talked to Aaron, who said he'd pass on the news to the girls, and to Pete, Brett and Laurie. I couldn't reach Michael's parents. Probably passing through a dead zone or something. Not sure what to do about that."

"Yeah, that's unfortunate. I'm not sure how to handle it either. Someone should probably meet them at the airport."

Gabi offered, "Do you want me to do that? I got to know them pretty well at the wedding. So—"

"I want to do it," Cassie said firmly. "When I married Michael, they became my mom and dad too."

We all stared at her, seeing the resolve in her eyes and realized that as hard as it would be, it was the right thing to do.

"Okay," I replied. "Then we'll all go to the airport together. We good with that?"

Gabi and Muriel agreed and started walking toward the exit. Cassie hung back, staring toward Michael's body.

With her hand pressed against the glass of the CICU, she sobbed, "Bye, my baby. I'm going to miss you so much," before turning away and staggering toward me.

There was nothing left there to see. Michael was gone.

CHAPTER 61

The next two weeks passed in a mind-numbing blur.

True to his word, Bernie took care of every single detail, a fact for which I intend to see him generously rewarded. Cassie didn't have to do anything except sign a few documents.

Meeting Michael's parents at the airport was nearly as difficult emotionally as seeing Cassie reacting in the CICU. I mean imagine flying clear across the country to support your son only to find out upon landing that he is already dead. Not the first time anything like that had happened to good people, but because it was family, we all felt their pain very deeply.

Two weeks to the day from when Michael died, we held a private memorial service at *Mosaic PB* in Pacific Beach, San Diego where Vanessa's sister, Laurie and her husband, Brett Hansen are the directors—a place Michael had endowed generously a year and a half before.

The members of the media descended like a pack of rapacious jackals, eager to photograph any unguarded moments and eavesdrop on less than circumspect conversations. As it turned out, they got nothing thanks to Pete Tolles "going cowboy" on them, or so he said. I had never seen the man truly angry before. And after observing the phenomenon, I can safely say that I never want to see it again.

I'm pretty sure the members of the press would agree.

The graveside service—conducted the day before at Mt. Hope Cemetery in San Diego—had been challenging. Given its location in an economically distressed, high crime neighborhood, it is about as unlikely a place for an international celebrity like Michael James Harvey to be buried as you can imagine. But, legendary detective novelist, Raymond Chandler is buried there, and Mr. Chandler had been a lifelong inspiration to Michael. As such, he had clearly specified in his will that Mt. Hope be his final resting place.

My long-time friend, and part time confident, Father Jack Mahoney, conducted the memorial service. It was heartfelt, relevant and, best of all, brief. He lauded Michael's career but spent most of his time praising his stature as a good and decent man.

And he was.

Cassie sat next to me throughout the memorial, keeping it together, but only just. When it was all over, and people began to mingle, the few close friends and family in attendance kept their interactions with her to a minimum, for which I was very grateful.

I was standing a few feet away from Cassie, when Vanessa's niece, Abby—my favorite little human on the planet—approached and asked me, "Jake, do you think Michael and your Abby have met in heaven yet?"

Out of the mouths of children.

"Well, honey, from what I hear it's a pretty big place. I mean I'm not sure there's a display board, or anything, that announces when people, uh, arrive. So, it might take some time for them to meet each other."

Her eyes widened in wonder.

"Do you think I'll go to heaven when I die, Jake?"

It occurred to me in that moment that I would much rather be passing a kidney stone than talking about heaven with an eight-year-old.

"I'm pretty sure you will, sweetie."

"And how about you, and Aaron, and Muriel, and Vanessa, and my family? Because if you guys aren't going to be there, I don't think I want to go."

Vanessa wandered by and rescued me.

"What's going on here?" she asked lightly.

"Oh," I replied, "Abby and I have just been discussing the vagaries of eternal life."

"Huh?" Abby said, her nose scrunched up.

"Heaven, baby doll. I meant to say that you and me have been talking about heaven."

"Ahhh..." Vanessa replied with a smile. "How about if we go find some cake, Abby?"

Abby nodded and started to walk away, but turned back and ran into my arms, burying her face in my neck.

"You'll be there, Jake," she pronounced with authority. "We'll all be there."

I sat Abby down wordlessly and watched her hurry away with Vanessa toward the refreshment table where Gabi was conferring with the caterers.

I felt a presence hovering behind me.

It was Aaron.

"I can't get my mind around this whole thing," he said sadly in the impossibly low growl that manifests as his voice.

"I know what you mean. It's like I keep expecting to see him come walking through that door any time now and that this whole, sorry ordeal will have been a bad dream."

"Well, it is definitely a bad dream, only I don't think we get to wake up from it. At least not any time soon."

"You talk to Tommy lately?"

"As a matter of fact," he replied, "he called me just before we left this morning."

"He doing okay?"

Aaron nodded slowly.

"He is. Thanks to Charles and Oksana keeping their promise, he is now a couple million dollars richer and enjoying an extended stay in Cabo San Lucas, Mexico." He paused, and then asked, "How about Orlov's sex trafficking ring? You hear anything from Gerry or Zack?"

"Both, actually. As of yesterday, that entire network was completely broken up based on the information provided by various members of the vory they were able to apprehend."

"And I don't suppose anyone has heard from Charles or Oksana?"

"Not a word. Then again, no one really expected to. It's funny, but I hope they have the opportunity to live out their days in peace."

A skinny, longhaired kid with a camera suddenly appeared in front of us and had just begun snapping pictures when he was lifted completely off the ground and shaken like a rag doll.

"Now, pardner, I warned you what would happen if you tried to sneak in here."

Pete had him by the collar of his shirt and the back of his pants. It couldn't have been very comfortable.

The kid was whining about freedom of the press and that he had a right to be there and to take pictures.

Pete said, "This is a private party, old son. You got no rights in here." Glancing around the kid's jerking frame, he asked, "Now what do you think I should do with this—"

"Interloper?" I provided.

"Yeah, that's it. This interloper."

"Oh, I don't know. I'd suggest you toss him through the front window, but then that would leave a mess—you know, blood and broken glass—and I don't want Brett to have to deal with anything like that."

Aaron leaned close and said, "How about you let me take him in the back room and teach him some martial arts?"

The kid's eyes bugged out and he shrieked, "Just let me go. I promise I won't bother anyone ever again. I don't even like this job. I'm an introvert, for God's sake."

Pete sat him down and roughly escorted him down the back hallway and shoved him out the rear door as people applauded.

"Okay," I said loudly. "Excitement's over, folks. Just an example of poor decision making and the unintended consequences thereof."

As people went back to their conversations, Aaron and I sat in a corner across the room where we could still observe our girls.

"She's amazing, isn't she?" he said, gesturing toward Cassie, who, at present, was holding Abby on her lap and rocking her. With eyes closed, Cassie stroked her hair as a small smile fought its way onto her face.

"Yeah, she is. But then, I'm prejudiced."

"Me too, bro. Me too." After a few moments he asked, "She going to be all right? I mean, really?"

A question I had already spent considerable time debating.

"I don't know, Aaron. I want to say, yes, but how can you be okay after something like this?"

"You tell me. I mean you've had quite a bit more experience at it than me."

"A sad and terrible truth."

"And, how about you?" he said.

"Well, having Gabi here through this whole ordeal has definitely helped."

"But?" he prompted.

"But...I don't know. I think Michael's death has reopened some very old and very deep wounds."

"Hmm," he breathed and then went silent.

"Does anything go with, 'hmm,' or is that it?"

"I was just thinking: been a while since you and Father Jack had one of your sessions. Might be a good time to get together."

I stared across the room toward where Father Jack stood talking to Brett Hansen. The best thing I can say about the man is that he's real. Which, in this age of shallow pretenders, is saying quite a lot.

"Perhaps you're right."

"Oh, you know I'm right."

"I actually *don't* know that, which is why I said 'perhaps.'"

"Man, come on. You need to listen to me and go talk to the man."

I sighed and turned partway toward him.

"Maybe I don't want to talk to him—or anyone else, for that matter."

"It'd do you good. All I'm saying."

"And what if it didn't?" I asked. "What if it just stirred things up even more than they already are and didn't solve anything?"

"That's not gonna happen and you know it! You just being stubborn, is all."

"I am *not* being stubborn!"

"Yes, you are."

Muriel appeared in front of us.

"Are you two arguing again?"

"No!" we said in unison, and then laughed.

"Love you, bro," said Aaron.

And I loved him back.

Love.

It was what had carried our friendship through these long years. It was what had carried Cassie through this unspeakable loss and would continue to carry her through whatever lies ahead.

I guess you could say that love carries *us*, so that *we* may carry on.

Carry on.

Maybe I would talk to Father Jack after all.

EPILOGUE

Mattie Malloy's was crowded on that early spring evening; conversation resonating between people of good humor and conviviality; the warmish air redolent with the scent of good booze and delightful aromas from the kitchen next door. I sat at the far end of the seventeenth century bar that had begun its life in Killeagh, County Cork, Ireland—the deeply burnished wood bearing the marks of countless souls who had gone before me, bellied up to its inviting contours, downing drinks and pouring out their stories.

Seated next to me was Father Jack, neatly sipping a glass of Bushmills single malt.

"Perhaps," he suggested, his voice resembling a spoken version of Rod Stewart's famous rasp, "if you weren't such an arrogant, stubborn bastard we wouldn't need to be having this conversation."

Father Jack Mahoney loves Jesus, but he believes the judicious utterance of profanity to be efficacious when the occasion demands.

"So, I'm stubborn because I won't fall in line with your arguably draconian belief system?"

"No, you are stubborn because you consistently allow your circumstances to dictate your theology rather than allowing your theology to elevate your experience."

I glanced sideways and frowned.

"You just make that up?"

"No. I heard it from some evangelical. Pretty good,

huh?"

I shrugged and took another sip of a better than average Long Island Ice Tea. It was my second of the evening. And, yes, it is a bit indulgent but given the subject matter of the conversation, I felt it was justified.

"Listen, Jake, your belief system has been shaped almost entirely in response to your experience—"

"Very little of which has been good," I interjected.

"All right. I will concede that point. However, I must hasten to add that you aren't the only soul who has been, from time to time, thrust into the maw of the dragon. I mean no one comes out unscathed, my friend."

I sighed and took another long pull on my drink.

"I know all that. But that's not my issue. My issue is that thing with the bottle of tears."

"From Psalms?" He thought for a second and then said, *"God has marked all of my sorrows; He has collected all my tears in a bottle and has recorded each one in His book."*

"That's the one."

"Okay, and what exactly is your complaint?"

"That! That *is* my complaint. So, you've got this supposedly all-knowing, all-powerful God who, according to Hebrew Scriptures, created the heavens, the world and everything in it, including mankind. And you're telling me that in the face of human tragedy the best he can do is 'collect our tears' and stick them in some damn bottle for observation? Are you kidding me? What the heck kind of help is that?"

But I didn't say, "heck." I used a word to describe human copulation that sounded somewhat like, "stuck."

I didn't mean to become so heated, but the liquor and the subject matter seemed to be conspiring to push me over the edge.

"Michael's dead, Padre," I continued. "And I'm supposed to comfort myself in the knowledge that God is gathering Cassie's tears for his collection?"

He sipped his Bushmills, wiped his mouth with a napkin and leaned against the bar, propped up on one elbow.

"On the face of it I will admit that it sounds...insufficient."

"Insufficient? How about disinterested and indifferent?"

"You're overreacting."

"Overreacting? Wait 'til I really get going."

He winked.

"*Princess Bride.*"

"What?"

"Vizzini—to the Man in Black in the poison scene. It's what he said."

"Who?"

"Vizzini." He gestured with his hands and then said, "Never mind. Look, I'm not going to argue with you, Jacob. You have a particular mindset as it regards this topic and the nature of mindsets is that they are, well...set."

He was right. My opinions regarding all things theological were now, and had been for a long, long while, pretty much set in stone. It's what happens when you lose the thing most precious to you in life, knowing that the God you serve could have stepped in and intervened at any time he chose.

But he didn't.

I took a deep breath and then blew it out.

"I respect you, Jack. You know that, right?"

"Without question."

"And I'm pretty sure you respect me."

He smiled, hoisted his glass and replied, "Hard not to respect a man who buys you single malt Bushmills."

"Granted. So, within the context of our mutual respect, please understand that my issue isn't one of unbelief. I wish I *didn't* believe! Life would be so much simpler. But I do, and therein lies my conundrum—believing that God is there; believing that he can heal, save, intervene, while at the same time observing and experiencing over and over again that he chooses not to. As a result, people die terrible, screaming deaths while their loved ones—who cried out to God on their behalf—are left slogging through the emotional ruins of their lives desperately seeking something, anything, that will help bring order to the chaos."

He seemed taken aback by my intensity. And rightly so, for it was a subject about which I was nothing if not intense.

Finally, after several moments' consideration, he said, "Can I tell you something I've never told another living soul?"

"Of course."

"Everything you've just articulated? I have uttered all of that, and more, during those dark nights of the soul that St. John of the Cross talked about. But at the same time, I find that there is something in the mystery that keeps me coming back. I mean who would want to serve a God that you have all figured out?"

"So, you're suggesting that by embracing the mystery of a non-interventionist God I will find sustenance for my soul?"

"That's exactly what I'm suggesting."

I took a long pull of the Long Island.

"Nice try, but no cigar."

He laughed and replied, "Oh well, it was worth a shot. So, how's Cassie doing?"

"Well, it's only been two weeks since the memorial service, and she's still an emotional wreck. Hell, Father, *I'm* an emotional wreck! A fact that is most likely self-evident."

He asked, "Do you find that there is day-to-day improvement, or does she seem stuck?"

"Stuck," I said, "definitely stuck."

"Hmm, that's not good. Maybe she needs something to distract her, you know, get her mind focused elsewhere than on her own, smothering grief."

"Agreed. But, I don't really know..." I stopped speaking, because I suddenly remembered a notion I'd entertained several weeks before while still in Florida. "Actually, there is something I was thinking about and just now remembered."

"Great, let's hear it."

"When we were all still in Florida and trying to fight our way through all the tumult, I realized that there is something I've been wanting to do for quite a long time."

"And, what's that, Jake?"

"Taking a long road trip."

"I love road trips. Where would you go?"

"South Carolina."

He raised his bushy, gray eyebrows in surprise.

"Really? Why there?"

I said, "My mom was born and raised in a little town up in the Blue Ridge Mountains, and I've always wanted to go but have never been."

"That sounds like a fascinating pilgrimage. And I assume you'd take Cassie with you?"

"That's what I've been thinking about."

"So, would you fly back to the east coast somewhere and rent a car, or would you drive from here?"

I pondered the question for a few beats.

"Well, that's what I don't know yet. Both ideas have merit. If we drove from here, I'd want to take my time. It's kind of like that old Simon and Garfunkel song that says something like, *I've gone to look for America.* On the other hand, it'd be a lot more expedient to fly back to, I don't know...maybe Miami, and drive up the coast from there."

He smiled around a sip of Bushmills.

"But then, are you really looking for expedience?"

No. I wasn't.

I was looking for healing, for both Cassie and me. And I reckoned by starting where my mother, Cassie's grandmother, *began* her life that, perhaps, I could trace the threads of our heritage and by so doing figure some things out. Because there were things that were in desperate need of sorting out and putting to rest. Without it, neither one of us had the slightest chance of moving on nor becoming the people we were supposed to be.

Cassie owed it to herself.

I owed it to myself.

And to Gabi.

I turned to Father Jack, stared at his rumpled, friendly face and said, "Thanks for listening, Padre."

"My pleasure, dear friend."

AUTHOR'S NOTES

With the conclusion of Tears in a Bottle, thus ends the saga of A Faint Reflection of Riddles, wherein Jake has had to wrestle through one of his most daunting challenges in a life that, seemingly, has seen nothing but challenges from the very beginning.

There are two pressing themes throughout this novel that I am quite sure some readers will find uncomfortable. Those being my continued focus on the proliferation of human trafficking and Jake's ongoing battle with the Almighty.

Human trafficking is a reality on the earth. It is global, it is prolific and, if extreme efforts are not mounted, will soon become pandemic. Some estimates place the number of known human slaves at over forty-five million. And when it comes to sex trafficking, the average trafficked person is a fourteen-year-old girl. My wife and I are actively involved in the fight to see this horror erased from the planet. Should you desire more information as to how you can help, please visit notforsalecampaign.org or other very worthy organizations that are similarly dedicated.

Regarding Jake's issues of faith, as is true with so many people, those issues are real, and they run very deep. Jake's statement that, "Oh, I believe in God. I'm just not sure he believes in me," should provide a clue as to just how deep. Some have inquired as to whether there isn't an autobiographical element fueling the inclusion of this thread. Honesty compels me to admit that, yes, I too have struggled at various points throughout my life. Indeed, who hasn't? So, don't look for this issue to be settled any time soon. In the end, the battle for one's worldview is well worth fighting for.

As always, the production of a manuscript is never a solo effort. So, once again, I offer heartfelt thanks to those faithful few who provided much-needed assistance on this project: Dr. Roselynn Irawan for walking me through the medical aspects of Michael Harvey's untimely death; Captain Sean Archer for all things aeronautical; my cover designer, Sarah Wagner for another winner. Thanks as well to my advance readers, Sharon Walling, Bob Book, and Phil Hoffman, for honest, expert input.

And, finally, to my ever-faithful editor, Cheryl Gollner, who is most likely the only person on the planet unafraid to go toe-to-toe with me to insure an authentic, viable and engaging manuscript…thank-you!

Jake and company have many more adventures to come, starting with "Acacia Grove: The Journey Home."

Thank-you for reading. Please keep it up…and, tell a friend.

R.G. Ryan

March 2021

Ocean Beach, San Diego, California

ABOUT THE AUTHOR

R.g. Ryan

R.G. Ryan is the author of the Jake Moriarity series of thrillers, The Voices In My Head (the biography of late Las Vegas entertainment icon, Danny Gans), and the popular Snapshots At St. Arbuck's series. He lives with his first wife on the coast of somewhere beautiful. Can sing a little.

BOOKS BY THIS AUTHOR

Watercolor Dreams

Eighteen-year-old runaway, Vanessa Phillips, knows a secret… and the secret knows her—knows where she sleeps and where she eats on the streets of Pacific Beach in San Diego, California.Crooked Las Vegas politician Harry Olivetti is willing to kill in order to protect this secret, and his two hired assassins are closing in leaving Vanessa nowhere left to run.To a city by the sea—where the world flocks for sun, sand and surf—comes legendary FBI missing persons consultant, Jake Moriarity…a lost soul in a desperate search to find this lost girl. Moriarity can save her, but first, he has to find her. And the only thing he has to go on is like a watercolor painting that has been left out in the rain with all the colors running together.

Finding Wonderland

Simone Ducharme is poised to be the next big thing in the world of jazz. In fact, according to industry insiders, it's almost a sure thing. Twenty-four, exotically beautiful and blessed with the kind of voice that seems to come along only once in a generation. But to stand where she now stood, in the live room of a legendary Hollywood recording studio—a studio that had been home to some of the most famous recording artists in history—required more than looks and talent. She also had an understanding of the music industry in general and the Jazz genre in particular that transcended her age and experience. In short, Simone was the whole package.Her producer, Lonnie Falcon—also jazz great Aaron Perry's producer —is confident her debut album will surpass one million units in sales and be the crowning jewel on his already illustrious career. But while polishing up her vocals on the album's final track, she simply vanishes while on a five-minute break from recording. But is her disappearance voluntary, or has she been abducted? Falcon only knows one man who can make that determination—Jake Moriarity.When Jake agrees to take on Simone's case, he has no idea that his search will uncover a secret past, a vengeful former enemy and lead him through long forgotten, subterranean ruins into a violent encounter with Yves Barreau...an honest to goodness dead man walking and the toughest man Jake has ever faced."Finding Wonderland" takes the reader on a fast-paced journey from the pristine recording studios of Hollywood to the gritty sands of Ocean Beach in San Diego where Jake is running out of time in a place that time has forgotten.

The Secret Of Gaspard

2:00 a.m.
Just outside of Toulouse, France, an obscure warehouse sits in the middle of a forgotten orchard. A monstrous evil is hidden away within its musty interior where four men have gathered in secret conclave. Powerful men—and ruthless beyond comprehension—they comprise the core of a multi-national cartel dealing in Holocaust art stolen by the Nazi's during World War II. The purpose of their nocturnal gathering is to determine the fate of one of their own.

Six hundred kilometers away, in Villefranche-sur-Mer, Jake Moriarity is enjoying blissful days and balmy nights in Gaspard Ducharme's Mediterranean family villa while he recovers from serious injuries suffered as a result of his conflict with Yves Barreau. Surrounded by his best friend and family, life is good and worries are few, for Gaspard Ducharme is a kind and generous host...who will be dead by morning unless Jake Moriarity can fight his way through more twists and turns than an Olympic Giant Slalom and save his friend.

The fast paced action takes the reader on a frantic journey from the Côte d'Azur of Southern France, to the Costa Brava of Catalonia, the deserts of Las Vegas and finally to the high rises of West Hollywood. And in the end, Jake Moriarity will be left wondering if he can trust anyone...including himself.

The Haunts Of Cruelty

On the trail of his most hated enemy, Jake Moriarity is deep in the Amargosa Desert. He is cut off from the FBI team that inserted him, severely wounded, running on empty and apparently hallucinating, because he just shot Paul Morgan in the head with a 12-gauge and then watched him get up and walk away.

Paul Morgan, the man single-handedly responsible for causing Jake's niece Cassie, to become addicted to heroin and then setting her up as his main girl in a Seattle escort service.

Paul Morgan, who has now kidnapped Cassie and is threatening to kill her while forcing Jake to watch.

Paul Morgan, whose life Jake should have ended when he had the chance, but didn't—a decision that has now come back to haunt him, cruelly.

In the Amargosa, life is hard—it's kill or be killed. Only, Paul Morgan refuses to die.

The Wood Between The Worlds

An obscure and ancient Turkish church where, if legend is

to be believed, thousands have been healed of all manner of disease and injury by simply walking through a door and into a small, candle-lit chamber.A renowned archeological team from a prominent Pacific Northwest university who have uncovered an ancient manuscript claiming to lead its possessor to a relic, the discovery of which would be the single greatest archeological find in history.A clandestine conclave of nine incalculably wealthy men ensconced in an obscure Swiss chalet. Their focus is also consumed with unearthing this self-same relic. For in their possession, the geopolitical, financial and ecumenical global landscape will be altered...shaken to its very core, with everything falling into their avaricious and diabolical hands.And Jake Moriarity in a desperate life and death race to secure the relic before The Nine. What's required is a clear-cut strategy. What he has is nothing more than a faint reflection of riddles. But even if he has to kill in order to bring it about, the relic must be protected...for it is The Wood Between the Worlds.

The First Stone

Bartholomew Bennet hadn't planned on living on the streets of the Burnside Triangle, addicted to heroin and pimping himself out. Far from it. A newly minted MBA in hand and a job with one of Portland, Oregon's most promising tech start-ups, Bart had arrived with hopes and plans for the future.And then, it all fell apart. The once bright, engaging twenty-two-year-old hipster was now a skinny, desperate, dying drug addict who would do anything for twenty bucks. And the saddest part of all? No one would be there when he died...not his mother, or his grandfather...Father Jack Mahoney.A thousand miles away in San Diego, Father Jack turns to his good friend, Jake Moriarity to find his grandson. What begins as a favor for a friend becomes a life and death dance with a master of the game as Jake stumbles headlong into a web of intrigue involving prominent members of Portland's wealthy elite, the judicial system, and the Russian mob. At the center of that web Jake finds Bart hopelessly ensnared, but he's not alone. Adolescent and pre-adolescent girls—some kidnapped, some sold by families, but all trafficked for sex—are also there, hidden in plain sight in the City of Roses. With action that is both taut and terrifying, this fast-paced thriller follows Jake Moriarity on a journey through the dystopian darkness of Portland's underworld where he comes face to face with a foe as formidable as Jake is fearless.

Snapshots At St. Arbuck's Vol 1

Snapshots at St. Arbuck's deftly captures quiet, personal human moments in one of the least likely of places—a bustling coffee shop. R.G. Ryan's observations and vignettes remind us that there are stories unfolding in front of us constantly and that perhaps all we need to do is sit still for a minute to hear and see them.

Snapshots At St. Arbuck's Vol 2

This is the second volume in author R.G. Ryan's Snapshots At St. Arbuck's series. These books offer "snapshots" of an amazing race...the race called humanity in their work-a-day comings and goings in coffee shops from Sydney to Barcelona and all points in between. Funny, poignant, heart-rending and uplifting they indeed present "Life...one sip at a time."

The Voices In My Head

Danny Gans poured his energy into everything he loved, from his family to his faith, from baseball to his career in entertainment. When it came time to document his life story, he poured his energy into this project as well. Sadly, one day after this manuscript was completed, Danny died. His inspiring story remains, offering a compelling mix of touching tales and life lessons. From the baseball diamonds of his youth to his sold-out stardom on the Las Vegas Strip, Danny charts the struggles and successes of his life. Along the way, he tells us of the heartwarming courtship of his wife, Julie, and his close relationships with his father and mother. An uncommon gift as an impressionist lifted "The Man of Many Voices" to the pinnacle of the Las Vegas entertainment industry, where he will be long remembered as a much-loved performer and a generous man. Here is the story of Danny Gans, told in his own voice, and from his own heart.

www.ingramcontent.com/pod-product-compliance
Lightning Source LLC
Chambersburg PA
CBHW030407180626
46812CB00005B/1965